Books by Paul Tobin

THE GENIUS FACTOR
How to Capture an Invisible Cat
How to Outsmart a Billion Robot Bees
How to Tame a Human Tornado

THE GENIUS FACTOR

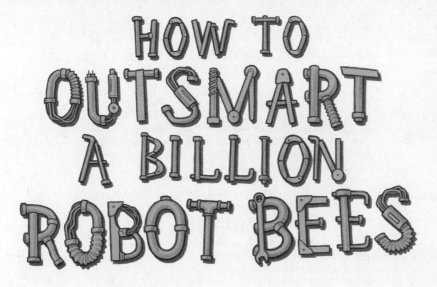

HOW TO OUTSMART A BILLION ROBOT BEES

Paul Tobin

illustrated by
Thierry Lafontaine

BLOOMSBURY

NEW YORK   LONDON   OXFORD   NEW DELHI   SYDNEY

First published in the United States of America in March 2017
by Bloomsbury Children's Books
Paperback edition published in March 2018
www.bloomsbury.com

Bloomsbury is a registered trademark of Bloomsbury Publishing Plc

For information about permission to reproduce selections from this book, write to
Permissions, Bloomsbury Children's Books, 1385 Broadway, New York, New York 10018
Bloomsbury books may be purchased for business or promotional use. For information on
bulk purchases please contact Macmillan Corporate and Premium Sales Department at
specialmarkets@macmillan.com

The Library of Congress has cataloged the hardcover edition as follows:
Names: Tobin, Paul, author. | Lafontaine, Thierry, illustrator.
Title: How to outsmart a billion robot bees / by Paul Tobin;
illustrated by Thierry Lafontaine.
Description: New York: Bloomsbury, 2017. | Series: The genius factor
Summary: Sixth-grade genius Nate Bannister, with his talking car Betsy and super-
powered pets Bosper the Scottish terrier and Sir William the gull, teams up with his friend
Delphine to stop the Red Death Tea Society from unleashing angry bees on the city of Polt.
Identifiers: LCCN 2016030008 (print) | LCCN 2016037457 (e-book)
ISBN 978-1-61963-897-6 (hardcover) • ISBN 978-1-61963-898-3 (e-book)
Subjects: | CYAC: Adventure and adventurers—Fiction. | Science—Experiments—Fiction.
| Genius—Fiction. | Bees—Fiction. | Humorous stories. | BISAC: JUVENILE FICTION /
Action & Adventure / General. | JUVENILE FICTION / Humorous Stories. | JUVENILE
FICTION / Science & Technology.
Classification: LCC PZ7.1.T6 Hom 2016 (print) | LCC PZ7.1.T6 (e-book) |
DDC [Fic]—dc23
LC record available at https://lccn.loc.gov/2016030008

ISBN 978-1-68119-604-6 (paperback)

Book design by John Candell
Typeset by RefineCatch Limited, Bungay, Suffolk
Printed and bound in the U.S.A. by Berryville Graphics Inc., Berryville, Virginia
2 4 6 8 10 9 7 5 3 1

All papers used by Bloomsbury Publishing, Inc., are natural, recyclable products
made from wood grown in well-managed forests. The manufacturing processes
conform to the environmental regulations of the country of origin.

Dedicated to Mom and Dad, and all the shoulders of the giants I've ever stood on

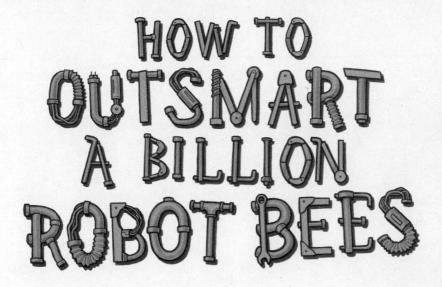

chapter 1

I do not know how the bumblebee got in.

It was Saturday.

This, of course, means it was time for my weekly Cake vs. Pie club meeting, where I get together at my house with Liz Morris, Wendy Kamoss, Buenaventura "Ventura" León, and Christine Keykendall. The purpose of this weekly meeting is simple: we debate which is better, cake or pie. I personally believe that cake is superior, but I remain open to the discussion, and to pie.

"Cake is moist," Wendy argued, as if that settled the matter.

"You think *this* isn't moist?" Liz said. She was holding up her fork to showcase an impressively balanced wedge of cherry pie, which was dripping off the edges and falling more or less onto her plate. Plus a bit on the table. And some onto her hand.

I said, "It does look moist." I was trying not to take sides, even though I am secretly on the side of cake. Well, *somewhat* secretly. Okay . . . not at all secretly, because I was in fact wearing my *"Cake is better than pie, dummies!"* shirt. Still, my job as hostess was to foster the debate, not settle it.

"Cake!" Ventura said. The word was partially mumbled. She was positively munching on cake at the time. Since I believe in committing to your opinion, you are only allowed to eat one thing during our meetings. You have to choose pie or cake. No lines can be straddled!

"Pie!" Liz said. She pointed to the cherry pie on the table between her and Christine, or Stine, as we call her.

"Don't just yell," I encouraged. "Debate!"

"Cake!" Wendy yelled. Voices were rising. I secretly love it when our meetings become boisterous.

"Pie!"

"Cake!"

"That's absurd! Pie!"

"Pie doesn't have *frosting*! Idiot!"

"Yeah, well . . . *cake* doesn't have *pie*!"

"Cake is best!"

"Pie forever!"

"Cake!"

"Pie!"

"Bumblebee!" Wendy said. It was the loudest yell so far.

I said, "Huh?" I admit that, at first, I was trying to put the word into context, as if "bumblebee" was slang for pie or cake. But it simply didn't make sense.

"Bumblebee!" Wendy yelled again. I moved on to wondering if either cakes or pies could be made out of bumblebees. Neither of them sounded delicious. Or particularly safe.

Ventura said, "Bumblebee!" So . . . it was catching. Everyone was yelling "bumblebee." We were in my basement with the steep stairway and the posters of glittering unicorns being attacked by monsters. My brother, Steve, bought the unicorn posters at the mall and painted the monsters on them. They were very well done and my friends loved them, but since my brother painted them I couldn't admit that I liked them.

"Bumblebee!" Stine yelled. She leaped over the back of the couch, shrieking in an amazingly loud fashion, reaching up and over and grabbing a pillow that she then attempted to throw either across the room at something, or else straight into my face. If she was trying to throw it into my face, then her aim was excellent. I tumbled out of my chair and fell to the floor. From this new position, on my back, I looked up at the table, to where the cherry pie plate was teetering on the edge, threatening to fall. I could almost hear it saying, "Delphine Cooper, remember how many times you've said that you love cake more than pie? I'm quite sure you do. Prepare for our revenge."

Luckily, I've been honing my reflexes ever since the day I was attacked by a giant cat during the first of what will assuredly be only the start of the adventures I'll be sharing with the genius, Nate Bannister. In the long weeks since then, in the months since we'd not only shrunk the cat but also defeated the Red Death Tea Society, I've been honing myself, training for hours and hours every single day, and learning to expect the unexpected. So, drawing on the magnificent results of those countless days of training, I rolled to one side with my phenomenal speed, straight into a table leg, jarring the pie off the table and down onto my head.

So I had pie in my eyes and my friends were running around screaming, "Bumblebee," and it was only then, a bit late, that it began to occur to me that there could be a bumblebee in the room. No problem. I know a lot about bumblebees.

"Don't provoke it!" I yelled out to my four best friends, all of them obscured by a veil of cherry pie over my eyes. "Don't, uhh, make any sudden moves or call it any nasty names."

"Are you serious?" Stine said. Her voice doubted that I could be serious. In her defense, it's seriously hard to look serious when you're covered in pie. I grabbed a towel (we keep several towels handy during Cake vs. Pie meetings, because we've learned that accidents *will* happen, if you count picking up handfuls of pie or cake and throwing them at each other as accidents), and I cleaned myself off and said, "Bumblebees really only sting you when they feel threatened."

The bee flew over and stung me on my forehead.

"Gasp!" I yelled. I could already feel my forehead turning into a melon. This is something that happens when a bee stings you. You balloon into something many times your previous size. Don't be alarmed by this. It's normal. Be alarmed by the intense pain, though.

"Gaaargh!" I yelled. I picked up a pillow and bit into it, because I've seen in television shows that people bite things in order to help them withstand pain. The pillow, unfortunately, didn't do me any good. So I picked up a piece of cake and bit into that. It didn't help with the pain, either, but it tasted better than the pillow.

I told everyone, "Don't worry about, uhh, aaargh, *so much pain*, don't worry about the . . . uhh, this cake is SO good, uh, but seriously . . . don't worry about the bumblebee. It can only sting once. We're safe now."

It was at this point that the bumblebee landed on my arm. And it stung me. Then it flew down onto my butt. And stung me. And then it landed on the back of my neck. And stung me. And then it returned to my butt. And stung me.

I made all the sorts of noises you might imagine, if you have a particularly vivid imagination.

"Grun!" I finally yelled, when the bumblebee barrage was temporarily over.

"What?" Stine said. She was frantically dancing back and forth. The bumblebee was buzzing in the air, cackling.

"Hrun!" I said. I wasn't speaking very well, probably because of the agony and the horror.

Ventura said, "I think she's telling us to run!" She'd grabbed up a quilt from the back of the couch, holding it in front of her like a matador facing a bull, if bulls were rude enough to fly and to sting you several times on the butt.

"Whatever," Wendy said. "Let's run!" I appreciated how she didn't care what I was trying to say. The important thing was the part about running.

We ran up the steps. Or *they* did. I was stumbling. As it turns out, having multiple bee stings on my butt does nothing for my foot speed. In mere seconds, I was alone with the bee, crawling up the stairs. I mean that I was crawling up the stairs. The bee was flying. Like they do.

My phone rang.

It was back on the table.

In the Bee Room.

Now, you might think I should've ignored my phone, but the particular ringtone meant that Nathan Bannister was calling (the ring is Godzilla's roar), and Nate is the smartest person in the world (I'm not kidding), and I had some questions I wanted to ask him about bees. I couldn't exactly ask the bee, after all, because *it* clearly didn't know *anything* about bees. Plus, I knew it would lie. Seriously, bees are liars. So I called the bee an unkind name, turned back for my phone, grabbed it, and then scrambled up the stairs. The bee zoomed over to me and became stuck in my hair (which is curly, and red, and does not frequently harbor bees), and I want to say that I am normally very brave, but I was considering screaming.

I made it up the stairs.

Through the kitchen.

Out onto the sidewalk.

Where I found Wendy and Liz, Ventura and Stine, all of them standing very still, looking at six rows of at least a hundred bumblebees that were hovering in precise military formation.

"Guh," Stine said.

"They normally do that?" Liz asked, pointing to the bees. She sounded skeptical.

"Wow, Delphine," Ventura said. "Your forehead looks like a melon." I nodded at this. It was true and there was little sense in denying it. Also, my head even *felt* like a melon. My butt, I might note, felt like I'd sat in a fire. In *two* fires, in fact. As for the lines of bees, they sounded like a titanic rattlesnake. The bee in my hair was positively enraged. The message on my phone, the one from Nate, the text from the smartest boy on earth, said, Hey, this might sound strange, but watch out for bumblebees.

Too late, I texted back.

The lines of bees moved closer.

🔅

We ran.

Our plan was to outrun the bees, but this did not prove successful. Our other plan was to scream. This secondary plan was *wholeheartedly* successful, but it did little (meaning, *nothing*) to stop the bees. Our third plan was to beg the bees not to sting us, but either they didn't understand English (which is likely) or else they were having too much fun to stop, which was even more likely.

As a final plan, I decided to call Nate, because he is very smart. By then I'd become separated from the others because I run faster, and also because the bees seemed to be following only me, meaning that whenever my friends took evasive maneuvers, they actually evaded, while I was only giving the bees a decent workout. So I just kept running. Occasionally cursing. Also that thing with the screaming.

Nate answered after the first ring, undoubtedly because he has a mathematical formula for when I'm going to call. He says that it has to do with prevailing weather patterns, the chemical makeup of the air at any given time, and lunar cycles. I have no idea what he means, but I rarely have any idea what he means and so that doesn't bother me. I like it, actually. Mysterious and incomprehensible friends are the best.

"Hey, Delphine," he said. "Are you being chased by bees?"

"Yes," I said. "I am being chased by bees." I'll admit that it came out a bit rushed and garbled, more like, "Yzzbeenchassbees!"

"I was afraid of that," he said.

"I am also afraid of it," I noted.

"Let me see where you are on the GPS tracker I have in your hair."

"Huh? I have a GPS tracker in my hair? What do you mean? It's not this *bee*, is it? Because I have a bee in my hair! You'd better *not* have put a bee in my hair!" At that point the bees were chasing me around and around the hedge in the Bellinghams' yard. I was hoping the bees weren't smart enough to understand that they could fly over the hedge, or that they could break off from their precise formation and surround me from all sides.

"Why would I put a bee in your hair?" Nate said, apparently thinking that he normally does things for a reason, which I can assure you is not true.

I said, "Grgargh!" because a bee had just stung my left arm, just above the bicep. It had, to my dismay, flown over the hedge after breaking off formation with the other bees. In other words, the bee had cheated. Never trust a bee. They are liars, cheaters, and stingers. It is an unfortunate combination.

"Ooo!" Nate said. "A bee just stung your left arm, huh?"

"How did you know that?"

"Because you said, 'Grgargh,' and that's the noise someone makes when a bee stings their left arm, just above the bicep."

"It is?" This was news to me. I suspect it would've been news to anyone on earth but Nate.

"It is," Nate said. "Have you tried running away?"

"Flargrah!" I screamed.

"Ouch," Nate said. "Stung you on the right leg, did it? Anyway, I was saying, don't try running away. A bee can fly at twenty miles per hour, and you can't."

"I can't," I admitted. "I can't even fly at all. Definitely not at twenty miles per hour. And how can these bees sting more than once? Isn't that cheating?"

"You're thinking of honeybees. They have barbed stingers, so they can only sting you once. Bumblebees can sting you as many times as they want."

"Piffle," I said. It's a word I use. In fact it's a *curse* word I use. One that doesn't get me in trouble.

"You'll be fine," Nate said. "No reason to curse like that. Except I suppose for how you keep getting stung by bees. Anyway, I'm tracking your location, and Sir William is almost there."

"Sir William?" I said. I was running across the lawn toward a sprinkler that was sending sprays of water all over the grass. To me, the water would be nothing but a chilling spray, but to the bees (*ha ha ha!*) the water droplets would be like a barrage of cannon fire.

Nate said, "Sir William Gull. He's my robot gull."

"I know who and what he is. I'm wondering how he's going to help." The spray from the water sprinkler was constantly rotating, so I had to keep leaping to the left and the right so that the bees couldn't sting me. Some of them tried, and the water brought them down, so that they were crawling on the grass, too wet to fly, buzzing and furious.

"Sir William can eat the bees," Nate said.

"Send him. Send that robot gull to me."

"You should see him by now. Look around." I did look around. I looked at the angry bees flying in the air and the furious bees crawling on the ground, scrambling like insect zombies across the grass, still trying to get to me. I saw Wendy, Ventura, Stine, and Liz, all of them inside a car, waving for me to come and join them, but they were too far away, and if I left the safety of the sprinkler the bees would either sting me to death or carry me off to their hive. I saw Kip Luppert . . . our classmate who often acts in the plays that Liz and I put on . . . riding by on a bicycle, practicing his lines for something I didn't recognize, talking about submarines and commando units, entirely oblivious to the bumblebee tragedy that was unfolding on the nearby lawn. I saw the Bellinghams' cat warming herself in the window. Her name is Pony. I think that's a good name for a cat. At one point a bee landed on the window, and Pony batted at it through the glass, but she did so in a particularly languid fashion, as if she couldn't care less what was happening outside.

So I saw a lot of things, but I did not see a robot gull.

"Where is he?" I asked Nate.

"Did you look up?"

"Of course," I said. "Duh." I hadn't actually looked up but decided against telling that to Nate.

I looked up. There was a speck in the sky. It grew larger. Soon, it was a gull, an entirely lifelike robot gull, only giving away its "not a real bird" identity by the speed it was flying. At probably a hundred miles per hour, it swept down on the bees.

"Sir William!" I yelled. "Over here!"

"Screech!" the gull yelled back. Sir William doesn't make the distinctive shrieking caw of an actual living seagull. Instead, he just pronounces "Screech!" like a word. In Nate's voice. I probably don't have to mention this, but it's disconcerting.

Sir William whooshed through the bees at high speed, opening his mouth, scooping up bumblebees as he sped through them. He landed on the side of the Bellinghams' house and stuck there like a spider for a few seconds (I suppose this would also be considered strange behavior from an actual living seagull) and swallowed the insects with a loud mechanical gulp. Then he sprang out from the house, taking to the air again, whooshing all around in a complicated series of aerial maneuvers that left me dizzy to witness. There were circles, ovals, rectangles, and slashes through the air, all of them faster than I could really see. Much too fast for the bees.

"How's that top speed of twenty miles per hour working out for you *now*?" I taunted the bees. The ones on the lawn grumbled angrily. The ones in the air had no time to spare for grumbling, because Sir William was coming for them, hunting them, swallowing them.

It was over in moments. I found it all marvelous, though it was still of no interest to Pony, the cat in the window. Nate and I once had an argument about cats. I claimed that the only things that ever interest a cat are naps and food, while he claimed that it was only food that truly interests a cat, because once you fall asleep you technically lose interest in a nap. After that, you're just napping.

Well, *I* wasn't going to be caught napping. I waved to get Sir William's attention, pointing to the bumblebees on the lawn, which I bet were really hoping I would forget about them.

"There's more bumblebees down here!" I said.

"Screech!" the robot said in what I assume was appreciation. He certainly did enjoy his bees. He'd already swallowed all the bees that had been in the air. Nearly a hundred of them. That's a lot of bees to have in your stomach. Far too many, from my viewpoint, because *zero* is my limit when it comes to swallowing bees.

Sir William landed in
the grass and then skipped
and darted all over the yard,
plucking up bumblebees and
swallowing them whole. I
could hear the buzz of the bees
inside him, making him sound
like a bad connection, or a rattlesnake, or a mechanical bird full of
irritated bumblebees.

"Screech!" he said when the
last of the bumble-
bees had been
swallowed. At that
moment my phone buzzed, vibrating, and of course I
thought it was a bee (they'd been buzzing, which is the
same thing as vibrating: making this an entirely understandable mistake) so I flung my phone quickly away
from me, wary of adding to my collection of horribly
distorted bee stings that had turned my forehead into a
melon, my legs and arms into what appeared to be the
first stages of a zombie plague, and my butt into something that looked like two butts.

My phone sailed across the yard and landed on the
windowsill. Pony, inside the window, moved an inch
back, then yawned. I waddled across the yard to the

sound of Godzilla's roar coming from my phone, which meant Nate was calling. Maybe he was going to offer me some sort of ultra-medicine that would cure my bee stings and instantly un-freak me?

"Hello?" I said after picking up my phone and losing a staredown with Pony.

"Delphine," Nate said. "We need to talk."

"Then it's a good thing you called me," I said. "Because we could do that. We could talk. Right now on the phone."

"It's about the Red Death Tea Society," he said. "Bring Sir William to my house." Then, before I could say anything, he disconnected.

"You're kidding me," I said to the silent phone, which was soaking wet from how I'd been holding it while standing in the spray of the lawn sprinkler.

"Screech!" Sir William said as I picked him up. He was equally soaking wet, and vibrating like crazy. I tucked him under one arm, fully aware that I was holding a high-tech container of angry bumblebees. I carried him out to the car where my friends were still cowering. Stine tentatively rolled down a window.

"Are the bumblebees gone?" she asked. Her eyes were darting in every direction.

"Yes," I said. "All gone."

"You're carrying a seagull," Ventura said.

"I do that sometimes." It wasn't the best cover story

I'd ever devised, but I was in pain and had a melon head and two butts' worth of bee stings. None of my friends were truly aware of how smart Nate was, and I had to keep it a secret. It wasn't all that difficult to pretend Sir William was an actual seagull instead of a robot. Nate built Sir William to pass almost any inspection. Although, I have to say, he was a little heavy. Or at least I was a bit weak. Sluggish. If for nothing else, I'd eaten a thousand pounds of cake (that's hyperbole; I'd eaten no more than five hundred pounds of cake) before all the excitement began. Unless you count eating cake as excitement. Like I do.

"Are you okay?" Liz asked.

"She doesn't look okay," Wendy said.

"Screech!" Sir William said.

"Oh, he sounds odd," Stine said. "Did he get stung?"

"Umm, yes," I said. My arm was starting to go numb from holding him. Too much vibration. "I think I'll take him inside and give him some medicine. And then I'm going to nap." My friends were warily getting out of the car, looking for bees. It's amazing how a little thing like getting attacked by hundreds of bees can make you paranoid about being attacked by hundreds of bees.

"Should I call my mom?" Wendy asked. Her mom is a doctor. I shook my head, which made me go dizzy, but I heroically didn't topple over, though I did drop Sir

William. He landed on the ground and cocked his head quizzically, watching me.

"Sure you're okay?" Stine asked. I nodded. This time it didn't make my head throb any harder.

"If you're okay," Liz said, "then tell me which is better. Cake or pie?"

"Cake," I said. "Duh."

"Wrong," Liz said. "We should get you checked out."

"How is she *wrong*?" Wendy scoffed. "Cake *is* better than pie. We all know that!" Ventura was nodding in a vigorous fashion, the way people can do when they adamantly believe in something and also haven't had bees transform their heads into a melon.

"Pie!" Stine yelled. She threw her hands up in the air, stomping on the sidewalk. "I'm not saying that cake isn't good, but it only comes in third, behind *pie* and *more pie*!"

"Idiot!" Ventura yelled.

"If liking pie makes you an idiot, then I'm the world's biggest idiot!" Stine yelled back, then paused as she realized that her words weren't quite on the mark.

I left the four of them on the sidewalk to battle it out.

I had a seagull to deliver.

I showered.

I put on fresh clothes.

I stared in the mirror to see what the bees had done. They hadn't changed my red hair, of course, and my eyes were still green and I still had freckles and I was still about four feet and seven inches tall, unless you counted the bumps from the bee stings, because then I'd grown another inch, at least.

I decided to wear a hat in order to disguise the horribly unappealing bee stings on my head, but, unfortunately, the only comfortable clothes I had . . . loose-fitting clothes to avoid irritating my countless bee stings . . . were my workout clothes, meaning that I eventually stepped out of my house looking like I was on my way to the gym carrying a vibrating seagull.

And that's when the helicopter landed in the street.

Five men with automatic rifles leaped out, yelling about securing the area, running here and there, ordering people to get off the street and back into their houses, even checking under cars, where I guess they thought people normally hide?

I stood transfixed in my yard. The rush of the helicopter's blades had blown off my hat, and it was bouncing down the street, tumbling farther and farther away, escaping.

A gray-haired man in a bright green suit stepped out of the helicopter after the soldiers had given the all clear.

The man was chewing bubblegum. He blew a bubble. While staring at me.

From the side of his mouth he said, "Delphine Cooper. Come with me."

The bubble popped.

chapter 2

The helicopter was huge, and I was strapped into a harness that was made for someone much larger than myself, which meant that I was basically dangling like a wind chime from the helicopter's interior, except instead of musical notes I was just saying "ooof!" each time the helicopter shifted and bounced me off the wall. The five soldiers were glaring at me as if they expected me to make a daring escape. The roar of the helicopter was that of a gigantic lion with something caught in its throat.

"Delphine Cooper," the gray-haired man said again. It was the third time he'd said my name. He hadn't said much of anything else, except he'd twice offered me bubblegum. I'd declined him the first time because I never take anything from strangers in helicopters. I accepted the second time, though, having decided I could use the bubblegum to aid in my eventual escape, as soon as the soldiers let down their guard. Unfortunately, I wasn't exactly sure *how* I'd use the bubblegum in any escape, so I was hoping the soldiers wouldn't let down their guard anytime soon, not until I was ready.

I was, as far as I could determine, being kidnapped. There'd been no discussion if I'd wanted to go with these men. No chance to contact anybody. When I'd tried to call my dad the man in the green suit had simply taken my phone away from me, putting it in his pocket, shaking his head as if I'd done something mean and he was disappointed in me. Then, one of the soldiers had nabbed Sir William from me, and another had picked me up, tossed me over his shoulder, marched me into the helicopter, and strapped me into the harness, locking it shut. In the interest of how my memoirs are likely to become required reading material, I'll say that I endured this treatment in a noble manner, not doing much kicking (I landed a few good ones) and mostly not swearing all that much.

So, I was strapped into a kidnap machine, and a man in a bad suit was staring at me as if I were a particularly difficult puzzle. The winds rushing through the helicopter were making my hair fly all about, and if I turned my head a certain way, and opened my mouth just so, then the wind made my lips flap like a dog with its head stuck out the window of a moving car. It made a noise like *flobble flobble flobble*.

That part was kind of fun.

"My name is Reggie Barnstorm," the man in the green suit said.

"That sounds made up," I mentioned. I blew a bubble with my gum. It was *choice*.

"It is made up," Reggie said. "You don't have the clearance to know my real name." He paused, and then with a sweep of his hand he indicated the other men sharing our luxurious helicopter accommodations. "They don't have the clearance, either, for that matter." None of the men responded. They didn't seem insulted. They just kept staring warily at me, and then at Sir William, even though he'd been stuffed into a lead box with a lid that had taken two men to lift.

"Why kidnap *me*?" I asked. "Is this about my science paper?" I'd written my last science paper about a benign virus that could be injected into cats in order to give them the ability to change colors, like chameleons. Nate had helped me with some of the more scientific aspects. To be more precise, he'd run everything past me saying, "I wish cats could change colors, like chameleons."

"It's about your association with Nathan Bannister," Reggie said.

"He only helped a little on the paper," I said, blowing another bubble.

"I'm not sure what paper you're talking about," Reggie said. "This has to do with the Red Death Tea Society."

"Piffle," I said. "Are you with *them*?" I was suspiciously sniffing the air, but there wasn't the slightest scent of tea, and none of the men were drinking any.

"Hardly," Reggie said, aghast. "Well, we *were*. But our goals differ now. You could say that we're at scientific odds with them. You could even say we're opposed to them. In fact, you could say that we're deadly enemies."

"Could I say who you *are*? Because *you* haven't. Altogether, with the kidnapping and the complete lack of introductions, you've been awfully rude."

"Oh," Reggie said, and the soldiers all echoed him, giving that sigh you give when you not only realize you've done something wrong but you've been caught doing it. I am unfortunately and intimately familiar with this sigh.

"Is a helicopter kidnapping traumatic to a young girl?" Reggie asked.

"Um, yes. A bit. Kind of. Completely and totally."

"I hadn't considered that," Reggie said. "We've all been flustered. Things have been happening rather quickly, of late. I suppose you might have noticed the bees?"

"Um, yeah," I said. "Somewhat. A little. Painfully and entirely." I was glancing meaningfully to my arms, where the bees had accomplished the equivalent of a bombing run.

"Oh," Reggie said, with that sigh again. He started to say something else, but the pilot called his name and he went up to talk with her. I, of course, stayed right there, strapped into my harness, bouncing off the side of the helicopter, which I believe is called the cabin, which doesn't sound right to me because cabins are in the woods, not in the air.

I kicked my heel back against the wall and asked the soldiers, "Is this called the cabin? Are we in the cabin?"

No answer.

"So, are you guys sworn to silence, like monks?"

No answer.

"So, that Reggie guy? A green suit? Who wears a green suit?"

No answer.

"Look! I can blow a bubble!" I blew a bubble.

No applause.

"I'll just play over here by myself, then," I said, looking around for any items that seemed like they could aid in my escape. It would've been handy, just then, if life were more like a video game, meaning that any necessary items would glow softly, signifying their importance. But . . . no, nothing was glowing, unless you counted my bee stings, which at least *felt* like they were glowing. Or burning.

"Could you at least play some music?" I asked the men. They just stared at me. Not music lovers, I guess. I tried to decide where Reggie and his men were taking me. And . . . why was he so familiar? Ever since he'd first stepped down from the helicopter, I'd felt like I'd seen him before. And what was it with the suit? Who wears a green suit? The only other time I'd seen a green suit was when—

"Oh," I said. The soldiers looked at me. Well, *continued* to look at me, but now with narrower eyes.

"Nothing," I said. But it wasn't nothing. I *had* seen Reggie before. He was one of the experts who'd come to our school to test Nate. So . . . now I knew. But what did it mean?

"Hmm," I said. The soldiers tensed, as if I was dangerous. I narrowed my eyes and tried to look menacing, but the helicopter shifted and bounced me like a sack of potatoes against the wall, and it's very hard to look menacing when you are a sack of potatoes.

I sighed.

I hung there, in my harness, on the wall.

From my angle, I could see outside the open door, all the way down to the city of Polt, far below. The wind was swarming through the cabin, investigating everything, sending my red hair flying. Not a single strand on any of the soldiers' heads budged. I wondered if soldiers train their hair. Do they make their hair lift weights, maybe do push-ups? Thinking of their hair made me remember the GPS tracker that Nate had put in my hair. I wondered if he was still tracking me.

"I am," Nate said.

Or at least it was Nate's voice. It *wasn't* Nate. *Couldn't* be. Because Nate wasn't there. Not in the helicopter. How could he be?

Nate said, "I calculated this was the time you'd remember the GPS tracker in your hair. I could see it in your eyes when you thought of it. Stay there for a minute; I'm going to get Sir William."

There was still no Nate to be seen. I decided I was hallucinating his voice. Maybe I shouldn't have chewed the bubblegum? Maybe it had some weird chemical in it, one that made me hear things?

The top of Sir William's lead box began to slowly rise in the air. The soldiers looked over to it, confused. It wasn't exactly the sort of thing that would blow around in the wind.

"Sir?" one of them said, trying to get Reggie's attention, but the roar of the helicopter and the rush of the wind devoured his voice, and Reggie didn't hear him.

The robot gull peeked out of the metal box.

"Screech?" it said.

"Sir!" one of the soldiers said, louder, trying to get Reggie Barnstorm's attention, frantically waving his hand.

"Screech!" the robot gull said, now perched on the edge of the box. He flapped one wing, as if waving back at the soldier.

"Sir!" another soldier said.

"Screech?" said the robot gull. It was then that I realized the problem.

"His name is *Sir* William," I told the soldier. "He thinks you're talking to him."

At that moment, Reggie came walking back and saw what was happening. He trembled, then peeled back the sleeve of his green suit to reveal an amazing array of electronics on the inside of the cloth, with multiple screens displaying streams of data. He studied them for only a second before gasping, and then yelled, "He's here! Bannister is here!"

"He is?" I said. "So I wasn't just hearing things?"

"I *am* here," Nate whispered in my ear. There was a flash of light and then my harness became unconnected. I fell down against the wall of the cabin, perilously close to the open door.

"Sometimes the cabin can be called a 'fuselage,'" Nate whispered to me. I still couldn't see him. I did not think it was the appropriate time to be discussing the proper names for helicopter parts. I did, however, think it was the appropriate time for *not falling out of a helicopter*. It usually is.

"Secure Delphine!" Reggie yelled. "And flood the cabin with—"

But whatever he was about to say, it was too late.

"Screech!" Sir William said, but this time he kept his mouth open.

And the bees flew out.

There was an immediate panic, because as any soldier can tell you, guns are not very useful against bumblebees, not unless you are a *very* good shot. Also, for a well-trained group of muscle-bound men, the five of them certainly did act frightened, but in their defense they'd had me to look at, hanging from my harness on the cabin wall, a clear illustration of *The Evil Bees Can Do*.

"Come on!" Nate said. He appeared beside me, wearing a wet suit, which is not proper attire for a helicopter. He took me by the arm and tugged me toward the open door.

"Long ways down," I told him. I hoped he'd noticed. I hoped he wasn't as panicked by the bees as everyone else.

"Sure," he said. "It's currently fourteen thousand

three hundred and seventy-nine feet to the ground. No problem. We'll just jump."

"Okay," I said. "Let's jump!" I've learned to trust Nate. No, scratch that, I *haven't* . . . but I've learned that it doesn't ever *matter* if I trust him or not. Everything still happens, and I'll only waste my breath talking about it, when I should be saving my breath for any screaming I might need to do while falling fourteen thousand three hundred and seventy-nine feet to the ground.

One of the soldiers tried to grab me, but several bees started stinging his face and he said, "Glaggt!" and fell over backward. The others were rolling around on the cabin floor, trying to get bees off them. Nate was tugging me toward the open sky. Sir William flew past me, and out the door he went. Reggie Barnstorm was yelling orders to everyone, including to all the soldiers, to me and Nate, to the pilot, and even to the bees, but none of us could hear what he was saying because of the rushing winds and the anguished cries of the men being stung by the bees.

"It's time to go!" Nate told me, urging me toward the door.

"Just a second!" I said. I had something very important to do.

I ran up to Reggie and grabbed my phone from his pocket. Then I took the chewed-up bubblegum from my mouth and stuck it on his forehead.

"There!" I said. "I'm escaping!"

With my Grand Bubblegum Escape Plan now in action, I ran back to the open door, grabbed Nate's hand . . .

. . . and we jumped.

So we were falling.

Totally expected.

Didn't bother me at all.

Nate said, "Could you not scream so loud? It hurts my ears."

"Sorry," I said. "Hadn't noticed I was screaming. Incidentally, the last time we were falling through the air, you had some antigravity cloth. You still have that?" I tried to sound as if such a thing were of little concern. After all, we were only fourteen thousand three hundred and seventy-nine feet off the ground. Well, a little less than that, now.

"No," Nate said. "Wow. I should have brought some."

"Yeah."

"Did they tell you who they were?" Nate asked. We were apparently finished with the whole "antigravity cloth" topic. To be honest, I thought it warranted more discussion. I'm not sure if I need to point this out, but we were still falling.

"You're screaming again," Nate said.

"Oh. Sorry. And, no, they didn't tell me who they were, not really. The man in the green suit, I've seen him before. He was one of the experts who came to test you that one day in school. He claimed his name is Reggie Barnstorm, but that sounds fake."

"It is. Sort of."

"Sort of?" We were falling through a cloud. It was wet. Was that why Nate was wearing a wet suit?

"Well, it's his real name, but he had all his official documents forged to a fake name. The same one."

"His fake name is his real name?"

"Yeah. Apparently, he thinks it confuses people."

I said, "I do admit I'm confused." Sir William flew past us. He was good at flying. As for me . . . ? Not so much.

"Reggie is the leader of the League of Ostracized Fellows," Nate said.

"I guess you're going to explain that?" We were falling through another cloud. Much like the first cloud, this one was wet. I suppose that makes sense, since clouds have that whole "rain" thing going on, but for some reason I'd always considered that clouds would feel like cotton balls.

Nate said, "The League of Ostracized Fellows was partly formed as a response to the Red Death Tea Society. They're ex-members of the Red Death Tea Society who had problems with the Society's philosophies of world domination through science. So they formed a splinter group, not only to stop Jakob Maculte, the leader of the Red Death Tea Society, but also to lead the world into a new scientific revolution. A peaceful one. Unfortunately, most of the League's members are, well . . . awkward. They don't fit into society as seamlessly as I do."

I discreetly coughed, which was easy enough to do, because it's not hard to be discreet when you're thousands of feet in the air.

Nate said, "I do respect the League, though. They have a lot of good ideas. The bottom line is, they're an organization of mostly amiable scientists and undeniable geniuses."

"I deny that wearing a bright green suit is the act of a genius," I told Nate. He only shrugged in reply. Our ideas of fashion do not often agree. I thought it best to let the topic drop. Anyway, I was having fun watching the wind rush through his hair. It almost made him look handsome. Not that I was looking. Well, I *was* looking, but *mostly* I was looking at the city of Polt. It was below us. I could see the amusement park. I could see the bike trails along the Farlton River (which Liz and I call the *Fart-Long* River, which I suppose says something about us, and why we're friends) and the tops of the buildings all along Trillip Avenue, where the antiques and vintage clothing stores are, and where I love to shop, though it's not exactly where I would like to fall. There seriously isn't a very long list of where I'd like to fall from over fourteen *thousand* feet. Nate and I were definitely going to have to start talking about how we were falling. It was becoming pertinent.

"The League has a lot of the smartest people in the world," he said. "Outcasts, mostly."

"Why?" I asked. I noticed Nate's lip tremble. It seemed to be something emotional, rather than any effect of the wind, which I might note was tremendous. I opened my mouth as wide as I could, and the wind swooshed inside, puffing out my cheeks and making them vibrate and wobble, sending me spinning a bit out of control. Nate tightened his grip on my hand and pulled me closer.

He said, "Well, being smart can be . . . difficult. I mean, socially." His lip trembled again. I definitely saw it. He looked sad. I hated seeing him that way. I thought of Polt Middle School, where Nate and I are both in sixth grade. I thought of how most of the other kids don't like to talk to Nate, how he's always sitting alone at lunch, how they call him Egghead, and how no one really pays much attention to him. I'm one of his only friends. People ask me why I spend so much time with him, and when I say it's because he's smart they look confused, like they can't understand why that would be interesting. I tell them . . . if you don't think *smart* is interesting, then you're *dumb*. Being friends with Nate is always an adventure. For one thing, Nate teaches me something new almost every day. Right then, for instance, I was hoping he would teach me why it was okay that we'd jumped out of a helicopter.

I said, "I get it. So, these guys formed a group of outcasts? What do they do? I mean, besides kidnap me, which is not what I'm hoping they do all the time."

"I think they were using you to get to me," Nate said. He unzipped his wet suit. The zipper was on the back, and he was having trouble with it. I was just about to offer to help when Sir William landed on Nate's back and tugged the zipper down.

"Okay," I said. "I've got questions. First, what do you mean they were using me to get to you? Why do they want to get to you? And why are you taking off your wet suit? And . . . you *are* wearing something *beneath* that, right? Lastly, and I hope you don't take this the wrong way, but I'm going to be mad if you're not going to do anything about us falling from the helicopter." I looked way up in the sky toward the helicopter. I'd quit looking down. It had been making me nervous. So I was only looking up. To the helicopter. Trying to decide if it was fourteen thousand feet above us. Because that would be bad.

Nate said, "The League knows they can't beat Maculte and the Red Death Tea Society. Not all by themselves, anyway. They've run hundreds of predictive models, and the result is always the same: alone, they'll be wiped out. So, they're trying to force me to join them. To *lead* them, actually. Reggie undoubtedly planned to hold you hostage as a way of pressuring me into acceding to their demands of taking a leadership role in the League of Ostracized Fellows. But I don't want to. They're always bickering about each other's inventions, and they're extremely comfortable being who they are, with being ostracized from society, I mean. I don't *want* to be comfortable with who I am. I think it's the duty of a human being to constantly challenge themselves, to push their limits, to become smarter. That's the way I want to be. I mean, Delphine, let me ask you, are *you* comfortable with yourself?"

"I'm not exactly comfortable with falling from the sky. Maybe I should have asked you about that first? You can skip ahead to it, if you like." By then, Nate was almost entirely out of his wet suit. Thankfully, he was wearing a shirt beneath it, a blue T-shirt with an image of Einstein and a cartoon word balloon saying "Think!" Also, he was wearing a pair of boxer shorts. They were green with cartoon drawings of toast. Not sure what that was all about.

He said, "Hold this a second, will you?" He tried handing me the wet suit, but the wind was too strong and it slipped from my grasp. It went up while we continued to fall down. Well, *it* was probably falling, too, but much slower, caught in the wind.

I said, "Oops."

"Ooo," Nate said. "We're going to need that."

"Oh," I said. "Well, I'll just go up and get it. Since I can fly."

"Great!" Nate said.

I said, "That was sarcasm, Nate."

"Oh. That's too bad. Because we really *are* going to need that."

"Then why did you take it off?" Honestly, my question seemed the height of reason. Speaking of height, we were losing it. We'd had an abundance of it at the start, but our supply was diminishing. I was beginning to be able to distinguish quite a lot of objects on the ground. None of them looked soft.

"It was uncomfortable," Nate said.

"So is falling from fourteen thousand feet. You have to adjust." The ground was rapidly approaching. Honestly, I was a bit bummed out. Nate and I began to spread out our arms and legs, to flatten ourselves as much as possible, trying to slow our descent enough for the wet suit to catch up to us, but it wasn't working. Luckily, we had an ace in the hole. Or, more exactly, a robot in the sky.

"Sir William!" Nate called out.

"Screech?" The seagull was flying some ten feet away from us. He made it look easy, but for all my panicked flapping, I wasn't even slowing my descent. I guess you have to start practicing to fly really early in life, or something.

"I need that!" Nate said. He pointed up to the wet suit. Sir William immediately soared upward, faster, faster, climbing higher and higher, until he was only a yard or two away from the wet suit. And then, with a tremendous burst of speed . . .

. . . he flew right past it.

"What the piffle?" I said.

"You're screaming again," Nate said. This time I knew it. I felt justified. It was a good time to scream. An excellent time to scream. Sir William just kept flying up, and up, and up, and . . .

"Oh," I said. "He thinks he's supposed to retrieve the helicopter."

"Well, that won't work. He'll just break it."

"He will? Wait, never mind. There isn't time for one of your explanations. Can't you contact him somehow? Bring him back? Call him on the phone?"

"Seagulls don't carry phones."

"No. I suppose not. Well, it's been good knowing you, Nate."

The ground was only a hundred feet below us. We were above the parking lot for the Cabaret Antique Store. There were a few cars there. A mother was holding her young daughter's hand, walking across the parking lot. The daughter was looking up at us like we were something she couldn't quite figure out. I wanted to tell her . . . don't worry, I can't figure us out, either.

Ninety feet. Eighty feet. Seventy feet. And so on. I closed my eyes because I decided it would hurt less.

There was a loud noise. Something like the roar of a robot elephant. Then, there was a jarring impact that was . . . soft? I kept my eyes closed. I wasn't falling anymore. I moved my left leg. It did not seem to be broken. I moved my right leg. It worked. I wiggled my butt, which wiggled as requested, though it complained of bee stings. I held up an arm to see if it worked, and it was at that point that something clamped onto my hand and I screamed.

I opened my eyes.

"What the heck?" Nate said. He was holding my hand. "I was just trying to help you up! Why did you scream?"

We were sitting on top of Betsy. Meaning Nate's car, Betsy. She's green and has a painting of Albert Einstein on the driver's door. Her license plate is WAIT4IT, which is something that Nate likes to say.

"Everybody okay?" Betsy asked. Oh, yeah, I should've mentioned that she talks and she's quite intelligent. I really like her. Even though she's a car, she has more personality than almost any of my classmates. I feel like I could have her over to my house some night. We could play video games. There's not really room on the couch for her, though. And I'm not sure my parents would understand me being friends with a car, and, also . . . *how was I alive?*

"How am I alive?" I asked Nate. He was jogging across the parking lot, to where the wet suit had flompled onto the concrete. If you don't think that "flomple" is a word, then you haven't heard a wet suit land on concrete after a fourteen-thousand-foot drop.

"Oh, ask Betsy," Nate said. This is one of the frustrating things about Nate. Sometimes he's so distracted that when someone asks valid questions, like wondering why they haven't been reduced to a two-dimensional pancake, his answer is to ask a car.

"Betsy?" I said. "Can we run over Nate? A little? I mean, I don't want to really hurt him. Maybe a bump on his head?"

"No." Her voice was slightly cold. I should've mentioned that Betsy is a bit sweet on Nate. I'm sorry that I keep mentioning facts that I forgot. I was still shaking from the fall and entirely confused by the whole "not being squished on the parking lot" thing. To be honest, my mind was super-flompled.

"I was just kidding," I told Betsy.

"Oh. Okay. Are you still curious about the reverse gravitational muon bombardment?"

"I don't even know what you just said."

"It's how I was able to decelerate your fall so that you were not dismantled."

"Some sort of force field?"

"No. That would be silly. It was a compressed deceleration field."

"Ha ha," I said. "Yeah. I'm not even sure why I said that thing about a force field. That really would be silly." I had no idea why that would be silly, but I didn't want to look stupid in front of a car.

Nate came walking back with the wet suit. He sure has skinny legs. Betsy's tires squealed as she quickly turned around. She was embarrassed, I think, to see Nate in his boxer shorts. Her windows tinted red.

"Got it," Nate said, holding up the wet suit in triumph.

"Okay," I said, not quite sure why we should be celebrating.

Nate told me, "We don't have to worry about falling from the helicopter now." I looked around. I was standing in the middle of a parking lot. Nobody else was in sight, excepting the mother and the young daughter, with the daughter trying to explain to her mother that Nate and I had fallen from the sky and that a talking car had caught us. The mother, not even looking our way, was telling her daughter that she wouldn't let her drink any more coffee if she was going to be having hallucinations.

A bumblebee buzzed past me, and that gave me a momentary panic, but the bee flew quickly on, out of sight.

I said, "Nate, we aren't falling anymore, so I'm not exactly worried. What could you have done with a wet suit, anyway?"

"It's one of my inventions. It can . . . well, I guess it doesn't matter now." He frowned, clearly disappointed that he couldn't show off his new invention, meaning that he was grumbling when he grabbed some clothes from Betsy's trunk, and he was peevish as he slid into his pants. He managed to make buttoning his shirt into an orchestra of sighs. Still, it was nice to have him look normal again, nice to see his flopping brown hair, his brown eyes, his nose that I kindly claim is not too big, the glasses that he made himself and that I honestly think are stylish, his normal checkered shirt, and the pants where he's scribbled endless equations and technical drawings. Yes, it was very nice to have him look his regular ol' self again. What I'm really trying to say here is that I was glad his legs (which I will describe as "skinny" and "pale" . . . because that's the simple truth) weren't showing anymore.

Beep. The noise was from one of the buttons on Nate's shirt. I only know this because the button glowed red at the same time.

"Uh-oh," Nate said. He looked down at the button. It was the third button on his shirt. All his buttons were buttoned. He's the only one I know who always buttons all the buttons. He tells me that everything has its purpose, and that if you don't use a button, it simply goes to waste. I haven't argued against him on this because the argument would serve no purpose and my time would simply go to waste.

I said, "Uh-oh? Is something wrong?" Nate looked up to me, then back down to his button.

"Here," he said, holding open Betsy's passenger side door. "Get in. We have to leave. Right now." He tossed the wet suit in the backseat and ran around to the driver's side. Betsy opened the door for him and he got in. Whenever we're in the car, the windows display images so that, to any onlooker, it seems like two adults are driving the car, rather than two sixth graders. It's just easier that way. Sometimes the projected images have us look like regular people, but Nate occasionally programs the illusions so that we look like, oh . . . Oscar Wilde or Napoleon or Cleopatra or, in one memorable instance, two polar bears. I'm not sure why Nate ever thought that last one was a good idea. It's not like onlookers would think, *"Oh, for a second there it looked like two sixth graders were driving that car, but luckily it's just a couple of polar bears."*

Anyway, Betsy actually drives herself. Nate and I are just passengers.

Nate seemed frantic as we got into the car, and he told Betsy, "Full speed home," and she sped away so quickly that I nearly tumbled into the backseat before I could get my seat belt on.

"Sorry, passenger Delphine Cooper," Betsy told me. "We will be traveling at high velocity." The parking lot was already a blur. Betsy is *fast*. Nate has told me that he installed a collider engine into the car. I'm not sure what that means, and he only chuckled when I said that I wasn't sure I wanted to be in a car that had a collider, because I don't want to collide with anything. His chuckle was the type you hear when someone thinks you've told a really good joke. I hadn't been joking.

"What's going on, Nate?" I asked as we sped out of the parking lot.

"My button glowed red and beeped. That means a member of the Red Death Tea Society is close by. In fact, I think maybe several members, since the button is still beeping."

It was. His button was going *beep . . . beep . . . beep . . .*
beep beep beep. I have to say, I'd never before considered
that a button could be ominous, but there it was, being all
ominous.

I said, "Well, that's bad news."

"Yeah." Nate's button was still sounding the alarm.
Beep . . . beep . . . beep . . . beep beep beep. "Lately they've
been sending me letters about how they'll stop at nothing to erase my 'menace,' or at least turn me to the tea
side."

"Letters? Actual letters? Like, in the mail?"

"That's right. They're on parchment. Lettered in red."

"I'm starting to wonder if I'm hallucinating this
entire day. This could all be a dream. Maybe I hit my
head when the bee was in my house?"

"No, it's real. Speaking of your head, it looks like a
melon. You shouldn't let bees sting you."

I said, "Yeah." I'm fully aware that it was a terribly
lame comeback to Nate telling me my head looked like a
melon (which is not something boys should do, incidentally, because it is rarely considered a compliment), but
I'd just noticed there were four cars following us. I mean,
there were a lot of cars following us, because we were
driving down the street (Betsy was doing all the driving),
but there were four cars in particular, each of them a
dark red (I'm just going to go ahead and say they were

the color of blood, because it sounds more dramatic) with a painting of a teacup on their hoods.

Beep beep, Nate's buttons sounded out, warning us of imminent attack. I looked in the mirror, and then I looked to Nate's button, and I nodded.

"Yeah," I told the button. "*Beep* it is."

"Four cars following us," I told Nate.

"Yeah. I know." He patted that glowing button. It beeped again, several times, apparently in some sort of code. I didn't let it bother me. Nate speaks math. Like, as a language.

Nate said, "Betsy? Can you slide out the medical tray?" I lifted my feet. I knew where the medical tray was because Nate had once sprained his ankle at a park when he was trying to make slides more fun. He'd put jet accelerators along the edges of the slide so that when somebody slid down they reached Mach 4. I'm not sure if that sounds like any fun at all, but I can tell you it wasn't as much fun as it sounds.

The tray slid out from beneath my feet.

"There's some bee sting ointment in there," Nate said. He was looking in the rearview mirror, at the oncoming cars.

"Good," I told him. "I want some bee sting ointment.

That is exactly what I want." I started rummaging around in the tubes on the tray. There were salves for burns (such as you might put on your butt, if you've been on a slide and were suddenly accelerated to Mach 4), and there were bandages you could put on your forearm (if, for instance, you accidentally did a cartwheel off the edge of your house while watching Nate install a satellite receiver), and there was a liquid that, when you rubbed it on your skin, you smelled like cinnamon. I guess that last one was really just perfume, nothing all that special and I'm not sure why it was in the medical tray, but I do like cinnamon. I put a little on.

"Ahh, here it is," I said. The tube of bee sting ointment had an illustration of a bee. Also, it was making a buzzing sound. "I like this illustration," I told Nate. He'd done it himself. I know his art style.

"Thanks," he said. He'd reached into the back and was grabbing the wet suit, and his face was twisted into his "thinking" expression.

"It made the ointment really easy to find," I said, rubbing some on my arms. "Plus, I could've just listened to the sound of the buzzing. How did you make the ointment do that? Some sort of sound chip on the tube?" I was holding up the tube, looking at it. The buzzing was louder.

"It doesn't buzz," Nate said. He'd taken out some sort

of remote control from his pocket and tossed the wet suit out the window. I didn't bother to ask what he was doing. That's useless. I did, though, decide it was going to be strange. I came to that conclusion based on prior experience with Nate. Most everything he does is strange, so you can reasonably expect that the next thing he does is also going to be strange. That's called a hypothesis.

"It does too buzz," I said, holding up the ointment tube, rubbing some on my melon-head. It was going *buzz buzz . . . buzz . . . buzz buzz buzz*. It was out of tune with Nate's button, which was still going *beep . . . beep . . . beep . . . beep beep beep*.

"No," Nate said. "I didn't make the tube buzz. Good idea, though!" He was watching the wet suit flutter in the wind. It was caught up in the wake of passing cars, whooshing back toward the four cars that were following us, and which, incidentally, should not have painted teacups on their cars if they were going to be a part of a secret society.

"Then . . . what's buzzing?" I asked.

Betsy said, "Passenger Delphine Cooper, I am detecting a life-form in your hair."

"You are *what*?" I said. It came out as a squeak.

"There's a bee in your hair," Betsy said. Of course there was. I'd forgotten all about the bee in my hair. I suppose that says a lot about how my day was going, because I am not normally the type of sixth grade girl who forgets a bee in her hair.

I tried to say, "That's no good. I don't want a bee in my hair. Can somebody please take it out?"

It came out more like, "*AHHHHHHHHHH!*"

"Don't scare the bee!" Nate said.

I tried to say, "Why shouldn't I scare the bee?"

But it came out more like . . . punching Nate in the arm.

"Guhh," Nate said. He's not really accustomed to physical combat. Not that it was really combat. It was more like he was just getting punched. You'd think he'd get used to it. We've been friends for a while now.

"Would you like me to help you with the bumblebee?" Betsy asked.

I said, "Yes." I was spinning around in my seat, trying to get a look at the bumblebee, but all my twisting and turning was mostly turning my seat belt into a giant cobweb, where I was trapped.

The air-conditioning kicked on, which confused me. Did Betsy think we could *air-condition* a bee out of my hair? Then, the whole car suddenly filled with the scent of . . . flowers. How was that going to help?

The bee flew out of my hair.

It hovered fatly in front of my face. It pivoted in place,

around and around, spinning like a tiny yellow-and-black tornado. It went, "Bzzz?" There was definitely a question mark at the end of it. I could hear it.

Betsy said, "I have flooded the car with the scent of calamintha and perovskia." The bee landed on the dash. Spun around. Obviously confused.

I said, "Huh?"

Nate said, "Calamintha and Russian sage, the latter being a more common name for perovskia, are two flowers that bees favor. Betsy is overloading the bee's hunting instincts."

"Bees have hunting instincts?" I did not prefer bees having hunting instincts. Nothing that was ever in my hair should have a hunting instinct.

"Sure," Nate said. He was still looking behind us, toward the cars. They were closing in. "Bees hunt flowers. Nectar. They're quite peaceful."

"Says the boy who *doesn't* have a melon for a head." The bee was now trying to fly into the air-conditioning vent, but the wind was too strong. It kept blowing the bee back.

Nate said, "Oh. Yeah. Well, the thing is, the Red Death Tea Society is obviously using the bees. Programming them with chemicals and mechanical quarks."

"Aren't quarks, like, the smallest thing there is? Even smaller than atoms?" When you're friends with Nate, you pick up a few stray bits of knowledge along with the random adventures and occasional injuries.

"Much smaller than atoms," Nate said. "*Much* smaller. The fact that somebody has actually managed to nudge them into mechanical shape is invigorating." Nate did indeed look invigorated. His cheeks were practically flush. He stuck his head out the window and waved back to the cars following us. They were keeping a safe distance, tracking us, even though we were now whooshing through the streets at a speed that I wouldn't think a human driver could match. We had Betsy on our side. Who did the Red Death Tea Society have on theirs?

The lead car was about a hundred feet back. I decided they were waiting for us to reach somewhere not quite so public, and then they'd make their move. We were zooming along Parade Avenue, with all the secondhand clothing stores, the comic book store, the bookstores, and the art galleries. It's one of my favorite sections of Polt, but it was going by so fast that I couldn't make anything out, especially while still struggling to unwrap myself from my seat belt.

"Catch that bee," Nate said. "We need it."

"Catch it how?" I asked. If it was a cricket or a grasshopper or a fly, I would've cupped it in my hands. This is because in such a situation a cricket would think, "*I'll make an irritating noise*," and a grasshopper would think, "*Hmm, guess I'll spit up some stinky juice*," and a fly would think, "*Guess I'll do some buzzing*." A bumblebee, however, would think, "*It's time for some top-notch stinging on the hands of this foolish sixth grade girl. You would think she'd know better*."

"I *do* know better," I said.

"What?" Nate asked.

"Nothing. But, again I ask, how am I supposed to catch the bumblebee?"

"Pet it."

"You're joking."

"I'm not. Betsy is spilling friendly scents into the air. The bee already likes us now, so just pet it, and it'll be your friend forever."

"Why would I want to be friends forever with a bumblebee?"

"Not really forever, actually," Nate said. "Bees only live for about a year. Usually less."

"Ooo, that's sad," I said, reaching out to pet the poor thing. It was still hovering in front of the air vent, and it bobbed up and down as I ran my finger over its back. It turned around and looked at me, which made me nervous, but it made a buzzing sound that was . . . friendly? Then, it darted through the air and landed on my shoulder. It seemed content.

"There," Nate said. "You caught her."

"Her?"

"Sure. Can't you tell by the buzzing?" Nate was entering a series of numbers on his remote control, glancing to me, glancing to the cars following us, and glancing up into the air, at something I couldn't see.

"You can tell by a bee's buzz if it's a girl or a boy?"

"Yes. Also, it stung you. Only female bees do that."

"Ooh. They're mean."

"You should name your bee."

"How about Melville?"

"That's . . . not very feminine. But it's okay, I guess."

"What do you think those guys are after, this time?" I asked, looking back to the cars following us. My bee pivoted on my shoulder, looking back along with me, already loyal.

"Umm," Nate said, unwilling to tell me something, which I always consider to be a bad sign. If I had any warning buttons on my shirt, they'd have been wailing like sirens.

"Nate," I said. "What have you done?"

"Umm," Nate said.

Betsy said, "Passenger Delphine Cooper, I might point out that today is Saturday the fourteenth."

"Yeah?" I said. "But what does that have to do with . . . with . . . oh. Oh no." I turned to Nate. He shrugged. The fact that it was Saturday the fourteenth meant that *yesterday* was the thirteenth. *Friday* the thirteenth. And that was a problem. Nate is so smart that he often grows bored, and to keep his mind lively he schedules himself to do three really stupid things every Friday the thirteenth, such as . . . in one recent instance . . . teaching math to a caterpillar. Sometimes his Friday the thirteenth experiments are fun. Sometimes they go awry. Spectacularly. From my side, I'm constantly puzzled why Nate does these things, but I've come to accept his oddities, because that's what friends do. After all, he never complains about my Cake vs. Pie meetings, or how I collect photographs of my meals whenever I eat macaroni and cheese at a restaurant (eighty-four of these photos, to date), and so we just . . . accept each other the way we are.

Which is slightly disturbing, I suppose.

Anyway, alerted by Betsy, I turned to look at Nate and said, "Yesterday was Friday the thirteenth."

"That's true," he admitted.

"Which means you probably did three really dumb things."

"I did," he said.

"Tell me about them," I ordered. I gave Nate the meanest look in my mom's arsenal, the one that could turn aside a tornado.

"Oh, okay," Nate squeaked. "I . . . ahh . . . I developed a deodorant that makes your underarms sweat more."

"You really do use your time wisely," I entirely lied, glancing back at the cars that were following us. "What's the next thing?"

"I made an Infinite Engine," Nate said. Melville, on my shoulder, buzzed in an inquisitive fashion, probably asking the same question I was about to ask Nate.

"What's an Infinite Engine?" I asked.

"Ooo!" Nate said, infinitely eager to talk about science. "I stabilized Nothingness after extracting electrons and neutrons from an atomic field, and bathed the field with gravitational waves, so that—"

"Bzzz?" Melville said.

"I know, right?" I told her. "But that's how he always talks. I think he's trying to say that he created a machine with . . . infinite energy?"

"That's right!" Nate said. "A small, self-contained, infinitely self-sustainable system. Limitless power! The possibilities are endless!"

"I see," I said. "And . . . I'm guessing one of those possibilities is that those guys in the cars back there want this thing, right?" I gestured to the cars following us.

"Um, yeah," Nate said, deflated that the news was turning bad.

"And what could Maculte and the Red Death Tea Society *do* if they got their hands on your infinite energy machine?"

"Um, bad things. The possibilities are still endless."

"Well, we can't let that happen, then. So let's hope we can lose the cars behind us, and—"

But it was at that point that I saw four more of the Red Death Tea Society cars. These new cars looked a lot like the other ones. *Exactly* like them, I suppose. Except that while the first four cars were *behind* us, the new ones were in *front* of us, roaring down the street in a line, side by side. There weren't any corners we could take. We were trapped.

"Hold on," Nate said. "This is going to be impossible."

He was enjoying himself, again.

The cars from behind were getting closer. Much closer. It looked like they'd just been waiting for their trap to close, for the other cars to block off our escape. Betsy was slowing down, having nowhere to go, and the four cars behind us were only a hundred feet behind, and I could see the drivers now. They were carrying guns. I'd known that was a possibility, but I'd still been hoping they were carrying tea.

"They have guns!" I told Nate.

"Idiots," Nate said.

"Why are they idiots?" I asked. It was comforting to hear they were idiots. I already had a genius-level friend, and felt no overwhelming need for any genius-level enemies.

Nate said, "Have you ever heard that saying about not bringing a knife to a gunfight?"

"Yes. It means that you should always be prepared, or something. But what does that have to do with—?"

"They brought guns to a wet suit fight," Nate said. He gave me the look of a person who was expecting me to say something like, "Wow!" or "Hah!" or "Hurray! We triumph!"

Instead, I said, "Huh?"

Nate sighed. His shoulders slumped. He said, "Wait for it, Delphine."

I did wait for it. Betsy had all but stopped on the street so there was little else for me to do, so I simply waited while the other cars came closer, closer, and I could see there were multiple men in each of the cars and that they were all wearing sunglasses and red suits and they were waving guns. They seemed exceptionally enthusiastic. They were only about hundred feet away. Fifty. Twenty. I was bracing for impact and gunfire.

And that's when it happened.

The wet suit swooped down from above. It was like an octopus or something, latching onto the lead car and grabbing tight, entirely covering the windshield. The car began to swerve and I could hear the driver shrieking, now driving blind, worried he would crash, except . . . he honestly didn't have to worry about running into anything on the street.

Because the wet suit became a *jet suit*.

Seriously, the jets kicked in and they were *powerful*. The jet suit nabbed the car up into the air and then dropped it on the next car, making a noise that I'll just describe by saying that it sounded like one car dropping on top of another. Add in a few exclamations of surprise, and you've pretty much got it.

The following cars slammed into the lead ones, creating a wall of smashed cars. Men began spilling out from the cars, jumping out, falling out, stumbling out. They were all waving their guns. Some of them were trying to shoot the jet suit, which had unhooked itself and was whooshing back toward us.

"Hold tight!" Nate said, which was unnecessary, because "holding tight" is something I always do when Nate is around.

The jet suit latched onto Betsy and grabbed us up. We began to rise into the air.

"Wheeee!" Betsy said.

"Guhll," I said, because it felt like it does when an elevator zooms upward much faster than you thought it would. Except in this case I hadn't thought there would be an elevator in the first place.

"It works!" Nate said.

"Did you think it *wouldn't*?" I screamed in a conversational tone.

"I estimated it had a sixty-three percent chance of simply tipping us over," Nate said. "The odds were against us."

"Guhll!" I said, because the jet suit was carrying us over the pile of wrecked cars, taking us twenty feet into the air. Since I'd recently fallen from over fourteen thousand feet, you'd think that a mere twenty feet would be meaningless, but it felt even worse.

"Bzzz?" Melville said. My bee was right in front of my face, making the buzz that she makes when she's confused (it really is distinctive) and flying in a circle. I decided she was perplexed as to why I was panicked about flying. If you can fly, it must be hilarious when other people can't.

I said, "I'm a little busy being utterly panicked, Melville. Can't you go sting the bad guys or something?"

She said, "Bzzz!" and zoomed out the window, just as the jet suit slid Betsy to a rolling drop on the street past the wrecked cars.

"Perfect!" Betsy said. Her wheels started spinning and squealing, and then we were racing off down the street. The crashed cars behind us had filled the entire street, blocking off the cars that had appeared in front of us, back when things had been only reasonably crazy.

Behind us, I could see the men from the Red Death Tea Society swatting at something, grunting in pain, running in circles, yelling curses, screaming out "Grgargh!" (which meant Melville had stung somebody's left arm), and "Flargrah!" (which meant my bee had stung somebody's right leg), and other noises like "Waghhrr!" and "Guhguhrr!" and "Yagghh!" . . . the meaning of which I did not know, but of course I could reasonably guess.

I tossed the tube of bee sting ointment out the window, and we sped off, leaving everything behind.

Let's talk about bees," Nate said. We were in his living room. Nate's parents, Algie and Maryrose, weren't home, so we could talk about anything without fear of them discovering how smart he is. Nate keeps it secret from them. Parents always want their children to be exceptional, but it makes them nervous when they are.

I was holding two invitations in my hands. One was from the League of Ostracized Fellows and the other was from the Red Death Tea Society. I looked up to Nate when he made a throat-clearing noise, trying to get my attention. He was serving refreshments. To be honest, it's not one of his higher-level skills. Because he's somewhat of a loner, he doesn't have much experience with having friends over, and doesn't have any idea of what to serve. This time, he was holding a cereal bowl full of olives, and he'd hollowed out three apples and filled them with chocolate. He also had tree juice. Yes. Tree juice. He said it was like orange juice, but from a tree. I drank enough of it to be polite and then asked him for some water and began picking out the chocolate from the apples.

"Bees?" I said.

"Yeah. Bees. Oh, I see you found my invitations."

"This one's really weird," I said. It was the one from the League of Ostracized Fellows. It was on stiff yellow paper, precisely folded, and had a letterhead illustration of two men standing back-to-back, but still holding out their hands as if to shake hands, just . . . in the wrong direction. The letter read . . .

League of Ostracized Fellows
PO Box 83 101 99 114 101 116
Norumbega

Dear Nathan Bannister

We would like you to . . . Oh. That was rude. I didn't even say "hello." Hello, Nathan. My name is Reggie Barnstorm. I'm the head of the League of Ostracized Fellows, though I should point out that I only won the election by three votes, so please don't consider my authority to be absolute. Still, a majority is a majority, and on behalf of our league I'm pleased to offer you a membership in our society. Your duties would include an annual processing fee of $50.00 (fifty) US dollars, a "substantial-benefit-to-mankind" scientific presentation of your invention at our spring and fall conventions, and a pledge to dedicate your life to battling the Red Death Tea Society, which has been responsible for an unfortunate percentage of the world's ills, and which has reduced our own membership by 72.58 percent during the last decade, owing to its plague of kidnapping, brainwashing, and outright "disappearances."

We hope that you'll agree to join our league, and I should point out that you would be entered into the rotation to provide snacks at our monthly meetings, and that three of our members have severe peanut allergies, so those are right out.

Lastly . . . there will be unfortunate consequences should you refuse. Did that sound rude? My apologies. It *was* a threat, though. And somewhat vague. We're still voting on any possible consequences. It's just a mess here. Sorry about that.

Sincerely,
Reginald "Reggie" Barnstorm
27th President, League of Ostracized Fellows

"Hmmm," I said, putting the letter down and then picking some more chocolate out from inside an apple. I was sharing the snack with Melville. She'd come flying into Nate's house about a half hour after we arrived.

Betsy had sensed her arrival, so Nate was able to open a cupboard door and deactivate the house's automatic defenses, allowing my bee to fly in through the door. I was so proud of Melville that I wanted her to have some chocolate, but she was far more interested in the apple. That worked out okay.

"Hmmm?" Nate asked. He was asking what my own "hmmm" had been about.

I tapped on the letter and said, "The League seems a bit . . . scattered."

"They're not used to interacting with others," Nate said. "It makes things weird for them." He was crumbling crackers over the bowl of olives, I guess to make it more appetizing? He shoved the bowl closer to me, and I pretended not to notice.

"So you turned them down?" I asked.

"Yes, though I did consider joining. But, really, some of their ideas are beyond ridiculous. Can you believe they're still working on a system of time travel based upon linked atomic twelve-point vector recontrol?"

"Ludicrous," I said.

"I know, right? It's like they're completely ignoring duality of infinite mass combined with zero length."

"First grade material," I said, trying to pretend I knew what we were talking about, but I'd apparently pushed it too far. Nate gave me a look. Then frowned.

"Sorry, Delphine," he said. "I forget that most people don't know this stuff. It's just . . . it's just . . . I get carried away whenever you're around. It's so exciting to talk with you!" I admit that something lurched in my stomach when he said that. That said, it was probably something to do with that tree juice I drank, not anything to do with Nate acting somewhat romantic, because we're not *girlfriend* and *boyfriend* no matter how much my friends taunt me (Liz is the worst), and it was only coincidence that Nate and I fell into a silence filled only with the sound of me blushing. Yes, I was blushing so hard that it was audible. It was making a *bzzzz* sound that . . .

Oh, wait. No. The buzz was Melville, happily devouring her apple. To cover up my embarrassment, I looked at Nate's invitation from the Red Death Tea Society. Like Nate had earlier mentioned, the letter was on thick parchment, with ragged edges. It looked very official, hand lettered with red ink. I sniffed the ink, worried it was blood, but it smelled more like jasmine. I looked up from the letter and Nate was inches away, holding a spray bottle, staring at me. He pulled the trigger, and a big burst of smelly water splattered all over my face.

My first impulse was to punch him.

I went with it.

"Guhhnk!" Nate said. He fell off the couch and landed on the floor. The spray bottle fell from his hand. Melville was hovering next to Nate, thinking about stinging him, but I waved her off. Bosper, Nate's Scottish terrier, came bounding into the room and looked to me, then to Nate (on the floor, rubbing his upper arm), and finally to the spray bottle that was rocking back and forth on the floor, slowly coming to a halt.

Bosper said, "Did Delphine do a punching?" I should mention that Nate "accelerated" Bosper's brain. He can speak now. And do math like nobody's business. He's much better at math than he is at speaking.

"I did a punching," I told Bosper.

"Bosper is going outside for a pooping!" he said, skipping across the floor and going out the doggie door.

"Why'd you punch me?" Nate asked, standing up, staying well out of range.

I pointed to my face. It was dripping wet.

"Oh," Nate said. He sat on the couch next to me, well within punching range again, but now understanding what had happened. "I should've explained why I did that. Whenever they send out letters, the Red Death Tea Society puts mind-control chemicals in the ink. I was worried your brain would be altered when you sniffed the ink, so I sprayed you with an antidote."

"Oh," I said. And then, "Yes. You should have told

me." I settled back on the couch, cracked open another apple for the chocolate, and read Nate's "invitation" from the Red Death Tea Society.

It read . . .

Red Death Tea Society
PO Box 44 65 61 74 68 0d 0a
Circle Nine

Young Boy Nathan Bannister . . .

Your membership in our society is demanded. Your inventions have sufficient merit that you will either join us or be eliminated. Refuse us, and, if need be, we will make the earth barren in order to eradicate your existence. Your only recourse is to submit to our society, to kneel before the Supreme Commander, or else the seas will boil, the mountains will fall, those you love will vanish, and you will hear nothing but the wails of sorrow that cover the land like ash. You have three days to comply.

. . . Jakob Maculte

PS: If you stop into our recruitment center before Thursday, we're serving Tieguanyin tea. The oxidation of the oolong teas is particularly wonderful.

I said, "They seem serious about their tea." Nate nodded.

"Also about eradicating you," I added.

Nate nodded, again, then said, "They'd rather not, though. Right now, I calculate Maculte doesn't have the confidence that he could take over the world. He's brilliant, but his thoughts are all based on math. He doesn't have the ability to calculate the unexpected."

"Well, it *can't* be calculated, right? That's why it's unexpected."

"Exactly, but he thinks I could do it. He believes that I think so far out of the box that the box doesn't exist, for me, and Maculte wants that kind of wild card in his corner. That way, the Red Death Tea Society itself would become too hard to predict. Too hard to stop."

"Hmm," I said, thinking of how Maculte might not be so happy with Nate joining the Red Death Tea Society if Nate then provided tree juice and cracker-covered-olive snacks in the break room. I was considering going into the kitchen and checking for anything more normal to munch on (Nate's dad, Algie, is actually a good cook, and often has leftovers) when my phone buzzed. It was a text from Liz, containing an image of her with Ventura, Stine, and Wendy. They were trying to look serious, but lack talent in that area.

The text read, Are you okay? Do we need to beat up any bees? (Please say that we don't. Bees are scary.)

I took an image of my melon-face and sent it along in reply, adding, Modeling career on temporary hold, but otherwise okay.

Liz texted back, Where are you? That's not your house.

I sent, Nate's place.

My phone immediately lit up with multiple texts.

Wendy wrote, Nate's? You guys . . . together?

Nate is a boy, Ventura wrote.

Hearts, Liz wrote.

Stine wrote, Gossip. Tell us everything.

Nate knows a lot about bees and bee stings, I wrote back to all of them. That's all there is to it. We're not dating. Where are you guys?

Changing the subject, are you? Liz wrote back. We're at the mall. You sure you're okay?

Fine, I wrote. See you tomorrow? Liz and I often get together on the day after our Cake vs. Pie meetings in order to decide if we've learned anything, to see if we feel any progress has been made, and mostly to apologize for all the really horrible things we've inevitably said to each other during the debate.

Tomorrow for sure, Liz wrote. Have fun with not-boyfriend. I thought about writing something in return, but Melville interrupted me, buzzing past my phone to land on my shoulder. She was making a sound like *zoww-wrrr*, which I'm pretty sure meant she'd eaten too much of the apple and was flying a bit heavy.

"Oh good," Nate said. "Your bee. Would you mind if I took a look at her?" I narrowed my eyes, moved a bit back, and put my hand in front of Melville.

"What all would that entail?" I asked. "You're not going to try to . . . *dissect* her, are you?"

"No. I just—"

"And you'd better not be thinking about bombarding her with any radioactive materials, or mutating her into a giant bee, or—"

"Why would I mutate her into a giant bee? That wouldn't be very smart." I could have answered with actual words, but sometimes that's just not necessary. Instead, I used the same expression that Mom uses on Dad when she's mad at him, and I slowly pointed to Proton, Nate's cat, sunning himself in the window, staring out at the world. Noticing the attention, Proton did nothing at all, because that's just how cats are.

"Oh," Nate said, properly chastened.

"Indeed," I said, pressing my point. Soon after I'd first met Nate, I discovered that he'd recently transformed his cat, Proton, into a giant. An absolute *giant*. Taller than buildings, crushing cars when he walked, stalking me during a rampage . . . that sort of thing. It was all part of Nate's "do three dumb things every Friday the thirteenth" initiative.

Nate said, "I won't need to hurt Melville at all. Wouldn't think of it. She'd probably sting me, anyway."

"She does sting," I admitted. "That's actually how I met her." I turned to look at Melville, and she had the good grace to be embarrassed. She turned away, buzzing anxiously.

"Here," Nate said. "Can you have her crawl onto my finger?" He held out his finger. I looked to my bee and said, "Melville, land here, please."

I tapped on Nate's finger with my own and then added, "And *don't* sting him."

Nate smiled.

I said, "Unless he *tries* something. Then get him *good*."

Nate frowned.

Melville buzzed away from my shoulder, making the *zowwwrrr* sound again. She really did need to cut down on the apple intake. She buzzed a bit hesitantly in the air, hovering an inch or so away from Nate's outstretched finger, then pivoted back to look at me. I nodded. She turned back around and landed.

"Thanks," Nate said. I wasn't sure if he was talking

to me or to Melville. He stood and walked to the nearest bookcase, grabbing a magnifying glass from a shelf full of Sherlock Holmes books.

He said, "This might be a little startling." As he spoke, he was bringing up the magnifying glass to study Melville, and, at the same time, Bosper came back through the doggie door.

"What's so startling about a magnifying glass?" I asked, walking over to Nate, seeing if I could peer over his shoulder and have a look at Melville, although I wasn't sure there'd be much we'd be able to discern. It was only a magnifying glass, after all.

Click.

That noise was Nate hitting a button on his magnifying glass.

And I was suddenly face-to-face with a ten-foot-tall bumblebee.

Yeah.

Right in front of me.

I said, "Gyahhhh!" as loud as I could. Apparently, it was right in Nate's ear, because he shrieked in pain. Bosper, meanwhile, came bounding to the attack.

"Dog bites bee!" the Scottish terrier yelled, jumping up onto the back of the couch and then leaping toward the monstrous bee with his teeth bared, chomping down on . . . nothing.

He fell right through the giant bee.

I noticed this, and I did think it was odd, but I was quite busy screaming at Nate.

I yelled, "You promised you wouldn't mutate her into a giant bee! That is, in fact, something *very specific* that you promised!"

Bosper, spinning in confusion on the floor, barked, "Teeth missed bee?"

"Bzzz," Melville buzzed. But it wasn't very loud. Definitely not as loud as it should have been. With a bumblebee that size, she should have been shuddering the walls and bursting the windows, but—

"Here!" Nate said. He was thrusting his finger in my face. Which was rude, especially in all the excitement and especially since he had a bee on the end of his finger.

Wait. A bee?

It was Melville.

"Bzzz," she said.

"Okay, what?" I said, looking to Nate. How could Melville be in two places, one of them regular and one of them giant?

Nate said, "If I tell you something, will you promise not to punch me?"

"No. But you still have to tell me."

"That's fair. Well, it's not, but I do think I owe you another apology. I should've told you that my magnifying glass is actually a microsphere nanoscope projector."

"Which means?" So far, it didn't mean anything about Nate *not* deserving a punch.

Nate said, "It means that when I held it up to Melville it captured a three-dimensional image, which it then enlarged to giant size so everyone could see it." I thought about Nate's words. They seemed rather scientific, but not so scientific that I couldn't understand them. I turned to the giant bee. I tried to touch it. My hand simply passed right through the image and the bee didn't so much as twitch, although Melville, on Nate's finger, made a *bzzz* of interest.

I said, "So . . . this giant bee is just some ultra-high-tech movie hologram thing?"

"Well, it's a bit more technical than that. You see, since light travels at—"

"You are answering yes or no, or you are getting punched."

"Yes," Nate said, rather quickly. "It's just a high-tech movie hologram thing."

All the tension went out of the room. I did punch Nate in the arm, but not anywhere near as hard as I could have. Proton, in the window, had never moved.

Bosper started chewing on the edge of a rug, declaring, "Bosper is making attacks on the rug!" Apparently, the danger had passed. Unless the rug counted.

I looked closer at the giant high-tech movie hologram of Melville, hardly barely at all terrified of it anymore. The mandibles were as long as my arms. The proboscis (that's the long sticky tongue-thing: I looked up the word) was slurping all around. The antennae looked like saplings twitching in a strong wind. Bees have compound eyes, and also three of what are called "simple eyes," much smaller ones near the top of their compound eyes. I guess that makes them five-eyed, but it's still mean to call a bee that. Also, do compound eyes count as more than one eye? If so, Melville was, like, a thousand-eyed, which sounds like some creature from mythology, something that a Greek hero would've used a magic sword to vanquish, instead of something that pollinates flowers and occasionally perches on my shoulder, ever since we became friends.

All in all, friend or not, Melville looked pretty horrifying. Her eyes were reflecting me a thousand times over, and there were even more reflections in the bits of metal that were . . .

Wait a minute.

"Bits of metal?" I said.

"Bosper is alert!" Bosper said, reacting to the tone of

my voice, letting the rug drop from his mouth and standing to attention.

"Right," Nate said, moving closer to the giant hologram. I resisted the urge to pull him back. I was so freaked out that I picked up the cereal bowl of olives and started eating them, one after the other.

"They're actually a metallic-crystalline compound substance," Nate said, peering closer at the giant image of Melville. She herself was now perched on my shoulder, buzzing in confusion.

"Hmm," Nate said, studying the weird metallic things, or the crystalline things, the "definitely *not supposed to be there*" things. They were covering the tops of Melville's front legs. Several metallic dots on each leg.

"Scent traps," Nate said. "Each containing approximately a mole of perfume."

"She's wearing perfumed moles?" That didn't sound right. That's something I would have noticed.

"Not that type of mole," Nate said. "That's something you would notice. No, in this case, a mole is a unit of measurement."

I said, "I suspect you are about to confuse me."

Bosper said, "Bosper is going back to chewing on the rug and not getting in trouble, okay? Is true? Okay?" He was skipping in place, leaping up and down. I used my foot to nudge the rug, and Bosper snarled and went into full attack mode.

Nate said, "A mole is the amount of any chemical substance that contains as many elementary entities as the atoms you would find in twelve grams of carbon 12. Pure carbon 12, of course."

"Of course," I said. "But . . . and this may shock you . . . I'm rarely searching for elementary entities at all, not in carbon 12, or carbon 1, or carbon 2, or even that rascal, carbon 3."

"You should!" Nate exclaimed. "It's lots more fun than any video game!" He was looking at me, more pleased than ever before. At first I thought he was just happy to be talking about moles, but then I realized he was thrilled that he'd been a good host, as I'd eaten the entire bowl of olives.

"So, what do these things *do*?" I asked, moving a finger through the metallic scent traps.

Nate said, "I designed them to release an arrangement of perfectly timed scents in order to modify a bumblebee's behavior."

"Wait. Hold on. Stop. Did you just say that *you* designed them?"

"Umm . . ." I could see the worry in Nate's eyes, and I could also see that he was worried about getting shoulder punched.

"Don't worry, Nate," I told him. "I promise I won't punch your shoulder. Just tell me the truth."

"Okay," he said, relaxing. "So . . . yesterday was Friday the thirteenth."

"Right. And you made that extra-sweaty deodorant, and you made the Infinite Engine, and you . . . you . . . hmm. You never told me the *third* thing you did." I could feel my eyes narrowing, almost out of my control. I could feel my fingers clenching into a Shoulder-Punching fist, totally within my control.

"Well, you know how your birthday is coming up?" Nate said.

"I do. I am totally aware. *Keenly* aware, in fact." I had a long list on my bedroom wall, a list of seventy-seven potential inventions I'd been hoping Nate would make for my birthday, such as a machine that senses the nearest cakes (although, to be honest, I'm enormously talented in that area already) or something useful on an everyday basis, such as pills that would make my brother Steve uncontrollably fart, or a designer jetbelt, so that I could soar through the skies. Really, with Nate's genius, the possibilities of amazing birthday presents was endless.

"I made you a present," Nate said. His eyes were glinting.

"Ooo," I said, thinking of the inventions on my wish

list. Maybe he made me *all* of them? Although, seventy-seven gifts was probably asking too much. I'd say . . . thirty would be sufficient. Maybe fifty.

Nate gestured to the giant hologram-thingy of Melville and said, "I've been adhering these scent traps to tens of millions of bees, so that they will fly in precise formation and spell out 'Happy Birthday to Delphine Gabriella Cooper!' across the whole of the sky."

"Really?" I said. My fist was clenching again.

"Really!" Nate said. His eyes were glinting again. They should have stopped.

"So, of *all* the things you thought I might want, *tens of millions of bumblebees* was first on your list?"

"No. I actually thought you might want a designer jetbelt, but it was Friday the thirteenth, so I went with the bees with the modified behavior."

I went with punching Nate's shoulder.

"Oww," he said. "You promised you wouldn't punch me."

"True," I said. "But then you modified my behavior. And let me ask you this. If they were supposed to sing me 'Happy Birthday' or whatever, why did the bees *sting* me?"

"Good question," Nate said. "Here, look at this." He was pointing to the giant Melville hologram, where I could see a small switch on one of the metallic traps.

"*This* isn't mine," he said. "It's Maculte's. I recognize his work. He's added a remote control device on all the bees, basically turning them into robots that he can force to do whatever he wants. Meaning, the Red Death Tea Society has corrupted your birthday present."

"Those fiends," I said, gritting my teeth.

"This is really dangerous," Nate said. "With tens of millions of bees under Maculte's control, the Red Death Tea Society now has an army that could terrorize the entire city."

"Well, so far, they've only terrorized *me*," I said. Melville buzzed in embarrassment. Nate nodded, working out some sort of calculation in his notebook, scribbling a series of numbers, letters, and peculiar symbols.

"Right," he said. "I calculate that Maculte was trying to use an attack on you either to distract me away from the Infinite Engine, or possibly even to intimidate me into giving it to them."

"Hah!" I said. "That would never work."

"It totally would," Nate said. "I couldn't allow you to be hurt. You're my . . . friend." He'd hesitated before he said "friend." I saw it. I heard it. I have to report it honestly, but I can just as honestly say that he was busily working out another equation in his notebook, and was probably distracted, and it didn't have *anything* to do with Nate possibly about to say that I was his girlfriend, because neither of us would ever even *think* about that.

"So now you're going to give away the Infinite

Engine?" I asked. "Just because bees stung my butt? You can't! The Red Death Tea Society is evil! And they only have tea, not chocolate. I mean, if they were the Red Death *Chocolate* Society, I could understand, and I can't say that I wouldn't be tempted to help them myself if they were the Red Death *Cake* Society, but—"

"I won't ever help them," Nate said. "And they can't have the Infinite Engine, ever. But I'll need to be more alert. I'll have to increase the security on this house, and on you. The robots will help." He gestured to the air, or I guess to some robots, or . . . something.

"Robots?"

"Oh, they're nano-robots," Nate said. He tapped on some papers on the dining table and said, "Take a

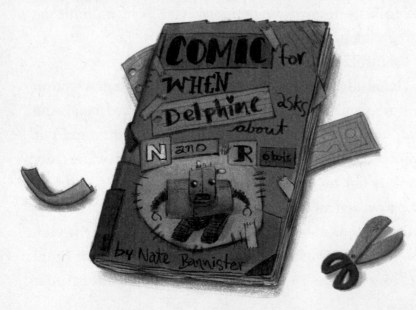

look at this." I picked it up. It was a handmade comic book titled *Comic for When Delphine Asks about the Nano-Robots*.

"You knew I would ask?"

"There was a 94.87 percent possibility."

"And you want me to read this?"

"Yes, please."

"You couldn't just tell me?"

He reached over and turned the first page, then tapped on it. I looked down. There was a cartoon drawing of Nate saying, *"It's more fun to make a comic!"*

"Okay," I said. "I *do* like comics." I turned the next page. There were a series of smiling faces, with arrows that said, *"Robots!"* pointing to them. I turned the next page. There was a single speck of black. A pinprick. It was labeled, *"Another robot, this time to scale."* Next to it was a line. The line continued off the right side of the page. I turned the page. The line went across both pages, and then continued on the next page. And the next. And the next. And the next. And so on. For twenty pages. Then, on the last page, the line was labeled, *"This line has been the thickness of a human hair, proportionate to that robot speck you saw several pages ago."*

"You made really small robots," I said, looking up from the comic.

"Bosper helped," Nate admitted, gesturing to the Scottish terrier. Bosper looked up, woofed, then ran a couple of steps closer to me, at which point he turned around and gave a warning bark to the rug. Satisfied, he turned back to me.

He said, "Bosper did good math and coughed up a quarter!"

"Good job with the math," I told him, reaching down to pet him. "But, quit eating quarters. They're not good for you."

"No?" Bosper said. He gave a hopeful look to Nate for, I think, permission to keep eating quarters. Nate shook his head. Bosper slunk back to the rug, plopped down, and started to chew on the edge. But his heart wasn't in it anymore.

I asked Nate, "So, these tiny robots, are they like the ones we had searching for cat hair?" Nate and I'd grown to know each other during the incident with the giant cat, the incident that was completely and totally his fault. It was terrifying at the time, but now, looking back, it was *still* terrifying, but also a bit fun. And it had involved microscopic robots looking for cat hairs, as these things so often do.

"That's right," Nate said. "Nano-robots." He gestured to . . . to the air again, I guess?

I said, "You mean they're here? All around us?"

"And *in* us. We inhale them. They're an early warning system and a security defense system, all in one."

"You made robots that I'm *inhaling*?" My eyes narrowed. My designated Nate-punching hand (it's my left) balled into a fist. I dredged up another of the expressions that Mom gives Dad. It's the one that makes him retreat.

"Uhh," Nate said. "Umm, well . . . yeah. But they're *really* helpful! You won't even know they're there! And now, the main thing is that, short of seeing us with their own eyes, the Red Death Tea Society members won't be able to find us in any way. No tracking us with cameras or satellites or with robots of any kind!"

"That's great, Nate, but . . . next time? Let a girl know before she *inhales robots*." I was staring at him. Making him nervous.

He said, "Uhh, enough about robots! So . . . the thing about the bees, Maculte's remote control device would need a series of localized transmitters to emit the coded scents, drawing the bees closer to Polt, and to us, contributing to the overall chaos and providing the Red Death Tea Society not only with a vast army, but a distraction from Maculte's true purpose of stealing the Infinite Engine. We need to disable the transmitters before Polt is totally swarmed."

"Okay," I said. "So, it sounds like you want me to break

things, and, Nate, I have to tell you, I am *very* good at breaking things. So, where are these transmitters at?"

"Maculte would want them mobile. And, disguised. And, close to us." Nate was jotting down equations on his pants as he spoke. "I'm thinking . . . he's probably used our classmates as transmitters."

"Our classmates? How?"

"By secretly linking the bee-controlling scent codes to our classmates' biorhythms, attuning the transmitters to their heartbeats, to their breathing, encoding the transmitters to work on our classmates' natural frequencies. We'll need to somehow disrupt them, to un-attune them, or else hundreds of thousands of bees will be drawn to Polt. Millions of bees, even. Then, the Red Death Tea Society could act with almost total impunity in the midst of all the pandemonium."

"I suppose it *does* make sense to use our classmates to cause chaos," I said. Our classes at Polt Middle School are not known for their lack of chaos, after all, though I'm normally proud to contribute to the overall commotion and consider myself to have a leadership role. "So . . . *all* our classmates, or only *some*?"

"I've narrowed it down to five," Nate said. "Based on a vector analysis of commonplace proximity alignments."

"Cool," I said. "Exactly what I would have done. Who are they?"

"Kip Luppert. Gordon Stott. Jeff King. Marigold Tina. And Tommy Brilp."

"And . . . would they *know* about these bee-transmitter thingies?"

"No. Maculte could have easily inserted the transmitters without their knowledge, so our classmates are perfectly ignorant. Um, I should have said 'innocent.'"

"Yeah. You should have. And now, how should we do this? If they've had these transmitters secretly implanted, how can we . . . what did you say, 'un-attune' them?"

"Ooo!" Nate said. "That's the fun part! All we'll have to do is knock them unconscious. Or put them to sleep. Or really do anything that overloads their bio-systems. Scare them, even. Or just get them really excited, like . . . by showing them cool math problems!"

"Math problems *would* be exciting!" I said, excited to have a chance to exhibit my assuredly world-class acting skills by pretending to be excited about math problems. Unfortunately, I kind of burped when I spoke, and that threw me a bit off. It also scared Bosper. I wondered if it had upset his bio-system. Could that be the solution to everything? I could just . . . run around burping in front of my classmates?

I burped again while thinking about burping. My stomach didn't feel so good. It had to be the olives, right?

Maybe the tree juice? What else could it have been? Other than having been nearly obliterated by bees, falling out of a helicopter, and inhaling tiny robots?

Nate said, "We'll have to protect the Infinite Engine from the Red Death Tea Society, but that won't be truly possible until we protect Polt from what I'm calculating could be a devastating bee army. I can't have the city in danger. I can't . . . I just can't have you in danger, Delphine." Nate was staring at nothing, blushing.

"Burp," I said. Or rather, I belched.

Nate said, "I never minded it so much when it was just *me* in danger, but now things have changed."

"Burp," I said. It was the wrong time, but burps never make appointments.

Nate said, "So, even though our priority is to stop Maculte from getting the Infinite Engine, we can't truly do that until we stop the bees. The ones you saw this morning are just the beginning. I won't have this city in danger! I won't have *you* in danger. I won't." He had an intense frown, and he thumped his fist on the table, scattering the letters, meaning the ones from the League of Ostracized Fellows and the Red Death Tea Society and . . . hmmm. There was a letter I'd missed before.

I picked it up.

"Oh," Nate said, watching me. His face had gone oddly

pale. I've seen him fall from immense heights and fight giant cats, but I've never seen him so anxious. Was the letter even worse than the death threats from the Red Death Tea Society? What could possibly scare him so bad?

I looked down to the letter.

And started reading. Out loud.

I read, "Dear Susan. Your smile makes my heart collapse into a singularity, such as that caused by the dilation of time inside a black hole's area of effect, owing to the relativistic effects of the immense gravity and the extreme speed of all matter being drawn into the vortex."

I stopped. Looked up.

Nate was having trouble breathing.

"What *is* this?" I asked him. The handwriting was . . . *his*. It was an unfinished letter. I kept reading.

"Your hair, Susan, shines like a quasar, emitting intense radioactive energy across the whole of the electromagnetic spectrum." I stopped. And I put down the letter.

"Oh gosh," I said, tapping on the letter. "Nate. Piffle. Is this a love letter to *Susan Heller*?" Susan is one of our classmates. She's one of those girls who shop as a lifestyle, and who probably thinks an adventure starts with a fifty-percent-off sale, and who was entering beauty pageants before she'd ever opened a book.

"No," Nate said. "It's not." He was twitching.

I said, "Nate. You're twitching." In response, he twitched more.

"It's okay, Nate," I told him. "I'm not mad. Why would I be? I mean, Susan isn't really very interesting, but it's no business of mine. You and I are just friends, right?" I gave him a friendly punch on the shoulder. He grimaced. I'd hit him a little too hard. Being extra-friendly, I guess. I opened my mouth to apologize, but I burped instead.

"Sorry about that," I said. Melville buzzed through the air and landed on my shoulder. I burped again. She flew away.

"Did you make some special burp-olives?" I asked Nate.

"Why would I do that? And . . . *how* would I do that?" He wasn't asking me the second question: he was talking to himself, clearly now considering the possibility of making burp-olives. Maybe it was something he could do on the next Friday the thirteenth, when he did his three not-so-very-smart things? Thinking about Nate's dumb things led me to thinking about the Infinite Engine, and about what Maculte could do with it. Then I had to quit thinking about that, because it gave me a sinking feeling. Also a burping feeling. Well, more like a *roaring belch* of a feeling. So, I burped. This time, Proton got up and left the room. I'm just going to go ahead and point out that while Bosper and I had been thinking we were fighting a giant bee, we hadn't made enough noise or commotion to scare Proton out of the room. But my belch did. So . . . you do the math.

I heard Bosper scurrying along on the floor, and then he was standing in front of me. Staring at me. His eyes were huge.

"Bosper?" I said.

"This dog is much impressed by the belching!" he said, leaping up onto the couch. "Delphine made thunder!"

"Okay, thanks," I said, waving him off the topic, though, to be honest, I felt a stirring of pride. Also, another belch. I let it rip. Bosper watched me with awe.

"Fourteen belches!" he said. "Fourteen is a companion Pell number, and an open meandric number, and the base of tetradecimal notation, and—"

"Yes. I *know* I'm belching a lot, Bosper. I can't help it." Melville came and landed on my shoulder, buzzing in querulous fashion, probably worried about me. Do bees ever belch? I was thinking of asking her, or asking Nate, and so I was looking to Nate just as he finally thought to switch off the button on his magnifying glass so that Melville's giant version disappeared, but . . . something else appeared instead.

Something far more hideous.

Maculte.

"Eww," I said. "Nate. Make that go away." I waved to the image of the smirking leader of the Red Death Tea Society.

"I'm . . . not doing this," he said. He was looking at his magnifying glass, clearly confused. It's not often I see Nate confused. I didn't like it.

"Hello, children," Maculte said. My skin went cold.

"Bosper makes attacks!" Bosper yelled, and he leaped for the hologram, and of course right *through* the hologram, and then smacked into the floor, tumbling to a stop.

"Bosper does not make attacks?" he said.

"It's just a hologram, Bosper," Nate said. "You can't bite it." Nate had shaken off his confusion and was now facing the hologram.

He said, "So I assume you've overridden my input data for the quad-laser control? That's how you're projecting your own image?"

"Of course," Maculte said. "And I assume you've understood that I've taken control of your trained bumblebees, and that I now have a vast army poised to strike?"

"Yes," Nate said. "Obviously." Bosper was now attacking the hologram again, chomping his teeth on nothing. Melville was buzzing angrily on my shoulder.

Maculte said, "You've failed to respond to my invitation to join my society, Nathan. And you've failed to hand over the Infinite Engine, as demanded. So now the time is up. The entire city will fall to a bumblebee plague, endlessly stung, succumbing to my army. All of Polt's citizens . . . eliminated. That is, unless you join the Red Death Tea Society and present me with the Infinite Engine, right now, at this very moment. You have no other options. Join now, or fall with the city." I'd been thinking that Bosper was being silly with the way he was biting at nothing, but . . . listening to Maculte, seeing that smirk . . . I found myself kicking at his intangible shins. And also belching.

Nate said, "How about instead of doing what you want, I fight? How about Delphine and I stop your bee army?"

"You don't understand, boy," Maculte said. "You have no bargaining chips. No recourse. Your time is up. We will commence our bumblebee attack in ten—"

"I predicted something like this," Nate said. "Which is why I've had Sir William, my robot gull, deposit a colony of genetically modified super-termites on your Ceylonese silver-tip tea crops near Nuwara Eliya in Sri Lanka."

"You've . . . what?" Maculte asked. His smirk had vanished. He was actually shivering.

"The termites will reach adulthood in a matter of hours," Nate said. "At which point they will be hungry. So very, *very* hungry. If I were someone who wanted to protect my tea crop, I'd be doing something about it, right away. Immediately. As in . . . now." Nate's eyes had narrowed like an Old West gunfighter's, and his smile radiated that sense of power he has, and I'm sure the drama of the moment wasn't overly diminished by the astounding volume of the burp I accidentally let fly.

"You . . . can't," Maculte said, staring in horror at Nate. He could barely give voice to his words. "I . . . you'll . . . this *isn't* over, Nathan." With that, the hologram vanished.

Nate turned to me and said, "Well, that's given us some time, but we'd best hurry." I either belched in agreement with Nate's thoughts, or I just plain belched. It was a solid one, either way.

Nate frowned at me and said, "I . . . don't think I should serve tree juice or bowls of olives anymore."

"Please don't," I said, patting my stomach.

"The chocolate in the apples, though, that was a good idea, right?" He looked so very hopeful that I couldn't possibly break his heart with something so callous as the truth about his snack-serving skills.

Instead, I did something much more soothing. I put a hand on his shoulder and I said, "Nate, let's go fight an entire army."

Nate and I were at Polt Pool, the best swimming pool in our city, largely because it's free and because Polt Pond (which is actually a lake, but "Polt Pond" is more fun to say than "Polt Lake") is sixteen miles out of the city and it's apparently a *huge* chore to drive children that far. Or at least to drive them home afterward, because parents are twitchy about having wet children in the car. I know this because it's one of my parents' lectures, along with "Seriously, don't forget to seriously clean your room, seriously" and "No, you cannot have a pet bear," the latter of which wasn't my fault because the bear cub followed me home after Nate and I had been in Polt Park (eight thousand acres of possible bigfoot sightings, by my own personal reckoning) and weird things tend to happen when Nate is around. I've mentioned this to him, and he contends that *I'm* one of the weird things that have happened to him. He meant it nice. And I took it that way.

Hmmm.

I wonder how my parents are going to react to a pet bee. At least bees don't cost much to feed. But all of that was for another time. What was important now was to protect the Infinite Engine (before we left his house, Nate went off for a bit and then told me he'd secured the Infinite Engine in the safest area possible) and of course we had to disable the transmitters before Polt was swarmed with bees.

So we went to the pool.

Jeff King was there.

He's entirely unlikable. A pest. His mother is mayor of Polt. This causes ongoing problems. Simply put, Jeff is a thriving menace. I haven't ever been able to convince Nate to send Jeff to the moon, but I *have* come close. And while I normally avoid having anything to do with Jeff, this time Nate and I simply *had* to get close enough to him to somehow disable the bee transmitter, before millions of bees attacked the city.

Nate and I were standing at the edge of the pool, watching what Jeff was doing. When some people go to the pool, they like to hang out with their friends, talking, paddling around, playing games. Other people like to swim, or dive in the deep end, sinking all the way to the bottom to get that uncanny feeling of isolation.

Jeff's a bit different. He likes to sneak up on people and dunk their heads underwater. He also really enjoys holding people underwater after he's dunked them.

"How are we going to do this?" I asked Nate. I was wearing my new one-piece bathing suit, the one with an image of a fluffy bunny on the front and a drenched bunny on the back. Nate was wearing a pair of swim trunks. They were black. Or green. Or red. What I mean is that the colors were constantly changing. One minute his swim trunks would be red and the next they'd be entirely green. I'd asked about that, and he'd said that it was an unfortunate though interesting side effect of all the mechanics woven into the fabric. I'd thought about asking what mechanics could possibly go into a pair of swim trunks, but Melville had buzzed meaningfully just before I asked. I'd looked to my bee. She'd buzzed again, and I'd realized she was right. I didn't want to know.

Nate said, "Follow my lead." He began walking toward the deep end, which is my favorite area. I love diving. There's something about that moment when you leave the diving board, and all you can do is fall. All the choices have been removed, and there's nothing left but the *action*. It's exciting.

Nate climbed up to the lowest diving board. It's

five feet above the water. He considered it, but kept climbing. I was glad. There's not much of a rush with a five-foot dive.

He climbed up to the ten-foot diving board, thought about it, but again kept climbing. I wasn't as happy about that, because that meant we were going to be diving from the twenty-foot board. Usually I'd be all for that, but two Sundays ago I'd tried a double flip from the twenty-foot board and had managed what was definitely history's all-time best belly flop. If you want to know what it felt like, I can tell you this: *you're wrong*, you do not want to know what it felt like.

But . . . I was still following Nate's lead, and so up we went.

"There he is," Nate said, pointing to Jeff King in the shallow end. There were maybe fifty people in the pool, not counting however many people Jeff was holding underwater at the time. So, make it sixty people, tops.

"Are we going to jump him from here?" I asked. It's true that Jeff was all the way across the pool, but I've learned not to underestimate Nate.

"Umm, no," Nate said. "That's a bit far. Although I've learned not to underestimate you. We only came up here to dive, though. I thought we might as well have some fun while we're at the pool, and I remember that you like diving."

"Do *you* enjoy diving?" I asked.

"I could," Nate said.

There was . . . something about the way he answered.

"You've never dived from a diving board, have you?" I asked. The thing is, the people who make fun of Nate in school, the kids who say that he's just an egghead and that he never gets out of the house, doesn't play any sports, and so on . . . those people are wrong. Nate *is* an egghead, sure, though I would never call him that, because it's somehow come to mean something negative, even though it means you're really smart. People *should* be smart. People should *want* to be smart. It's fascinating. It means there's always something new happening in your mind, which is more than I can say for most people, and if I ever did have a boyfriend, I'd want him to be a lot like Nate, or in fact *exactly* like Nate, except *not* Nate. Of course.

And, back to the topic at hand, Nate *does* get out of the house. A lot. And he participates in a variety of sports. They're just not . . . regular sports. This is, after all, a boy who'd once, on a Friday the thirteenth, taught sword fighting to a mouse. I suppose that's a sport, but not even Polt Middle School . . . where we are normally considered somewhat offbeat . . . has a sword-fighting team for rodents. So, no, Nate doesn't play football, or baseball, and while he does enjoy watching me at soccer practice, he's not what you'd call an athlete. So, yes, this was his first time diving in a pool.

He shrugged, ran to the end of the board, bounced once, and then did nine flips, entering the water with barely a ripple. Melville let out a huge *bzzzzzz* of applause.

"Hah!" I said, looking down at him once he'd surfaced. "If you think you can beat me with a paltry nine flips, you're absolutely right! There's *no way* I can beat that!"

"I think you're missing the point of trash-talking," Nate said, treading water twenty feet below me.

"You'd better hope I miss *you*," I said, leaping off the board. I did a very respectable two and a half flips on the way down. What was less respectable was that I was trying for three flips. Still, there wasn't a ripple when I entered the water. Because it was more like a tidal wave.

"Grahhh!" I said, but just in my mind, because on my recent horrific dive I'd yelled out a certain word (whatever word you're thinking of, it was worse), and of course yelling things underwater is not the work of a genius. This time, I knew better.

I plunged about ten feet down into the water, then kicked back up to the surface, right in front of Nate.

"That looked like it hurt," he said.

"Owww."

"Did you mean to do that?" he asked.

"Owww."

"You need to hug your legs more when you're spinning. And tuck harder, because it gives your flips more power."

"Owww."

"Diving is just math, really," Nate told me. "Executing a dive is merely transforming an equation into physical form."

"Owww," I said. Melville let out a sympathetic *bzzzz* and landed on my head. Nate started to say something else, but Melville buzzed out a warning to him, and then, together, the three of us swam over to the shallow end.

Time for business.

-💡-

"Let her up, Jeff," Nate said. Jeff King was currently holding Emelia Soney's head underwater. Emelia is four years old and aspires to be a pony. There isn't anything about her, as far as I know, that should make anyone want to dunk her head in a pool, other than that she cries when it happens. Some people are into that. I have a name for those people, but I am not allowed to say it at the dinner table. Or in the kitchen. Not the living room, either. Or my own room, the laundry room, the hallways, bathrooms, closets, yard, car, streets, sidewalks, or anywhere at all, though I *had* screamed it when falling from the helicopter at fourteen thousand feet above the ground and so far I wasn't in trouble. Maybe I'd found a loophole.

Jeff King turned around when he heard the authority in Nate's voice. Jeff's shoulders were slumped, knowing he was in trouble, but when he saw it was only Nate talking to him, Jeff broke into a big chubby smile. His head-dunking hand quivered in anticipation.

"Or else I'll be mad," Nate added. A ripple went through Jeff's body, and his smile became even more enthusiastic. I knew what he was thinking.

He was thinking that he couldn't believe his luck.

He was actually being *challenged*.

By *Nate*.

"Thank you," he whispered.

-ℚ-

So, Jeff King dunked Nate. Just reached out and grabbed the top of Nate's head like one of those arcade claw machines, the ones where you always think you're about to grab the absolute best prize, but then the claw is clutching nothing but air. Except in this case the claw (meaning Jeff's hand) actually *did* grab the absolute best prize (meaning Nate's head) and instead of dropping that prize into the chute, the claw plunged it underwater.

I think maybe I've lost control of my analogy. What I mean is that Nate was dunked underwater. And held there. Likely drowning. My first impulse was to yell for Candy Crable, the lifeguard, but of course she was all the way on the other end of the pool, flirting with a group of boys, oblivious to what was happening. It was all up to me. I grabbed Jeff's arm, but he was like a rock. I couldn't force him to let Nate back up, but I struggled for a bit, nonetheless, or at least I struggled until there was a menacing *glunk* sound that turned out to be Jeff's other hand grabbing my head.

"So much dunking!" Jeff said. There was something like a giggle.

"Dunking all the time!" he said. He was steadily pushing my head underwater.

"All this dunking is so . . . so wonderful!" I think maybe he was starting to weep out of pure joy. He really *was* in his element. I, however, was not. My head was barely out of the water.

"Whooosh!" Jeff said. And he pushed down.

"Whooosh!" the water said, as it thematically whooshed up past my mouth and my nose, rushing over the top of my head.

And then I was being held underwater, looking over to Nate.

Nate gave me a thumbs-up, which I thought was out of place. I mean literally out of place. *Underwater* is not the place for a thumbs-up. And then I noticed that Nate wasn't having any trouble breathing, which is kind of odd because not only *should* a normal sixth grade boy have trouble breathing underwater, but he shouldn't be trying to breathe underwater in the first place. Such things are just not done.

Nate's fingers were tapping on the side of his shorts (they were currently black) in what I at first thought was a nervous gesture, but then I noticed he was actually typing. There was a keypad on the side of his shorts. Nate was entering a string of numbers and then he said, "It's okay if you breathe."

I said, "It's no use talking underwater, Nate. I can't possibly understand you."

"You just did, though. And you talked back, too."

"Yeah." I shrugged. No sense in trying to understand it. I figured Nate was going to explain what was happening soon enough.

Right on cue, he said, "I'm using kinetic water flow to

promote oxygen patches and eliminate dangerous nitrogens."

"That's truly excellent," I said, not having any idea what he was talking about.

"The nano-bots I talked about earlier, they make it easier for you to adjust."

"Of course they do," I said, as if I were someone who had understood something, which I was not.

"Your body wants to continue on a single evolutionary path," Nate said. "But the nano-bots open other possibilities, other paths. Like breathing underwater."

"Thanks for the help, nano-bots," I said, giving them a thumbs-up. It was at that point that I noticed Jeff King was wearing swimming trunks with pictures of horses and monster trucks, neither of which are particularly known as aquatic, and therefore do not belong on swim trunks. I also noticed that, despite how Nate and I weren't fighting against our class bully (why struggle when you can breathe water?), Jeff himself was seriously thrashing around, struggling with all his might. I wondered what was up with that.

Nate began saying something about his tiny robots, the ones I'd apparently breathed in at some point, telling me they were processing our vastly reduced oxygen intake in some way, but I became more intent on the legs of everybody else in the pool. That's all I could really see.

A bunch of legs. Skinny legs. Short legs. Thin legs. Long legs. Hairy legs. Tattooed legs. There were a lot of legs. And *all* of them were doing the same thing . . . moving as fast as they could to the edges of the pool, hurriedly leaping up and out of the water, fighting for the ladders and that sort of thing. Everybody was suddenly in a *big* hurry to leave the water. Everyone except Jeff King.

"What's going on?" I asked.

"Not sure," Nate said, noticing the mass exodus along with me. "Let me do some calculations." His fingers began tapping on the sides of his swim trunks again. He frowned. Looked around. Nodded. He reached out and poked Jeff King in the leg. Nodded. Entered some more numbers.

Then he looked to me.

"Where's Melville?" he asked, looking around as if my bee might be swimming below the surface of the water, perhaps after having dived off the high board, neither of which is something that bees ever do.

"Not . . . below water," I said.

"Of course not," Nate said. I think he was embarrassed. Sometimes he gets so caught up in the higher calculations that he forgets the lower truths.

By then the only people left in the entire pool were me, Nate, and then Jeff King, who was still holding us underwater. Where had everyone else gone? And why? It was very strange.

Nate said, "I'm calculating a 97.9 percent chance that Melville got mad about you being held underwater and went on a stinging spree."

"Ooo," I said.

"Hmm," I added.

"That's not good," I stated.

I reached up to Jeff's hand and slowly disengaged his fingers from my hair. He didn't resist my efforts. Once I was free of his hand, I moved to one side, and surfaced.

I looked around.

Took in the situation.

I sank back down under the water.

"What's going on up there?" Nate asked.

"I calculate a one hundred percent possibility that your hypothesis about Melville going on a stinging spree was correct."

"If it's a hundred percent, that would technically make it a fact, not a possibility."

"Then it's a fact that a lot of people have big red melon-shaped bee stings on their arms and shoulders and faces," I said. "And, see this . . . ?"

I pointed to Jeff King's legs.

"Yes?" Nate said.

"This is one hundred percent of Jeff King that's *not* covered in bee stings."

"Ooo," Nate said.

"That's what Jeff keeps saying. Except in a much higher voice. Like a painful whine."

"Did you see Melville?"

"Yeah."

"Where is she?"

"Perched on Jeff's face."

"Did you tell her to quit stinging him?" Nate asked.

"No."

"Oh. You didn't?"

"Should I have?"

"It would've been the nice thing to do."

"I know that."

"Oh," Nate said. I decided it was probably best if we left the pool, so I reached over and worked Jeff's fingers out from their clutching grasp on Nate's hair. Again, Jeff didn't resist. Once we were free, I stood up with my head out of the water. Jeff's face was entirely swelled up with bee stings. Melville was circling him like a tiny, angry plane. A tiny, angry, *heavily-armed* plane.

"That's my bee," I told Jeff.

He said, "Aghhhh." It was a whisper. Melville, spotting me, gave a buzz of joy and landed on my shoulder.

"Been stinging people?" I asked her. I was just making conversation. It was, after all, entirely obvious what she'd been doing. She gave a noncommittal buzz, as if she was worried that she might get in trouble over what she'd done. I just shrugged. She'd certainly overreacted . . . since the pool was currently surrounded by possibly sixty people, most of them sporting bee stings . . . but I couldn't blame Melville too much for stinging Jeff, and why had everyone gotten out of the pool and just gathered around, anyway? Why didn't they keep running? It's not like Melville was only guarding the *water*. If anything, once everyone got out of the pool, they were even easier to sting.

"That crazy mad bee is on your shoulder!" Candy

Crable yelled. She's in her early twenties. Short hair. She reminds me of someone I'd see in a television commercial about surfers. She was frantically waving a flotation device back and forth, which I suppose she thought would ward off any imminent bee attacks.

"Oh gosh," I said, pretending I was in danger, because I certainly didn't want everyone to know that Melville was *my* bee, that *I'd* brought her to the pool, and that everyone getting stung was, you know, sort of *totally* my fault. Above all else, that had to be kept secret.

"No problem!" Nate shouted to everyone. "The bee is hers! It belongs to Delphine! Delphine Cooper! She brought it to the pool!"

He turned to me and said, "There. That should calm everyone down."

Well.

It didn't.

☀

Nate and I were able to escape the enraged mob, though not because we are superior climbers or first-rate runners. We weren't necessarily faster than everyone else when we were running across the parking lot, and we definitely weren't more agile when we were scrambling over the chain-link fence, because I had to help Nate climb, and by the time we made it to the top there were several people who almost grabbed us, like in the horror movies where the heroes barely escape the zombies.

The truth is, Nate and I would've been brought down from behind if it wasn't for Melville dive-bombing anyone who came too close, or if Betsy, Nate's car, hadn't heard our distress call (which was me yelling distressful curses at the top of my lungs) and zoomed forward to meet us, not even stopping as we piled into the back (Betsy had flung open her doors) and squealing away from the parking lot with Melville riding on the front of the car like a hood ornament.

Anyway, Nate and I did make our escape, and we did run fast, and I would seriously like a video of me climbing that fence, because while Nate didn't do all that well (he claims his hands were still slippery) I think I probably set a world record in the combined Climb & Scream event.

And I'm absolutely sure I took first place in the Punching Nate in the Arm for Announcing the Bee Was Mine competition.

chapter 5

We were blocks away when it hit me that we'd not only left all our normal clothes behind, but that we hadn't managed to disable Jeff King's bee transmitter.

"Oh dang," I said.

"Already on it," Nate said.

"Already on what?" I asked. We were zooming through Polt's fashion district. There were fashionable people loitering about, which is what fashionable people do. I mean, almost everyone loiters about, just on a casual basis, but fashionable people do it on a very conscious and even professional level.

Nate said, "Well, I could tell by your increased irritation levels that you'd remembered how we left all our clothes and belongings behind, and that we, in your mind, weren't able to disable Jeff King's transmitter."

"In my mind?" I said. "What do you mean by that?" Nate was behind the wheel (Betsy was doing all the driving, of course, and projecting an image of a distinguished gray-haired man behind the wheel) and had asked Betsy to turn all her fans on high in order to dry us quicker. It really wasn't working all that well, but Nate's hair looked nice blowing in the wind.

He said, "It's just that we *did* disable the transmitter."

"We did?" I was rolling down the window because I could tell that Melville was tired of riding on the hood. Not surprising, I suppose, because she must have been exhausted after stinging so many people.

"Because of her," Nate said, pointing to my bee as Melville flew in through the window and landed on the dash.

"Because of her?" I said.

"Well, all we needed to do was disrupt Jeff's biorhythms in order to un-attune the transmitter."

"Yeah?" Nate has a tendency to *teach* me answers rather than *tell* them to me. I know it's best for me in the long run, but I was sitting in a car wearing nothing but my sopping wet bathing suit and I was in an entirely "short-term" frame of mind.

"So, even a single bee sting could accomplish that."

"Oh," I said, remembering what Jeff looked like after

Melville was through with him. "Yeah. I see what you're saying. He certainly *did* look disrupted."

"Yeah," Nate said, smiling. "He did."

"But what about our clothes?" I asked. "What did you mean when you said you were already on it?"

"I've dispatched Sir William to collect them," Nate said.

"You did? You *do* know it's not normal for robot gulls to go into locker rooms and take clothes, right?"

"They won't know Sir William is a robot."

"You *do* know it's not normal for a gull of *any* type to go into a locker room and take clothes, right?"

"Sure. But I don't like being any kind of normal, and you don't, either."

"Hmmm," I said. "You've won this debate." By then we were pulling over to the side of the street, just short of all the booths and tables for Polt's Saturday Antique Market, a street fair where an amazing array of furniture and art and trinkets from the past were for sale.

"What are we doing?" I asked Nate.

"Well, we'll need clothes, and the nearest place is here. You don't mind vintage clothes, do you?"

"I *love* them," I told Nate, already jogging through all the various booths, because the fabrics on vintage clothing are always so strange, so colorful, that whenever I wear them I feel like I'm the star of a movie or a television show, either of which was preferable to my current feelings of being sopping wet in a bathing suit with bunny decorations.

So I pressed through the crowds of eager shoppers and I ran past all the vendors who were aggressively trying to make sales, hurrying past all the antique furniture and the vintage collectibles and the booth selling handmade chocolates, finally stopping at a tent with racks of vintage clothing. There were skirts, Capri pants, and amazing shoes, and hats and gloves and shirts and stockings still in their packages from the 1960s. Nate had barely begun looking at trousers before I'd assembled a small selection of no more than eighty items that I wanted to try on, and I was searching for a dressing room when the woman running the booth stepped in front of me.

"Excuse me," she said.

Her tone was unpleasant.

Her eyes were narrowed.

She was a short woman with big glasses perched on her nose, and the sound of her voice was so chilling that everyone around us, all of the other shoppers in the tent, went silent. Even the other vendors . . . the ones at the nearby tables who were yelling about all their fabulous items for sale . . . went quiet. It was *so* quiet that I could hear the water dripping from my swimsuit.

"Perhaps you could come back at a time when you're *not* a puddle?" the woman suggested in her unfriendly tone, tugging at the clothes I had in my hands. From the corner of my eye, I could see Nate coming forward, ready to help, holding out his *special* credit card, the transparent one with the golden elephant's head symbol, with Nate's name below it, along with a row of numbers and a big fat letter A. It's called a gold elephant card, and there are only three of them in the entire world, because in order to have one you have to be unthinkably rich. In fact, you have to be *so* rich that nobody will ever yell at you for trying to buy clothes even if you're dripping water everywhere.

"Here," Nate said, whispering, holding out the credit card so that the woman could see it, but his voice was so hushed that she didn't even look in his direction. Why was he *whispering*? It was clearly time for decisive action.

I took the card from his hands.

I held it up where everyone could see it.

And, as I was saying, "Don't worry! We have a gold elephant card!" I could see, from the corners of my eyes, Nate's own eyes going wide as he waved for me to stop.

As I finished my loud declaration, Nate's shoulders slumped.

Then . . . the entire market went silent.

The woman with the big glasses immediately quit pulling at the clothes I was holding. Her mouth was hanging open. Seconds ticked by. And still, there was just silence, which felt *extra* silent considering how all the vendors had been causing such a clamor, yelling for everyone to buy things.

Then, from out of the silence, from a couple of tables away, I heard a voice.

"Did someone just say she had a *gold elephant card*?"

"I think so," said a different voice from maybe twenty feet away.

"Here? In our market? A *gold elephant card*?" That was a man's voice from several rows away. His voice sounded . . . hungry.

"Where *is* it?" another voice asked. "I have things to *sell*!"

It was then that people began peeking in the tent. A crowd was gathering. A crowd of vendors. A crowd that was shambling forward. A crowd that was staring at the credit card in my hand, the one that Nate was quickly taking away from me, trying to hide it before . . .

. . . the crowd surged forward.

So Nate and I were running again, and Melville was again stinging people, trying to keep the crowd from catching us, much as she'd done at the pool when Nate had foolishly yelled out the totally wrong thing at the totally wrong time, which was entirely different from how I'd yelled out something entirely understandable.

Nate and I had to leap over tables and dash past booths, running through the crowds while all of the vendors were reaching out for us like zombies, so that we were barely able to grab a few pieces of vintage clothing (and eleven handfuls of homemade chocolates) and make our frantic escape, scrambling over a wall while the crowd surged behind us, yelling about all the cool things they could sell to the owner of a gold elephant card.

Fifteen minutes later we were back in the car and I was wearing coffee-colored Capri slacks and a yellow button-down shirt with matching yellow shoes, holding an incredible purse from the 1920s that was absolutely covered in glittering stones but somehow still subtle. Nate looked dashing in vintage slacks, shoes, and a dark brown sweater. Melville was flying all over in the car, looking at us from different angles, playing the role of an insect fashion critic. I had to wonder what bees know about fashion. A lot, probably. They pretty much rock that "black-and-yellow" look.

"Hmmm," Nate said. "Look at that." He pointed up through Betsy's windshield. I leaned forward and peered into the sky. There was a black speck, high in the air.

A helicopter.

"Is that . . . ?"

"Reggie Barnstorm and the League of Ostracized Fellows. Yes. Looking for us, I'd expect. Betsy, could you magnify?"

In the next second, Betsy's windshield acted like a magnifying glass, and our view of the black speck became a large black dot, and then a helicopter, and in only moments I was looking at an image of Reggie Barnstorm and his green suit standing in the open doorway of the helicopter, a few bee stings evident, blowing a bubblegum bubble as he held a strange device out the door. It looked like a 1990s cell phone with a small satellite dish.

"What's that?" I asked Nate.

"He's scanning for us. Looking for our DNA signatures and other trace identifiers."

"He doesn't look very happy," I said. In truth, he looked mad. He was energetically scowling.

"No," Nate said. "The nano-bots in our systems disguise us. There's no way he can find us like that. *They* can't, either." At this last, he gestured outside, to where two men in red suits were stomping along the sidewalk, pushing people out of their way, using a similar device to the one Reggie was holding.

"The Red Death Tea Society," I said. The men were both holding cups of tea. "You sure they can't find us?" My stomach was turning over, again.

"Positive. Like with the League of Ostracized Fellows, the nano-bots will disguise us. And Betsy's holograms make us appear like other people through the window, and even make her look like an entirely different car. So *they* can't see us, but *we* can see them. We can work undetected."

"Okay," I said. "But, let's get out of here. Where's the next transmitter to disable?"

"Gordon Stott is at Popples," Nate said. Popples is a burger restaurant. You put in an order (I prefer the Turkey Meteor) and then sit at a table where a series of hidden conveyor belts soon whisk your order to you, with the food popping out of a trapdoor in your table like a jack-in-the-box.

"How do you know he's there?" I asked.

"Tracking," Nate said.

"Tracking?" I asked.

"Tracking," Nate said, more emphatically this time.

"Driver Nate," Betsy said. "I believe that passenger Delphine would enjoy an explanation of what you mean."

"Huh?" Nate said. "Oh. Yeah, I guess that makes sense." I nodded, reaching out a hand to touch Betsy's dashboard as a gesture of appreciation. Just as I did, the windshield went black for a moment, and then the view of the outside world was replaced by a detailed map of Polt.

"What happened to the windshield?" I asked. I wasn't overly concerned with how I could no longer see out of the car. I mean, maybe that's something I'd normally panic about (in fact, it is *absolutely* something I'd normally panic about), but since Betsy just drives herself, I was guessing she could see.

Nate said, "It's not a windshield. It's an interactive thought pad."

"Thought pad?"

"It's like a touch pad, except you don't need to touch it. You just think about what you want it to do, and it registers your command."

"And, how does it do that?" I asked.

"Would you understand if I told you about linked nuclei harmonization?"

"I don't even understand your question about whether I understand what you're talking about."

"Okay then, just . . . just make believe that tiny robots are in your brain, relaying your thoughts to the screen."

"Is . . . that true?"

"Hmmm," Nate said. "I suppose it's possible. Once I created my nano-bots they had a small chance of developing individual intelligence." He waved off the thought with a quick gesture and said, "But that's not exactly how the technology is based. It's . . . uhh . . ." He hadn't stopped for his usual reason (meaning that I wasn't showing my particular expression of confusion, the one where Nate knows it's useless to continue) but because the windshield had suddenly gone all wonky. It was now just a series of fuzzy colors with repeating patterns, a chaos of reds and blues and greens and so on. Looking at it made my head hurt. It made no sense at all.

"What's up with all the flowers?" Nate said. He was squinting at the windshield.

"Flowers?" I asked.

"Yeah," Nate said, tapping on the windshield. "This is a bed of flowers. Well, it's how a bee would see a . . . Oh. I get it." He turned from the windshield and looked to Melville, who was buzzing in the air a few inches away from the windshield, occasionally thumping against it, then retreating with that buzz of hers that I've come to understand means confusion or frustration.

Nate said, "Interesting. The windshield is picking up Melville's thought patterns. I'll need to study that later. Hadn't thought it was possible!" He was positively radiant. A bit handsome, too, in those new clothes of his. He was dressed exactly like I would prefer my boyfriend to dress, if I had a boyfriend, which I don't.

"How come you can see like a bee?" I asked.

"Oh. Remember when I put on that mechanical dog's nose?"

"Yes," I said. "It was the first day I met you."

"Right. I've streamlined that technology so I can smell like a dog can, all without wearing the nose."

"Bees are not dogs," I said, happy to throw a little science in Nate's direction, for once.

"No. They're not. But I enjoy developing skills, so as long as I was working on the dog's nose I invented a way to see what insects are seeing, and also sonar like a bat, and I can sometimes jump like a kangaroo."

"You're like . . . the best crazy person I know."

"Thanks!" Nate said. He gestured to his bag in the backseat and added, "I use pills for the abilities. Kind of. They're more like tablets with nano-bots inside that give me temporary powers."

"So if I swallowed one, then I could do all these strange things, too?"

"Yep. I could make some for you, if you'd like."

"Naww. Don't bother. I don't want any super-cool abilities."

"Oh. Okay." He shrugged.

"Uhh, Nate?" I said. "You really need to create a tablet that gives you the ability to detect sarcasm. But, do that later. Now, we should find those transmitters before the city is overrun with bumblebees."

"Right," Nate said, and his brow furrowed for just a moment, and the map of Polt came back on the windshield.

Melville buzzed in disappointment, landing on my shoulder. I carefully petted her.

Nate said, "Here's where the rest of the transmitters are at." The map had four red dots. The first was at Popples, a dot that Nate said represented Gordon Stott. And there was another red dot at Tommy Brilp's house (Tommy, obviously, and it was actually over his garage), and another at Plove Park (apparently, it was Kip Luppert), and there was a dot for Marigold Tina at Polt Middle School, the home of the Crimson Pterodactyls.

"Nice," I said. "So you're tracking our classmates with the transmitters."

"Sure," Nate said. But just like I've grown to understand what Melville means when she buzzes in a certain way, I've also come to understand certain tones of Nathan Bannister's voice. This time, the undercurrent of Nate's voice was saying, "Sure. Although there's more to it that I'm not telling you."

"What are you not telling me?" I asked.

"Oh, uh . . . it's not only our classmates with the transmitters I'm tracking." He tried to stop talking but I gave him a Delphine Special (my best glare) and he reluctantly added, "I guess I track the rest of our classmates, too." Many more red dots appeared on the map.

"And?" I said. I still wasn't liking Nate's tone of voice.

"And the rest of the entire school," Nate admitted. Lots of new dots on the map.

"And?" I said. Melville buzzed next to me, adding in what was, I'm quite sure, a very menacing bee frown.

"And most of the rest of the town," Nate conceded. The map basically exploded with red dots, far too many of them to make any sense of it. They almost buried the map.

"Kind of creepy, Nate," I said. "But for now, let's just take it down to our friends with the secret transmitters, and deal with them one at a time." He nodded, and the map returned to having only four red dots, and then the windshield screen showed a crystal-clear view of Popples, the restaurant. I wasn't sure why.

"Why is it showing that?" I asked.

"Because that's what's outside," Nate said. "It's not projecting mental images anymore." He tapped the windshield and said, "Just glass, now. We're here." Nate opened the door and got out, heading for Popples. Melville flew out the window and hovered, waiting for me. I stuck my head out the side window and, sure enough, we actually were at Popples.

"It's a strange world," I said.

"It sure is," said Betsy, the car.

chapter 6

Welcome to Popples," the woman at the counter said. "What would you like?"

"Some sanity," I said, emphatically.

"Excuse me?" she asked, raising an eyebrow.

"Nothing," I said. "I mean, just some Popples fries and a lemonade." This time, the clerk only nodded and began entering my order in the register. She was a bit old to be working at a fast-food restaurant. Possibly in her late twenties. And she was too ... too *something*. She looked like she belonged strolling through Paris's Left Bank fashion district, because she was somehow managing to make even the Popples uniform (green and red, with an image of a cow and chicken looking bewildered while being catapulted into space) look stylish.

She had black hair, a sharp nose, and immaculate skin.

Her name tag said "Lorie."

Melville didn't like her.

"Oh, you have a bee?" Lorie said. There was the briefest of hesitations as she frowned at Melville on my shoulder. "Should I kill it?"

"No," I said.

"Bzzz," Melville said, with a bit of menace.

Nate said, "I'll have a Turkey Meteor and a glass of ice water, please. Also . . . a side order of Popples potato poppers."

"Sure thing!" Lorie said, still frowning at Melville.

While we were waiting for our food at the counter, I looked around the restaurant, searching for Gordon Stott. It wasn't a very long search, because it wasn't very crowded. There were three men sitting together, all of them in dark suits, wearing sunglasses, intently staring at a basket of chicken poppers on the table in front of them. Occasionally, one of them would reach out and eat one. They didn't look my way, and they weren't talking at all.

At another table were three women dressed like teenagers in some music video, except they were at least a decade too old to be dressed like that. They were loudly talking about classes in their high school, and events in their high school, and teachers in their high school, and so on.

But . . . no Gordon Stott.

"Is that bee a *pet*, then?" Lorie asked.

"A friend," I said. Melville buzzed in appreciation.

"How strange," Lorie said, but I was barely looking at her, because Nate was subtly trying to get my attention.

I should explain about Nate and his subtly. Much like how sarcasm goes completely over his head, subtly is also lost to him. While he can apparently grasp the very nature of the universe, the theories of subtlety remain far too complex for the genius that is Nathan Bannister. So while most people who wanted to act subtle would have cleared their throats in a meaningful way, or perhaps tugged on my shirt, Nate had a different tactic.

He said, "Delphine, I need to talk to you privately, without her overhearing us." He pointed to Lorie. She raised an eyebrow.

I said, "Well, that's real subtle, Nate."

"Was it?" he said. "Good. I was worried."

"I was being sarcastic."

"Oh. I missed it."

"Yeah. You did." I pulled him away from the counter, then whispered, "What did you need to talk to me about?"

"Tea."

"Did you want me to order some for you?" I asked. "I

thought you just wanted water?" I turned to Melville and added, "How about you? Do you want anything?"

Nate said, "I don't want tea. I meant that I believe we've walked into a trap."

"No. We walked into a fast-food restaurant. It's almost the same thing, though."

"I mean . . . the Red Death Tea Society. I think . . . they're here." When he said that, my stomach flipped a bit. I tried to look subtly around the restaurant, and I like to think that I have a bit more ability in that area than Nathan Bannister. I had Melville fly off my shoulder and buzz across the seating area, with me following her around, making it seem as if I was trying to get her to land on my hand, but in reality just using it as an excuse to get a better look at everyone.

And I realized Nate was right. The men at their table and the women pretending to be in high school, they had the horrible lean menace of assassins. They were furtively staring at us, or pointedly *not* looking toward us, and they were clenching their fingers and they positively reeked of tea.

The Red Death Tea Society was there in the restaurant.

And we were in trouble.

"Hmm," I said. Then I looked over to Nate, back at the counter, and gave him a subtle nod of my head.

"Find anything suspicious?" he called out.

"What? Uh, *no*! Just, uh, looking for a place to sit. That's all I'm doing."

"Did you notice how everyone is drinking tea?" Nate said, loud. I'd been hurrying back to him, trying to stop him from saying anything else that would blow the game, but with that, I slid to a stop. And, yes . . . I *had* noticed that everyone was drinking tea. The men in their suits, the women pretending to be teenagers . . . they all had extra-large cups of tea. They were all assassins, and Nate was right; we'd walked into a trap.

Lorie strode out from behind the counter and locked the front door. Was she one of the assassins?

"I suppose you know who we are," she said.

"I don't have the slightest idea," I answered. Maybe if Nate and I pretended we didn't know who we were up against, then we could catch them by surprise and—

"The Red Death Tea Society," Nate said, looking around the seating area. He paused, then gestured to Lorie and said, "You're Luria Pevermore."

"Huh?" I said. "She is?" Luria is the brilliant but deadly chemist, second in command for the Red Death Tea Society.

"Of course," the woman said. With that, there was a slight wrinkling in the air, like ripples moving across the room, and a disguise fell away from Luria, revealing her true self. We could see her wide mouth, her green eyes, and high cheekbones. A few freckles appeared on her cheeks and arms. Her hair changed from black to red, like mine, though hers was darker. I wouldn't say it was more luxurious or any silkier, but, well, okay . . . it was. Mine curls a bit.

Her smile went darker. Smaller. Crueler.

The men in the suits stood from their table, holding their teas in one hand and some particularly interesting pistols in their other hands. The weapons looked like science-fiction ray guns made of glass, and I was somewhat curious to know exactly what they could do, but not at all interested in any demonstrations.

"And I suppose the two of you know how we managed to surprise you here," Luria said, gesturing to Popples.

I said, "I don't have the slightest idea."

"Of course," Nate said. "You must have used pulsed light to refract your signatures." I slid closer to Nate and nodded with what he'd said. Pulsed light. Refracted signatures. Of course. It seemed so obvious, now. (I had no idea what he was talking about.)

"And do you understand what's going to happen now?" Luria said. She'd walked a few steps closer. Her shoes squeaked on the tiles, and the sound matched that of the straw in her plastic cup when she sipped her tea.

The three women who were pretending to be teenagers had torn away their horrible fashions to reveal dark red bodysuits that hugged their every curve, and also every curve of all the weapons they had stashed all over. Their eyes were narrowed, intent, not even taking their gaze off Nate and me whenever they had a drink of their tea.

I raised my hand.

Luria looked to me.

"Yes, Delphine?" she said.

"Can I go to the bathroom?"

"Now?"

"Standoffs make me queasy."

"You'll have to hold it," Luria said. Her every move was like that of a snake. I was trying to decide if she was exceptionally limber or if she used special tablets similar to Nate's, except that while his could make him see the world through a bee's eyes, her tablets made her as sinuous as a snake.

Eww. I don't like snakes.

I was trying to come up with a good way to go to the bathroom (this was not the first stage of an amazing escape plan: it was the first, only, and quite *desperate* stage of an "I need to go to the bathroom" plan) when I heard Melville buzzing. She'd landed on Nate's hand. From the corner of my eye, I could see that Nate had worked a black pill of some sort out from his pocket and into his fingers. Then, quite casually, he let his hand drop at his side, holding the pill between two of his fingers. Melville grabbed the pill and took to the air. Flying. Slowly. I could tell she was straining. The pill was almost as big as she was.

"What do you want?" Nate asked Luria. "You already know I'll never give you the Infinite Engine. Just leave us in peace."

"No," Luria said. "No, never that. It's true that Maculte holds tight to his hopes of you joining us, aiding us, but . . . I've studied you, Nathan Bannister. You don't see the world the way I do. The way *we* do." She gestured to the others, with her hand barely missing the unnoticed Melville as my bee lugged the tablet through the air.

Luria said, "And because you don't see the world properly, because you're no good with tools, because—"

"Nate's really good with tools!" I said, speaking up because one of the women in the bodysuits had noticed Melville and was starting to frown, and I needed to distract her. Also, Nate totally *is* good with tools. Not only hammers and saws and that sort of thing, but the last time I was over at his place we'd been in his tree house (one of his four laboratories, and the one with the best ventilation and the most squirrels) and he'd showed me a set of tools that looked like tiny metal squids or something, with just . . . weird things flailing all over. They were tools of his own invention. And he was good with them.

Nate told me, "Luria means other people. She calls them 'tools.'"

"Oh," I said.

"Precisely," Luria said. "Compared to my intellect, a normal human is no more intelligent than a rubber mallet. It would insult my genius to treat them as my equal. It's the duty of the Red Death Tea Society to educate others."

"Educate them?" I said. That didn't sound so bad. Education is good, right?

"She means treat them like slaves," Nate said. "To show them their proper place. Maculte and Luria believe that it's the duty of anyone they believe is less intelligent . . . meaning everyone else . . . to *serve*. The ultimate goal of the Red Death Tea Society is to construct a servant class. To assign numerical codes that quantify everyone's worth, and to force them to stay within the boundaries allowed by their assigned numbers."

"Oh," I said. "*That* type of evil." Melville was still hefting the pill across the room. She'd had to take a rest stop, landing on a table. There was a very small *click* when she landed and the tablet hit the table. I could hear her gasping for air, clearly exhausted from carrying the pill. It would've been like me trying to pick up a refrigerator and then running with it.

Luria said, "Nathan, you may have managed to distract our leader for a time, but his work continues. While he's eradicating the termite infestation in our tea crops, I've been entrusted with continuing to destroy this city. And you along with it. You will be dissected. Your brain studied. Probed for its secrets. Why should I simply steal the Infinite Engine when I can steal the brain that made it?"

"Boring," Nate said. He yawned, covering his mouth with his hand. I was the only one who noticed him swallowing one of the black pills, using the yawn to disguise what he was doing. Melville, meanwhile, had taken flight again. She'd pushed the pill to the edge of the table, grabbed it with her legs, and then launched off into the air, falling almost to the floor before adjusting to the weight and regaining some height. I could hear her straining.

"Boring?" Luria said. She'd taken out a small device, one that looked like a pencil made of braided wires. "Then let's see if we can't make this more exciting." She slid the device along the top of a table and there was a horrible sound, like when a muffler is hanging low off a car, grating against concrete, dragging on the pavement. There was a tiny puff of smoke. The table fell in half.

There was a smell of fresh bread. It was a pleasant smell, not acrid at all.

"Congratulations," Nate said. "You've invented a passably interesting saw."

I said, "Sorry, but I seriously *do* need to go to the bathroom." Nobody paid me any attention, though I guess even if I'd been excused to go off to the toilets, there was no way that I was going to leave Nate alone. Luria had been talking about . . . dissecting him? Seriously? I was shuffling closer to Nate, wanting to protect him, but he was a good ten feet away. The woman in the bodysuit, the one who'd noticed Melville, was walking closer, openly staring at my bee as Melville strained across the room toward me. Melville was only a yard away from me, and I thought about stepping forward, but at that moment Luria reached out and clamped a hand on my shoulder.

She was cold.

Like, cold . . . *wrong*.

"Brrrr," I said, shivering, and it did *not* help with how seriously I needed to go to the bathroom. I thought about saying something about how cold Luria was, but then I abruptly had a really good view of the cutting device in her hand, because she put it on my forehead, right between my eyes.

There was that strong smell of fresh bread. But it wasn't so pleasant anymore.

"Not *just* a saw," Luria said. "It's also a quark-level scanner. When it divides material, such as Delphine, it scans at the same time, revealing secrets at a subatomic level. Would you like an exhibition?"

"I seriously have to go to the bathroom," I said. Very softly.

"What?" Luria asked, leaning down. She put her lips right to my ear and started to whisper something, but it was at that moment that Melville stung Luria on her lower lip.

"Glakkk!" Luria yelled. There was a generous helping of agony in her voice. If she'd been somebody else, I would have sympathized. But she wasn't somebody else. She was the only woman I'd ever met who'd clamped a chillingly cold hand onto my shoulder and talked about dissecting my brain.

So, instead of sympathizing, I yelled, "Hah!"

And then I said, "Gurgle. Huck! Hghh!"

This was because when I'd first opened my mouth to yell, "Hah," Melville had dropped the pill halfway down my throat. I'd immediately started to choke and cough. My eyes were watering, but I still noticed Nate digging into his pocket for something. And then the men with the strange glass-like weapons opened fire, and a beam of light hit a chair next to me, missing me by inches.

The chair turned to smoke and ash.

It was . . . gone.

"What the piffle?" I said. "That is entirely not good." The pill slid a bit farther down my throat as I spoke, but it still wasn't what anyone with any reasonable knowledge of how to take a pill would consider as "swallowed."

I needed something to drink.

Luria was holding her lip and trying to swat Melville out of the air, so I took advantage of her distraction and nabbed the cup of tea from her hands and had a quick drink, washing the pill down my throat.

The rude men opened fire again, and the three women started gymnastically flipping over the tables and chairs, charging closer, but then . . .

. . . all the lights went out.

I mean *all* of them.

I mean the overhead lights were gone.

The sunlight from the windows . . . ? Gone.

All the light.

Everything.

Gone.

It was pitch black. *Space* black. Extra *super*-black.

I asked, "Did everybody else just go blind?" The last thing I could remember seeing was Nate holding up a device he'd taken from his pocket. It looked like a black lollipop, like one of those horrible lollipops that taste like licorice. Except this one put out a burst of sparks and then . . .

. . . yeah.

Everything was black.

"Wait for it," I heard Nate whisper. He was right next to me. He reached out and held my hand. I heard Melville buzz to a landing on my shoulder.

"Stay calm!" I heard. It was Luria's voice. "This is obviously some trick of Bannister's. It won't work. Don't let them leave alive. Everyone, block the doors."

"How? I can't see." This was a man's voice, somewhere out in front of me.

"Wasn't there a back exit?" Another man's voice.

"Spread out, keep our hands linked." This was from one of the women who'd been pretending to be teenagers.

"Are we . . . are we blind forever?" This was another man's voice, and I have to admit I was somewhat interested in the answer.

"It will only last ten minutes," Nate said, but he was only whispering to me. How had he found me in the darkness? In the *absolute* darkness?

"Can you see yet?" Nate asked. "You swallowed the tablet, right?"

"Yes. I mean, at first I was choking and then I had some tea to wash it down and . . . and . . ."

"Yes?" Nate said.

"That was some really good tea."

"Oh. Yes. They do make excellent tea. Smells like a citrus blend. Luria makes the teas."

"Should I compliment her? Would this be a weird time to do that?"

"This would be a weird time to do that."

"Yeah. I figured." Nate was still holding my hand, guiding me around the tables and the chairs and the various members of the murderous society of assassins.

I said, "So, you can see?"

"No. I memorized the layout of the entire room. I always do. You never know when it will come in handy. But, we should both be able to echolocate pretty soon."

"Say again?"

"Echolocate. The way bats navigate. We'll essentially be able to see shapes. We won't have full definition, not the way we normally do. Instead, we'll sense sound bouncing from all solid objects, echoing back to our ears, and we'll 'see' in that manner."

"You've turned me into a bat?"

"No. And just temporarily. It's not as if you look like a bat. You're still as beautiful as ever."

I wondered if Nate could see me blush. I mean, do bats know when their friends are blushing? Would it be more socially awkward to be ignorant of a blush, or less? It probably wasn't a topic to bring up with the others in the room, as they were generally trying to dissect us.

Nate and I were moving through the restaurant, but it felt like we were heading away from the door. Luria was shouting orders, and I could occasionally hear the awful noise of one of those glass pistols firing (the noise was like an electric chicken being startled), and she was ordering the men to quit panicking, telling them that Nate had likely used some sort of disruptor (it was, Nate explained to me, a coordinated swarm of our nano-bots charged with interrupting light to everyone's ocular receptors) and that she would solve it quickly enough and, until then, just move toward where they remembered the exits and guard them, and it was at that point that one of the men started yelling, "I've got him! I've got Nate," and there was the sound of a struggle, with chairs and tables crashing, and I looked in the direction of the noise, and . . . I saw them.

Sort of.

What I saw was shapes. No colors at all. It was still just blackness. But . . . blackness in the shapes of tables and chairs and . . . the men. I could see how two of the Red Death Tea Society assassins were wrestling each other, each thinking they'd caught Nate, and I thought it was really funny.

Then the whole room suddenly smelled like freshly baked bread.

"What's happening?" I asked Nate. I was still getting accustomed to the bat-vision. I could see Luria coming closer through the tables and chairs, walking way too confidently in the darkness and easily ducking an outstretched hand from one of the men as he tried to feel which way he was going. But everything I could see was just . . . shapes. Like black paper figures on a background of darkness. And that bread smell was everywhere.

"This is how bats see?" I asked Nate.

"Some of them. But much better than this. Most bats see the way we normally do, though. Their echolocation is in addition to their regular vision, which is actually pretty good."

"Huh," I said. I'd never known bats had two types of vision. No wonder they're so sneaky in the air. I concentrated harder on using the bat-vision (or . . . *half* of a bat's vision, I guess) and saw that Nate was tapping that pencil thing of Luria's all over a wall. I couldn't tell what he was doing, though. My best guess was that he was writing some nasty graffiti about the Red Death Tea Society, which was something I could definitely get behind, but it was maybe not the best use of our time right then? I was on the verge of telling Nate my personal opinions on the benefits of "running away" versus "writing clever graffiti" when Luria interrupted us.

Because she was so very close.

She was reaching out to grab Nate, and he hadn't noticed her. She was moving so silently, and he was faced the wrong direction, with no way to see her. How could she even see us? Did she have bat-vision, too?

Even in all the blackness, I could see her smile.

Then Nate, all without looking back, held up a tiny spray can over his shoulder and pressed the trigger. There was a burst of compressed air, a billowing cloud that looked like a ghost to my bat-vision, and Luria shrieked.

Loud.

She stumbled backward, hopping on one foot and bellowing a string of words that I'm quite sure would've impressed my brother Steve, who prides himself on his curses.

"What did you just do?" I asked Nate, watching Luria fall over backward, holding her foot.

"Toe-stub spray."

"You're going to have to explain that," I said.

"Hold on a moment," he said. "I'm pushing this wall over." He put his hands on the wall and shoved. A huge section of the wall fell over, leaving a gaping hole.

"You're going to have to explain that, too," I said.

"In a minute," Nate said. "We're in the middle of a dramatic escape." He grabbed my hand, and we tromped over the fallen wall into an alley outside. I'd have thought that there would be light now that we were outside, but it was still bat-vision. Nate was obviously accustomed to it, though, because he was racing us along at full speed, running through the alley and out into the parking lot.

He said, "Toe-stub spray stimulates neural synapses to trigger the exact same pain receptors associated with stubbing your toe."

"You're serious? Toe-stub spray? You were actually sitting around your house one day and decided you needed to make a spray can full of toe-stubs?"

"Well, I was in my tree house when I made the decision, but otherwise . . . yes. And if you're wondering about me pushing the wall over, I sliced through the wall using Luria's cutting device."

"Good idea."

"It was the best course of action, since they were guarding the normal exits. It's funny, really."

"What's funny?" I asked, hoping he wasn't going to say it was funny how people were using strange weapons to try to disintegrate me, because I did not find it humorous.

"It's funny how they were so concerned about the regular exits," Nate said. "It's that way all throughout the world. Everyone tries to do things in the normal way. To follow along with the herd. To say the same things. To act the same way and go through the same doors. It might be an easier way to live, but it's not nearly as satisfying. It's much more rewarding to create your own doors and blaze a new path."

"Bees," I said. A strange response, I'll admit, and it confused Nate.

"Bees?" he said.

"Specifically, those," I pointed up.

There was a swarm of bees in the air.

A blimp-size swarm of them.

We were obviously taking too long to disable the bee-summoning transmitters. The swarm had tens of thousands of bees. If Nate and I weren't able to un-attune the transmitters, who knew how many more bees would swarm the city? This was not looking good.

Speaking of how things were looking, to my bat-vision,

the swarm looked like a swirl of dots, constantly merging into larger shapes, collecting together, then moving apart, tens of thousands of individual black spots acting as one. I'm not sure I'd have recognized them as bees except for how I'd grown attuned to the shrill buzzing of their wings.

Melville zoomed up to meet them but only went a couple of yards before she stopped, buzzed in an inquisitive and confused manner, and then zoomed behind my back, hiding.

"That was not reassuring," I told her. "I thought they were your friends?"

"She's not part of the swarm anymore," Nate said. "She's part of *our* swarm now."

"We're a swarm?" I asked, watching the bees (and thus all their stingers) zooming closer. "I don't feel like a swarm. I feel like target practice for a blimp-size army of impolite bees."

It was at that moment I heard the peeling of car tires on the parking lot, and then Betsy, our car, was barreling closer, racing the quickly descending bees, putting on an amazing burst of speed and sliding to a stop next to us.

Her door popped open.

The bees were only a few yards away.

I dove inside.

"Safe!" I said. But . . . the door was still open. Nate was still standing outside. He was absolutely *not* diving to safety. He was only leaning inside the car, grabbing for his canvas messenger bag, the one with patches of Nikola "über-genius" Tesla, Isaac "apple to the head" Newton, Jim "I created the Muppets" Henson, and Albert "bad hair" Einstein.

"Get in the car, Nate," I said. To be honest, I screamed it. This had the unfortunate side effect of improving the clarity of my echolocation, so that I could now see the oncoming swarm of menacing bees with far better definition.

"Just a second," Nate said. He still wasn't getting in the car.

"We are not debating," I told Nate. "We are getting into the car." He was rummaging through his bag. It was full of various plastic vials, tiny ones.

"Hmmm," he said. "The labels are difficult to read when I'm seeing only with echolocation. I'll have to keep that in mind for future experiments."

"Yes, Nate," I said. "You do that. But here in the present, how about you get in the car and we close the door? Unless you're thinking about letting the bees inside the car, too? Giving them a ride somewhere?"

"Is this one of those times when you're being sarcastic?" Nate asked.

"This is one of those times when I'm screaming in fear," I said. Or rather I screamed it. Fearfully.

Nate was murmuring, "'Speed-Reading Pills.' 'See Ghosts Pills.' 'Talk French Pills.' C'mon, c'mon, where are they?" He was hurriedly pulling bottles of pills out from his bag and tossing them in the backseat.

"'Make Any Animal a Zebra Pills,'" he said, tossing another bottle into the backseat. This one bounced off my head. I grunted a bit in displeasure, but Nate didn't react to it. This was possibly because my soft grunt was disguised by my roaring scream of fear. In defense of my scream I should point out that the sky had turned into a solid mass of swarming bumblebees, and they were zooming toward us. The lead bees were now only a few feet from us, and the bees to the rear of the swarm were a good hundred yards back, and in between the front bees and the rear bees it was all just . . . more bees.

"'Shower Pill,'" Nate said. "'Toad Finder Pill.' Where's . . . ooo, here it is!" He popped the cap off a bottle and quickly swallowed a pill. Then he tossed another of the pills in my mouth, which was easy for him to do because I was still doing that one thing I'd been doing. Screaming, I mean.

"Glunk," I said, swallowing the pill, just as Nate took my hand and pulled me outside the car, directly into the giant swarm of bees.

Not exactly the move of a genius.

chapter
7

So, the bees were upon us. All around us. I couldn't see anything. Echolocation wasn't doing all that much good besides giving me the mildly comforting knowledge that Nate was standing next to me, but that everything else was bees.

I heard Betsy calling our names, and she was even cursing at Nate (the first time I'd ever heard her do such a thing, as she really does have admirable restraint), and then after a bit I couldn't hear anything except the overwhelming roar of the bees.

I said, "Ouch!" when the first bee touched me, because I was positive I was going to get stung, having experienced the agony of bee stings only that morning.

I said "Ouch," when the second bee touched me, too.

I said "Ouch" and "Piffle" and a few more things as a

seemingly infinite number of bees landed on me, crawling all over me, but there's no reason to go into everything I said because it was almost entirely foul, and it was whispered for the most part, owing to how I had a precise limit as to how far I was willing to open my mouth. That limit, which I was strictly enforcing, was . . . *less than enough space for a bumblebee to crawl inside.*

So, yes, I was whisper-cursing, and I was bumblebee bombarded, and I was whimpering, and I was likely doing a "bees don't touch me, please" dance that my brother Steve would have absolutely loved to post on the Internet, but what I *wasn't* doing was . . .

. . . getting stung.

Huh.

The bees weren't stinging me.

Weird.

While my morning had proved that I wasn't the most knowledgeable person in the world, bee-wise, I'd definitely had one major bee belief cemented as fact: bees *sting*. But these bees . . . *weren't.*

I could feel Nate press something into my hand, another of the pills from his messenger bag, and I managed to ask, "You want me to take this pill?" all without opening my mouth more than half the height of a bumblebee.

"Yes," Nate said. "Please do."

So I took the pill, pushing it past my lips rather than opening my mouth, only then realizing that Nate had spoken clearly, and that I'd heard him clearly, despite the constant tornado-level buzzing from the bees.

"Did you take it?" Nate asked. "And don't open your mouth, just . . . think the answer."

"Uhh, yes?" I said. Or, rather, I thought I said. I mean, I didn't say anything . . . I just *thought* about saying it.

"Great!" Nate said. "I suppose you want an explanation."

I thought about saying yes. I mean, I didn't just *consider* saying yes, I actually *thought* of saying it.

"Excellent," Nate said, apparently having heard me. Then there was a pause and he said, "Hmmm. You're getting the hang of it, but . . . did you know that you're thinking of a lot of curse words?"

"Yes," I said. Or, thought. Whatever.

"Oh," Nate said. "Well, here's the deal. Almost all of our senses, our smell, taste, our vision, they're based on chemical reactions, but hearing is an entirely mechanical process."

"WE ARE SURROUNDED BY A FAT BLIMP OF BEES!" I said.

"Ugh," Nate said. "Could you turn your brain down a

bit? You don't have to worry. We're safe. The first pill we took made us members of the bee swarm. They consider us as a part of them, now, and won't sting us."

"They don't notice that we're, like, a million times bigger than they are?"

"No. They're not very smart. Well, actually they are, but they're not very smart in *that* way. It's strange how sometimes people can be very smart in a lot of ways, but completely oblivious in other ways."

"Like the way some geniuses never detect sarcasm from others, or perfectly justified panic from their friends?"

"Sure," Nate said. "Those could be examples, I guess." He clearly wasn't putting two and two together and coming up with "Delphine is talking about *me*."

He said, "The thing is, we're safe in here. And we're hidden from Luria and her minions, but I had us swallow the other pills so that we can talk."

"We're not talking, we're only thinking about talking. How can this possibly be working?"

"I was explaining that. Also, quit worrying about all this being a hallucination caused by having been stung sixty million times by the bees."

"How did you know I was thinking about that?"

"Again. I'm explaining." He took me by my hand and we began walking toward . . . somewhere. Being encased inside a blimp-size swarm of bees was really messing with my sense of direction.

Nate said, "The second pill we took made some temporary minor changes in the arcuate fasciculus, which is a nerve tract connecting various language centers in our brains, and it . . . OUCH."

"Ouch?"

"You were just thinking about punching me, about telling me that Day One of Delphine's Life in the Bee Tribe is not the proper time for in-depth explanations of why we can hear and understand each other's thoughts."

"True. But . . . it hurt you?"

"I could feel the punch. It triggered the proper pain sensors that . . . OUCH."

"This is awesome," I said. "So I just think about punching you and . . . ?"

"OUCH," Nate said.

"What I meant by that last mental punch," I said, "is that all I needed you to say is that we can hear and understand each other's thoughts, not some complicated explanation of exactly *why* that is, because I'm not going to understand it anyway. Now, why are we inside these bees in the first place?"

"Because if we can move closer to Luria and the others, we can overhear what they're planning to do."

"Oh. Okay then, I have a question."

"I love that you have questions. Most people just accept things the way they are, never questioning what's happening to them."

"In defense of other people, they're rarely encased in giant swarms of bees, which *does* tend to bring up a few questions, like this one . . . We've turned invisible before, so I know you have the technology to be entirely undetectable, you know, *without* bees."

"True," Nate agreed. But that was all he said. I would've thought a genius could detect where my question was going, but I was apparently going to have to explain.

I said, "Well, then . . . why didn't we just do that? Wouldn't that have been easier than becoming a part of a bee tribe?"

"Easier isn't always better."

"But it *is* always better to be *not* encased in a giant swarm of bees," I argued. I was well aware that I was debating with a genius, but I felt like my reasoning was unshakable.

"Adventures are always better than not-adventures," Nate countered.

Urrgh.

My weakness.

Nate knows that I'm generally considered adventurous. Well, I'm more commonly considered "troublesome," sometimes "problematic," and occasionally "red-haired and dangerous," but for now let's just define it as adventurous.

"Okay then," I said. "Bees. I love them. More bees in my hair, please. I want them crawling on my arms and face. It's so awesome." I didn't really have anything personal against the bees, so I was hoping that none of them would drown in my sarcasm.

"It is awesome!" Nate said, as he has never been in any danger of drowning in my sarcasm. "Seeing life through someone else's eyes is an amazing perspective. I mean, since we took the pills, these bees think that you and I are exactly the same. We're just other bees to them. They can't tell us apart. They don't notice that your hair is red or that you're so pretty; they just think you're a bee. Same as me."

Hmmpf.

Pretty?

I was silent.

"Huhh?" Nate said. "Your thoughts are blank. Did I say something wrong?"

I was silent.

"Hmmm," Nate said. "This is odd. The pill's duration should still be in effect, but I can't hear you. Are you okay, Delphine?"

I was saved from having to say anything (I was

holding back a mental blush, which is uncomfortable) by Luria suddenly speaking, not more than ten feet from us, outside the swirling mass of bees.

"Nathan has to be around here," she said. We could barely hear her, since she wasn't speaking directly into our minds, meaning her voice was nearly drowned out by the tremendous buzzing roar of the swarm.

"Do we truly need him?" a man's voice asked. "Why can't we just steal the Infinite Engine from his house?"

"It's too well guarded. Between the defenses he's constructed and that dog of his, any direct assault will fail."

"A jar of peanut butter is enough to distract the dog, and as to the house's defenses, we can infiltrate with Project A."

"Untested," Luria said. "But, yes . . . it could be of value." Nate and I, safely hidden in the bee swarm, were trying to edge even closer to Luria. The bees weren't bothering any of the assassins of the Red Death Tea Society. In fact, two of the women in the spandex suits walked right through the swarm, which parted around them, forcing Nate and me to step quickly out of their way when we understood what was happening. It wasn't all that difficult once we noticed the different flow of the bees, a change in their flight patterns. There was a current to being in the swarm, and the longer we stayed inside, the more we understood it. Maybe we really *were* becoming part of the tribe? Understanding their ways? I'd probably end up as the head of the Bee Student Council, and I'd make a bunch of bee friends, and we'd all go to the movies together, and I could have them over for my Cake vs. Pie parties, and we'd all laugh about the time they crashed the party and stung me again and again, turning my face into a melon.

"What's Project A?" I asked Nate.

"No idea."

"Any guesses?"

"Science never guesses."

"I guess that's true, but you're not science . . . you're Nate. So, any guesses?"

"Not really. But the arrival of this bee swarm means we're clearly going to have to speed up the process of disabling the bee-summoning transmitters, though at the same time we should probably go back to my house and protect the Infinite Engine. I'd like to switch on all the extreme defenses."

"Extreme defenses?"

"Sure. The rugs. The doorknobs. Our mailbox."

"Doorknobs don't sound particularly awe inspiring, Nate."

"Wrong. I invented doorknobs that—"

But the topic of doorknobs would have to wait,

because it was at that moment that Luria said, "Well, if we're going to break into Nathan's house, we have to keep him busy elsewhere. It's time to implement the full scale of Project B."

Almost immediately, an intense odor washed across the parking lot, slamming into my nose despite the wind from the millions of tiny wings surrounding me. It smelled like a flower . . . but a *vast* field of flowers, or possibly one super-huge monster flower, a fifty-foot flower that had neglected to wear deodorant. The smell was overpowering.

"Uh-oh," Nate said.

"Uh-oh?" I asked.

"Luria is ordering the bumblebees into action," Nate said, grabbing my hand and hurrying us across the parking lot. But we'd only gone a few steps when the entire swarm of bees whooshed up into the air, leaving Nate and me entirely exposed.

Nate and I could see normally again, so for one moment we could see Luria talking with the other assassins, explaining how a tactical squad would deal with the danger of the doorknobs at Nate's house, and then suddenly the bees were gone and Nate and I were standing there completely in the open and Luria turned to me and met my eyes with a quizzical expression. Her gaze narrowed. She began to frown. Even sneer.

"Hey there," I said. I gave her a little wave and asked, "What's all this about *doorknobs*?"

Let me tell you about our escape.

So it turns out that there were other swarms of bumble-bees. There were, in fact, *swarms* of swarms. There was a swarm in Polt's industrial district, and one menacing Polt Middle School, and another at Polt University ("*Where Polt Pride Patrols*") and the tech school and *all* the other schools, as well as at our city parks, the swimming pool (where several unfortunate swimmers had already felt the cruel sting of fate . . . in this case meaning the cruel sting of Melville), and there were other swarms at the police station, the fire station, the post office, the mall, the entire shopping district, and so on and so forth.

There was even a swarm above my house, where Mom and Dad were sitting down for a late lunch, and Mom was just in the act of texting me when the swarm began trying to get in through the windows, so that Mom sent me a text of, Delphine, it's time for lunch. Where are . . . OH NO! BEES! SO MANY BEES!

"Why did you type out that thing about the bees?" I asked my phone, but it didn't answer and then I dropped

it anyway, because I was being violently bounced around. Nate and I had managed to make it to Betsy, our car, and she was trying to whoosh through the lobby of Polt Paramount, our city's largest movie theater. We couldn't be blamed for driving a car inside a movie theater, as we were trying to lose a herd of bees. Also, the sign at the front door had said, "No pets," but hadn't specifically said anything about cars. If they didn't want people driving cars through the lobby, they should have posted a sign.

I do admit we hadn't bought Betsy a ticket.

I reached over and punched Nate in the arm.

He said, "Oww," and then nodded at me in the way that people do when they understand what you *meant* to say, rather than what you *did* say. Or, in this case, what you *punched*.

He said, "I'm calculating a nearly one hundred percent chance that you're worried about your family."

"I am," I said. "Even Steve." My brother Steve was probably why Nate hadn't calculated an *entirely* one hundred percent chance that I was worried about my family.

"I'll send Sir William to your house," Nate said. "He can emit a subaudible shriek that will disturb the bees, confuse them, make them flee the area, at least for a surrounding block."

"Yes, do that," I said. "Make the bees flee." With that said, I crawled back over into the front seat, as I'd bounced into the back during a particularly tight corner Betsy had taken while trying to avoid running into a wall. I'd been in the theater lobby before, lots of times, and I'd always thought it had about four walls, but now they suddenly seemed to be everywhere, popping out at the most inconvenient times.

"Friend Delphine," Betsy said. "Please sit closer to Nate." I scooted a bit closer to Nate, wondering what Betsy was talking about. Why would she want me to move closer to Nate? After all, she gets a bit jealous over him. Okay, more than a bit. In fact, she has a complete crush. It's embarrassing. I myself would never act like that.

"I am monitoring reluctance on your part," Betsy

said. "That is not wise, friend Delphine. Please do not be so shy. Time is of the essence."

"You want me even closer?" I asked Betsy. I was already sitting almost right up against Nate. We were zooming around in the lobby, with people jumping out of our way, and with bees swarming us, and with spilled popcorn likewise swarming us, and with the theater manager (Harold Freymeyer) having crawled up onto the candy display case, from where he was ordering an usher to throw us out.

"We will be taking the stairs," Betsy said.

"The stairs?" Nate said, then, "Oh!" He put his arm around me and hugged me tight, pulling me as close as possible.

"Whuu?" I said. My brother Steve often talks about taking his various girlfriends to the movies. He always tries to kiss them. I couldn't help but wonder if Nate was trying the same thing. But . . . Nate *certainly* knew that he and I are only friends, and that kisses were entirely out of the question, even though my brother Steve claims that horror movies are the best times to kiss girls, and while it's true that Nate and I weren't at a horror movie, we definitely were at a horror *reality*, being attacked by precisely 27,562 bees (Nate had counted them, somehow), which I suppose could make people even more likely to kiss?

"I'm not kissing you!" I told Nate.

"We're shrinking!" he said.

"I'm confused!" I said.

"Me too," Nate said, staring at me.

"Get ready!" Betsy yelled.

"For what?" I asked. I was still confused. *Very* confused, even. "Are you talking about kissing?"

"Nate is not kissing you!" Betsy said. There was a touch of something extra in her voice, and I was wondering about that, and very much wondering if anybody could explain to me what was going on, and then I yelped because Betsy was . . .

. . . Betsy was . . .

. . . getting smaller.

"Is Betsy getting smaller?" I asked.

"Yes," Nate said. "Didn't I say we were shrinking? And why did you think I was going to kiss you?"

"Why are you holding my hand?" I countered. He was holding my hand.

"I didn't know I was!" Nate said. He dropped my hand. Then he blushed and glanced out the window, which was covered in bees. While he was distracted, I reached out and took his hand again. I have an excuse for this. I wanted any comfort I could grab. Let me again mention the 27,562 bees.

"Don't hold hands!" Betsy yelled, and then she puffed

out a cloud of smoke from her butt (I suppose it was her muffler, but mufflers are on regular cars, and butts are for talking cars), and the bees started choking and coughing and cursing (I may have imagined this), and then Betsy was aiming for the stairs up to the balcony seating, stairs that were way too narrow for a car. We were doing about thirty miles per hour. If you don't think that's fast, trying going that speed in a movie theater lobby, in a shrinking car.

Thump thump thump.

Those were the sounds we made going up the stairs. Betsy (she's made of unstable molecules that she can manipulate at will) had shrunk just enough for us to make our way up the stairs, which came as a shock to Denis Medri (one of my brother's best friends) and Abby Shaw (one of my brother's girlfriends, so ... *hmmm*) as they came down the stairs together.

"What what what?" Denis said as he noticed a car driving up the stairs toward him at high speed.

"Eeek eeek EEEK!" Abby screamed as Betsy shrank even more (I ended up half in Nate's lap) and we squeezed past them, gouging the wall as we passed and tearing down an old movie poster for *The Heartbroken Wolf Man*, shredding it entirely. A large piece of the poster stuck to our now-tiny windshield, with the forlorn wolf man staring in at us.

"Bees!" Abby screeched, when the bees reached her.

"Bees! Bees!" That was Denis.

If they said anything else, I didn't hear them, because we were back to the *thump thump thump* of the stairs and then we reached the balcony area and Betsy triggered a grappling hook that attached to the chandelier hanging over the main seating area and we were suddenly swinging out into the void.

"Gahh!" I said. An appropriate response.

"Hold tight!" Nate said, hugging me.

"Let go of him, Delphine!" Betsy said. "You promised me you weren't dating!"

I said, "This isn't dating! This is being terrified! And *he's* hugging *me!*"

"I'm monitoring an excess in your body temperature!" Betsy said. "According to the dating manuals Nate has given me to read, that means you're thrilled to be in his arms!"

I looked to Nate.

"You've been giving her dating manuals?"

"Yeah. I thought maybe she could teach me about dating, if . . . if she knew more about it."

"So, you thought it would be smart to learn about dating from a car?"

Nate decided to stay silent, which was the one true genius thing he'd done in recent memory. Betsy released her grappling hook from the chandelier, and we went sailing out over the crowd, and by "sailing out over the crowd" I mean "falling toward the crowd," who began running around in panic, like chickens terrified by a fox, if the chickens happened to be a couple of hundred people enjoying a movie, and the fox happened to be a car falling from the ceiling.

I rolled down the window, leaned out, and yelled, "Excuse us."

A bee flew in the window.

"Oh, right," I said. "Bees." I rolled the window back up as quickly as possible. But now we had a bee in the car. It was making a buzzing sound. It didn't sound angry or menacing. It sounded . . . happy?

"Melville?" I asked.

She buzzed again.

"There you are!" I said. "I missed you!" She'd been lost in the frantic escape from Popples. I thought about hugging her but it's really hard to hug a bee, so when she landed on my shoulder I reached out a finger and petted her, very gently. She made a buzz that sounded like a sigh. I could sympathize. It had been a long day, and I could only hope that things would calm down and get better. Then I looked up to see that we were headed right for the theater screen, which was just then showing a squadron of fighter jets engaging an alien spaceship.

There were all sorts of explosions, and I wondered if we would make a similar explosion when we hit the screen at a speed of *Way Too Fast*.

"Look out!" I told Betsy.

She swerved, and we drove partway up the wall, sending me bouncing over my seat into the back, where I landed gracefully on my face. Melville was buzzing in irritation, and I was doing much the same thing. By the time I managed to get back into the front seat Nate was scribbling a series of calculations on the windshield (Betsy was giggling, because it apparently tickled) and we were roaring up the theater aisle toward the lobby, with an usher waving at us with his flashlight, ordering us to leave while nimbly leaping into the seats, on top of my brother Steve.

"Oh, hi, Steve!" I said as we sped past, but I don't think he noticed me, because he'd spilled his cup of soda all over his lap, and there was ice and gasping involved.

Soon we were out into the street, and the bees fell out of sight, lost in the cloud of smoke that Betsy was leaving behind.

We'd made it.

"There," Nate said. "That wasn't so bad." There was a popping sound as Betsy returned to her usual shape and her normal roomy interior, meaning I didn't have to sit so close to Nate anymore. I slid back over to my side, feeling the aches and pains of the hundreds of bruises on my arms, legs, chest, butt, forehead, and in a general accumulation of areas that can be summed up as . . . everywhere.

"That was actually very painful," I told Nate. I tapped on the calculations he'd drawn on the windshield and asked, "What's this? Part of our escape plan?"

"A new popcorn recipe," he answered.

"You . . . you spent all that time working on a new popcorn recipe?" I was sputtering.

"No. Just this section." He circled a few of the equations. "Theater popcorn is always too salty and buttery for me, so I've devised a popcorn that salts and butters itself based on the voice commands of the user."

"You've developed voice-activated popcorn?" I said, making it clear that I didn't think it would be very useful.

"Sure!" Nate said. "It should be very useful. There have to be other people out there like me."

I said, "No, Nate, I don't think so." Melville landed on my shoulder and made a sound that I'm just going to go ahead and translate as a knowledgeable chuckle.

We were driving at good speed down Wood Street at that point, the street with all the artist colonies, where they display handmade crafts on the sidewalks. Well, on blankets, actually. But the blankets are on sidewalks.

We were roaring along fast enough that several of the blankets were flapping in the wake of our breeze.

Tapping on the windshield, I asked, "So, what are the rest of these calculations?"

"Ooo!" Nate said. "I'm glad you asked. Right now, it looks like Project *B*, the one Maculte and Luria were talking about, was actually Project *Bee*."

"Cleverly named," I said. "I bet Maculte names his pet dog 'Dog.'"

"He doesn't have a pet dog. Dogs don't like him. Cats, either. Or, you know, most any animal. But the point is, Project Bee is in full operation, and we have to stop it. Look at this." He tapped the roof of the car, and Betsy turned it transparent, so that we could see up to the skies, where there were huge swarms of bees soaring through the air.

Hundreds of swarms.

Each with millions of bees.

Project Bee.

Nate said, "They're trying to keep me away from my house, causing so much chaos that I won't be able to protect the Infinite Engine, but I've got a plan. It's a bit risky, but we have a seventy-two percent chance of stopping the Red Death Tea Society if . . . " He paused, frowned, smudged out a number on the windshield, and then wrote in another number. "Okay, make that a *sixty*-two percent chance of stopping them, but it's going to be dangerous, and hazardous, and treacherous, and perilous, and—"

"Those are all synonyms for the same thing, Nate. I get it. It's going to be absolutely death defying. So . . . what's the plan?"

He paused.

I don't like it when he pauses.

He took a deep breath.

I didn't like that, either.

He said, "It all comes down to *this*." He tapped a finger on the windshield again, there on all the numbers he'd written, amid the various squiggles and so on. I noticed that several of the equations had arrows coming off them, and all of the arrows eventually pointed to one thing.

A drawing.

A drawing of . . . a girl?

"Hey!" I said. "That looks like me!"

And then I said, "Oh. Great."

chapter
8

My phone rang.

An unknown number.

"Hello?" I said, answering the phone.

"Delphine, please. Oh, that was rude. Hello. This is Reggie Barnstorm, twenty-seventh president of the League of Ostracized Fellows. Could I please speak to Delphine Gabriella Cooper? She's the girl with the bee stings."

"That's me," I said. I looked over to Nate, with him behind Betsy's wheel, still scribbling equations onto her dash and her windshield, with Betsy still occasionally giggling, because she's ticklish.

"Oh, splendid," Reggie said. "Of course, 99.45 percent chance of you answering your own phone, but one never knows. One never knows."

"One never knows why you're calling me, either."

"Ha! I see. You've turned my own words against me." There was a pause. A long one.

"You still there?" I asked.

"What? Oh! Yes! I was writing down your joke, in case I could use it in a speech. I'll give you credit, of course, if there's any applause. There's usually not."

"Still don't know why you're calling me," I noted.

"Just so. Just so. The reason is, this thing with taking you up for a ride in the helicopter. We've had a meeting and, after looking up some things on the Internet and holding an informal poll, we've learned that kidnapping is considered socially awkward."

"Awkward is one word for it, yeah."

"We apologize."

"That's great. I guess." Melville came and landed on my phone, trying to eavesdrop. Her wings were tickling my ear.

Reggie said, "Well, to be honest, it was a fifteen to twelve vote for an apology. By no means unanimous. But not bad. We served hamburgers."

"Why?"

"Because they're tasty and—"

"No, why did you think I needed to know that? And also, never mind. Are you going to try to kidnap me again?"

"Probably not. Fifteen to twelve vote and all that. Instead, we have an offer. If you could stop Maculte and the Red Death Tea Society, we won't bother you anymore. Also, and this is embarrassing, but we could use some help in other areas."

"Such as?"

"Fashion tips. We have our upcoming League ball, and we'd collectively like to learn how to dress nicer, and, since we assume you're the one who advises Nate, and since he's the best dresser we know, could you help us, too?"

I looked over to Nate. He actually *was* dressed nice, thanks to our trip to the antiques market, but I was thinking of how he *usually* dressed, with his green-and-orange-checkered shirt and the pants where he's scribbled hundreds of math equations along with what seems to be a cartoon of an elephant farting. Even the nice shoes we'd grabbed from the antiques market were already scuffed, and his glasses currently had two notes taped to the left temple.

"You think Nate dresses well?" I asked Reggie. My voice was a whisper. Of disbelief.

"Don't *you*?" Reggie asked. His voice was a squeak. Also of disbelief. Melville had buzzed away from my phone and was hovering in midair, looking to Nate and then back to the phone. I shrugged.

"Maybe we can work together," I said into the phone.

"Fantastic!" Reggie said. "I suppose the first thing I'd like to know is, what's the best type of tie to go with shorts and sandals?"

"I meant that Nate and I will stop Maculte, since we'd planned on stopping him anyway."

"Oh." I could tell Reggie was disappointed.

"And don't wear a tie with shorts," I added, trying to be helpful. "Ties are formal, and shorts are decidedly not."

"Oh, *my* shorts are unquestionably formal," he said. "They're made of velvet."

I stared at my phone for a bit . . . thinking of velvet shorts . . . and then, with Melville buzzing in horror, and with me fighting for breath and not knowing what else to do, I simply hung up.

"Who was that?" Nate asked.

"Reggie Barnstorm. Leader of the League of Ostracized Fellows."

"Hmm," Nate said. "Nearly three minutes after I predicted." He reached up to one of the notes taped to his glasses, tugged it away, and crumpled it up.

We drove on.

-ᗤ̈-

Betsy and I dropped off Nate at his house. Bosper came running across the yard as we pulled up to the curb, bouncing and bounding in the manner of all terriers, except also excitedly talking, which is something I'm still getting used to.

"Who's a good boy?" Bosper said. "The dog has done some chewing!" I noticed there were several shoes in the yard. Men's shoes. They looked a lot like the ones I'd seen on the men from the Red Death Tea Society. Then I noticed a broken teacup and a dented teapot on the sidewalk.

"Did someone attack the house?" I asked Bosper.

"Who's a good boy?" he said. It was a bit more plaintive this time. He looked over at one of the shoes.

"So, someone *did* attack the house?" I asked, again.

"Who's a good boy?" Bosper said. He was now whining.

"Oh!" I said, finally understanding my role in this conversation. "You! You're a good boy!" Bosper began leaping around again, nodding his head. Barking. The usual terrier occupations.

"Bosper likes the shoes!" he said. "This dog was barking and biting! And sometimes Bosper was farting, but that is okay!"

"It is," I said. "I do it all the time. Did you chase all the men away?"

"Except shoes," Bosper said. He made what was, I think, a terrier smile. It involved way too much saliva. He continued bounding around, talking about biting (he really does enjoy biting) and how he should get chocolate (which is not good for dogs, even ones who are very talented at math), and I petted him for a bit (which he *did* deserve, though I kept my hand away from his saliva-dispenser), and I looked at all of the shoes in the yard and wondered what we should do with them, because they looked like something that would need to be *explained*.

"Hide those shoes, if you could," I told Bosper.

He was still jumping and leaping and spinning in the grass, but . . . he stopped suddenly.

Freezing into position.

"Delphine is the good friend," he whispered.

"True."

"We have a secret."

"True."

"Bosper will bury these secrets in the yard."

"Okay, you do that," I said, because I wasn't sure what else to say.

He reached out one paw, looking around in a furtive manner (which does not work for terriers, because they always look suspicious anyway), and scratched at the grass and the soil.

"The hole has begun," he whispered. But at that point Nate had reached the front door and called for Bosper to get inside.

"We have to protect this house!" Nate said, opening the door and letting Bosper inside. "We can't let them get the Infinite Engine!"

"And . . . Delphine?" Nate said, standing in the door, looking out to me.

"Yes?"

"*You* protect the city. Find a way to stop all the bees, and don't let things descend into chaos."

"Sure," I said. "Fine. Excellent. *You* protect a single house. *I'll* protect the rest of the entire city. That's totally fair." I was withering the very air with my sarcasm.

"Okay!" Nate said, and closed the door behind him.

I sighed and walked back to the car.

Betsy and I were three blocks away when my phone beeped. It was a text. From Nate.

It read, When you said "that's totally fair" . . . was that sarcasm?

I took a picture of me giving a thumbs-up and sent it back to Nate.

I was almost proud of him.

chapter
9

When I was eight years old I went to Rock Camp. It's where I first met Liz Morris and we became friends despite how, one night, sitting around a campfire . . . drinking lemonade and eating chocolate that we'd accidentally put too close to the fire and which was nearly liquid . . . she'd confessed something that I found repulsively shocking, a deep and hideous secret that nearly shredded our growing friendship into pieces.

She likes pie more than cake.

But we were able to overcome this incredible flaw in her character, and we've been best friends ever since. It's not *Liz* that I need to talk about here, though. It's where we *met*. At Rock Camp.

Rock Camp is not a camp where everyone gets together and talks about rocks, though I do find rocks to be fascinating and would definitely go to a camp where we scoured the soil for the prettiest rocks and various other buried treasures. But, *this* Rock Camp was all about learning to be in a band. Playing drums. Singing. And learning guitar.

I'd wanted to be a lead singer but the camp counselor had listened to my audition (Rock Camp was in a valley, and the "stage" was on a huge overlook, a natural rock platform that jutted out over the forest below) and had told me in no uncertain terms that I was frightening the bears, the rabbits, the deer, the raccoons, the squirrels, and even the turtles that hang out near the pond. Apparently, my voice is far too "enthusiastic." Anyway, after this crushing disappointment I tried to learn guitar, and I did get the basics, and I have a guitar in my room, but it only hangs on the wall because every time I play it Steve comes into my room and either tells me that his ears are bleeding or that Snarls, our cat, is hiding beneath his bed, hissing.

So I don't play much. But I do play a little. Even if all I can really do is play three chords in a manner that Ms. Brakehelm, head instructor for the Rock Camp for Girls, claims made the turtles leap off their logs and dive into the pond.

But I *can* play.

And that's important.

Because it saved the city.

Betsy and I were trying to avoid the bee swarms. It wasn't easy. Despite how she could drive much faster than the bees could fly, there were always more swarms. So, by outrunning one, it always seemed like we were running into another one. By then I was receiving reports on my phone. They were sent by Sir William, the robot gull, who was not only protecting my family, patrolling the house, but tracking swarms of bees all over Polt, using a sophisticated radar of Nate's own devising.

The bees, it seemed, were everywhere.

I *needed* to disable those transmitters.

"Up ahead!" I told Betsy. There was a huge swarm of bumblebees moving like a fat ribbon through the streets. We were back in the arts district where all the various sidewalk vendors (the potters, the clothes makers, the jewelers, and so on) were scattering as the bees descended, with the unfortunate people yelling out things like . . .

"Glaggt!" The sound you make when a bee stings your face.

"Grgargh!" The noise you make when a bee stings your left bicep.

"Gett-gaww!" And . . . that would be the right bicep.

And there was also "Flargrah!" . . . which is the scream from someone being stung on their right leg, and "Oh, I *hate* bees!" . . . which is a yell that could've been from almost anyone, owing to how bees aren't exactly well loved, probably because of that whole "intense pain when they sting you" thing.

Everyone was running inside the stores and the apartment complexes, and the bees were starting to cover the buildings like a thick writhing blanket, trying to find a way in, and I could tell from the various shrieks coming from within the buildings that our fine city of Polt has not properly bee-proofed our buildings. Still, there were fewer bees *inside* the buildings than outside, and since Betsy and I were about the last ones stupid enough to be moving along on the street, the bee horde collectively took a deep breath, turned their attention our way, smiled in malevolent fashion, and bellowed, "Let's *get* her!"

"Look out!" I yelled to Betsy, because we were headed straight for the swarm, which was now headed straight for us.

"I see it, Delphine," Betsy said. There was a certain tone in her voice. A bit . . . unfriendly.

My phone beeped.

A text.

From Nate.

It said, Forgot to tell you, Betsy's engine is different now.

I texted back, Okay.

I waited for his next text.

Nothing.

I texted, Nate . . . go on. Why did you tell me that?

Two seconds later, he texted, Oh! Because I'd always wanted to change her engine to a centripetal force generator system, meaning that she's powered by being in motion, so that the faster she drives the more energy she creates, but the math was difficult (I needed to solve Poincaré's smooth four-dimensional conjecture), and then the real problem was that Betsy's emotional modulator grew proportionally harder to control.

I texted, Okay, first . . . you type fast, and second, how did you solve the problem with Betsy's emotional modulator?

Didn't. That's why I texted you. Be careful. Betsy could be . . . interesting.

Wait. What?

Have to go. House being attacked. Bosper says "hello." Good luck.

None of that was anything I wanted to hear about, so I was about to text Nate a photo of me decidedly *not* giving him a thumbs-up, when I heard Melville frantically buzzing. She was on the dash, looking through the windshield, to where the huge swarm of bees was only a hundred feet from us, and then fifty feet, and twenty, and ten, and then . . .

. . . and then . . .

. . . the windshield turned to an image of when Nate and I had been hugging, when we'd been in the theater lobby and Betsy had been shrinking.

Betsy screeched to a halt and said, "Delphine. We need to talk about Nate."

I said, "Betsy, we are currently being attacked by bees. You're my friend, and I enjoy talking with you, but maybe this isn't the best time?"

The car started to shiver. I couldn't see out of the windows anymore because Betsy had changed all the views on the windows, treating them like they were computer screens, which I guess they are. There were images of me hugging Nate (which, again, we *only* did because Betsy was shrinking), and there were images of Nate walking along a sidewalk (with Bosper marching along behind him), and there were images of Nate riding a unicorn through space while Betsy watched him from a passing asteroid, which is something I'm positively completely and *almost-nearly* sure has never happened.

"Nate is so handsome," Betsy said. She softly revved her engine, which I guess is the automobile equivalent of a sigh.

"Handsome," I said. "Sure." Nate has a big floppy collection of dark brown hair. His nose basically dominates his face. He made his glasses himself. I'm not a big fan of checkered shirts, but Nate definitely is. His pants always look dirty because of the equations he's forever writing on them. His eyes are the brown of dark coffee. He's not overly muscular, or overly tall, or overly anything at all, except overly . . . Nate. That's something about him that I've noticed. Most people I know are only about forty percent themselves: the rest is a collection of the latest hot actor or the most popular singer, guided by peer pressure into trying to look the way they're "supposed" to look . . . but Nate is always Nate.

Entirely Nate.

I suppose I could call him handsome.

I also suppose I could mention that there were now so many bumblebees on the car that it was actually rocking back and forth, bringing forth questions I've never before asked myself, like . . . How many bumblebees does it take to tip over a car? I thought about texting Nate (these are the sorts of things he knows) but decided against it, since he'd said his house was being attacked, meaning that our texts would look like this . . .

"Hey. I'm being attacked by bumblebees." That one would be from me.

"Sounds unpleasant," Nate would text back. "I'm currently being attacked by a society of genius-level assassins who are trying to take over the world."

"Ooo," I would write back in sympathy.

"Also, they want to cut open my brain," Nate would add.

"Ahh, piffle," I would say, because that's what you say to friends when their archenemies want to dissect them.

"Maybe we should each concentrate on stopping the bees and the assassins rather than texting each other?" I would then write.

Nate would text back, "Okay, Delphine. Incidentally, you're inconceivably pretty and your singing voice is awesome, because you're *supposed* to be overly enthusiastic when you're singing rock songs."

"I *know*, right?"

That's the only way I could possibly envision our conversation going, so maybe it was best to just pass for now, especially since bees were trying to get in through Betsy's windows (no luck there, because they were up all the way) and to come in through some of the vents, which was unfortunately a bit more problematic. Melville was desperately flying around, chasing the invading bees back. Every time another bee tried to come in through the vents she would sting at them, or at least scold them in bee language, but she was being overwhelmed. Betsy could've easily reversed the vents and whooshed the other bees away, but she was lost in dreamland.

"Nate is so handsome," she repeated. "I love his hair."

"Sure," I said. "Did the two of you really go to space?" I tapped on the image of Nate riding the unicorn. Becoming friends with Nate has restructured my view of the impossible.

"No. I made that image. Isn't it wonderful?"

"Yeah. It's great. Hey, change of topic. Did you notice we're being attacked by bees?"

"I thought about making Nate's nose smaller in the image, but then I realized it's part of his charm."

"Yeah. Killer bees. Millions of them. Getting in through the vents."

"Why does Nate like being with you?" Betsy asked. Her voice had gone a bit stern.

"Oh, probably because of the way I defend myself against killer bee attacks. Nate enjoys that."

"He does?"

"Sure!" I said. "What boy doesn't?"

The vents suddenly whooshed into life, blowing air outward, vacuuming away the bees that were starting to crawl inside. I had to leap forward and cup my hands around Melville, because she was almost caught in the violent air currents. She buzzed gratefully in my hands. Betsy started honking in an overly excited manner, and at that point my hair began to float around me, almost like I was in water, with strands and locks of my hair fluttering up, sticking out.

"What's happening?" I said.

Betsy said, "I'm emitting a mild electric charge, covering my exterior. The bees will find it annoying."

"Oh! Don't hurt them!" I said. After all, they weren't really evil bees or anything like that. It was just that Maculte and the Red Death Tea Society were using them, having once more corrupted one of Nate's experiments, forcing the bees to act against their will by use of chemicals.

"I will try not to hurt them," Betsy said. "At least not physically. But emotional harm runs even deeper. Betrayal from a friend is the harshest cut of them all."

"And . . . I don't know what you're talking about," I said. But I kind of *did* know, because now the windshield, where Betsy was showing the view of Nate and me hugging, had become animated, like a GIF, so that Nate was repeatedly reaching out to grab me and pull me close.

Betsy made a growl. She revved her engine again, now much lower in tone.

I said, "You're mad about that *hug*? We needed to do that because you were shrinking!"

"Was I? And just *why* do you think I was shrinking? Do you think it's because I'm no longer wanted? That I wasn't so much shrinking as . . . shrinking away?"

"Well, no. I thought you were shrinking because that was the only way we could fit up the stairs."

"Have you ever heard Nate laugh?" Betsy asked in a wistful tone. "It's so masculine." Her voice had gone dreamy again. I didn't think it was the best time to point out that Nate's laugh wasn't exactly masculine. I honestly do like his laugh, but it's more like a duck being squished than anything else.

"Boys!" Betsy suddenly yelled. "They're all so mean!" She emitted a powerful blast of her horn, with a long, mournful tone.

"Look, Betsy," I said. "I'll make you a deal. Let's fight off the bee invasion together, thereby saving the city of Polt, and I promise that whichever one of us does a better job, Nate will give them a kiss."

"Hmm," Betsy said, considering my proposal. "Interesting. You know, I am much better equipped for bee fighting than you are."

"It's true. Look, I'm still melon-headed." I touched my forehead, where there was still a huge bump from the morning's bee attack. Melville buzzed in embarrassment, and Betsy's rearview mirror swiveled as if to get a better look at me.

"Would . . . would Nathan agree to such a contest?" Betsy asked. There was a touch of eagerness in her voice.

"Let's find out," I said. I grabbed up my phone and texted, Betsy and I are having a contest. We're bee fighters. Whoever does the best, you have to kiss.

I showed the text to Betsy, holding it up to the rear-view mirror.

Then I sent it to Nate.

Five seconds later, he texted, Sure.

I said, "Wow. I thought he'd at least ask for an explanation. But that's settled. Betsy . . . let's fight bees."

"Of course," she said. "And I hope you'll play fair."

"Definitely," I said. "And, you too!"

"No," Betsy said. "I think not."

All the doors locked.

And Betsy laughed.

-ᘐ-

So, here's how you fight bees when you're trapped inside a talking car that's trying to defeat you in a bumblebee butt-kicking contest.

You don't.

What you *do* is you get tossed all around when she ramps off the side of a building and soars into the air, slamming herself through a bee swarm while emitting a blaze of electrical discharges that stuns the bees and sends them plummeting to the ground.

What you do *after* that is struggle into your seat belt, because you realize it's going to be a bumpy ride.

And *then* you yell "Piffle!" when your seat belt suddenly disengages, because the car thinks it's funny you're being bumped around, because she believes you're stealing her boyfriend, even though he's *not* her boyfriend, and you're *not* stealing him in the first place.

Then, quite soon after that, you find yourself airborne and flung into the backseat, where you bounce around like an easily bruised Ping-Pong ball. As you struggle to get back into the front seat, you'll notice the car is now spraying a chemical that attracts bees (basically a billowing cloud of sugar) and also spraying, seconds later, a second chemical, after all the bees have gathered together.

"What are you spraying?" I asked Betsy.

"A chemical that makes creatures into your friend. Perhaps I should use it on you." Her voice was not friendly. I was hoping the wind would change, and maybe *she* would get caught in the cloud.

Looking behind us, I could see that the bumblebees were having some sort of a group discussion. They'd quit following us and were instead just flying around in circles. Were they friendly circles? I couldn't tell.

"There!" Betsy said. "I've just defeated one hundred seventy-two thousand and fourteen bees! I now lead you by, let me check my calculations and see what you've been doing . . . ahh, that's right . . . *nothing*. So I lead by one hundred seventy-two thousand and fourteen bees."

"How did you count them?" I asked.

"Cross-indexing scent signatures with wing vibration frequency. How else?"

"I don't know. Maybe ask their names? And this contest isn't fair! You locked the doors!" I have to admit that when I'd thought up the contest, I'd actually *wanted* Betsy to win because she was clearly jealous (although, of *nothing*) and I really didn't want any kisses from Nate, anyway, but now my competitive instinct was fully roaring, because Betsy was *cheating*.

"My apologies, Delphine," Betsy said. "I will open the doors."

All the doors flung open. We were at least thirty feet in the air just then (after ramping off a series of construction supplies for the new Polt Auditorium) and just about to soar through a new swarm of bees. I honestly have no idea how smart bees can be, but I was willing to bet that every last bee in the swarm would notice the helpless target that was bouncing around inside the wide-open car.

"Close the doors!" I yelled. Betsy immediately closed the doors.

"Make up your mind," she said. The doors locked shut.

Betsy again sprayed the sugar cloud, attracting the bees even closer, but this time she emitted the electrical surge, stunning the swarm. I could hear them grunting and groaning (buzzing, I mean, but I knew what they meant), and Melville, perched on my shoulder, made a soft buzz of sympathy.

"Why didn't you use the 'friend' chemical again?" I asked Betsy.

"Because I have no more supply. And you are now two hundred eighty-three thousand six hundred and twenty-seven bees behind in our contest. Do you wish to declare your surrender?"

"I wish to declare that I have not yet begun to fight," I said, sitting helplessly in a locked car from which I could not escape, with only one bee inside.

Just Melville.

She was buzzing at me.

She'd landed on Nate's messenger bag. The one that contained his gym clothes and also an assortment of tablets and pills he'd invented. Pills that had all sorts of amazing abilities.

Hmmm.

I reached out and picked up the bag, with Melville nodding in approval. Rummaging inside, I found "Outer

Space Breathing Pills," and those "Lightning Breath Pills" that I'm afraid of, and I found some allergy pills. None of these seemed like they'd help very much, so I kept searching, grabbing bottle after bottle.

"Ooo!" I said. "'Shower Pill!'" I was sweating. Heavily. It was gross. I swallowed the pill and instantly felt much fresher, though there weren't any bursts of water from nowhere or anything like that. Too bad. I went back to sorting through the pills. I found some "Make Any Animal a Zebra Pills," and some "Chameleon Pills," and a bottle labeled, in Nate's very precise handwriting, as "Big Muscle Beefcake Time." I very carefully returned those pills to the bag. They sounded a bit too peculiar, and possibly dangerous.

"Ahh!" I said, finding another bottle. "'Intangibility Pills'! Just the thing for a trapped sixth grader!" I hurriedly swallowed a pill, which was large and green and apparently made of chalk and sandpaper.

Nothing happened.

Well, it made my throat hurt, and there was a strange noise in my stomach, like I'd swallowed a clock. *Tick-tock, tick-tock, tick-tock*.

"Bzzz?" Melville questioned. She was hovering in front of my face. She wouldn't land on me anymore because I kept getting tossed around whenever Betsy took a quick corner or launched herself into the air, making it far too dangerous for Melville to come near me. She didn't want to get squished. I suppose nobody really does.

"Not sure," I answered in response to her questioning buzz. "Nothing seems to have happened."

My phone beeped.

It was a text.

From Nate.

It read, Wait for it.

"Huh?" I said, looking at my phone. "What does he mean? Is he . . . ?" But at that point my stomach made a new noise.

Tick-tock, tick-tock, tick-tock.

GLURGLE.

And then I fell through the bottom of the car.

chapter
10

Falling was weird. I wasn't doing it very fast, because I was mostly intangible to gravity as well. I felt like a leaf, falling gently, and it might've even been fun except the bees saw me instantly and collectively decided, "That looks like a *magnificent* target!" So they came buzzing toward me in a swirling mass, trying to land on me or sting me or annoy me as best they could, but . . . nope.

"Hah!" I yelled at them. "Delphine Gabriella Cooper is intangible!"

They were only flying through me, accidentally flying into one another and knocking their little bee heads together, buzzing in irritation and getting fuzzy.

Wait.

Why were they getting fuzzy?

My phone rang.

It was Nate.

I could tell by the ringtone.

Godzilla's roar.

But I couldn't answer my phone because my hand kept moving right through it. And everything was getting very, very fuzzy. And . . . dim.

"Hey, Delphine," Nate said from my phone. "Hope you don't mind that I overrode your phone's controls and made it accept my call, and then put me on speakerphone. My calculations show that by now you probably can't touch your phone, because you took an intangibility pill."

"What's happening?" I yelled. But I couldn't even hear myself.

"I've also determined that there's a one hundred percent chance you just asked me a question, since you're always asking questions, which is one reason you're so interesting. Unfortunately, I can't hear you." He paused.

"Why can't you hear me?" I asked. I'll point out that I wasn't blaming him, because I couldn't even hear myself.

"The reason I can't hear you . . ." There was a pause. Nothing. Then a sharp sound, and I could hear him breathing. Bosper began barking in the background. I heard a pounding noise, a burst of something electrical, and then Nate was back.

"Sorry about that," he said. "Still being attacked. Now, the reason I can't hear you is because you're almost entirely intangible, meaning your vocal cords can't produce sound waves. That's also why you're probably having trouble seeing right now, because your eyes work by channeling light from the pupil to the retina, which is basically a big lump of light-sensitive neurons called photoreceptors. They change light into electrical stimuli that . . . well . . . you probably want me to get to the point."

"I do want you to get to the point," I said, fully understanding that he couldn't hear me, but at the same time knowing he would hear me anyway, somehow.

"Wow, I can almost hear you saying it," Nate said. "Weird. Anyway, you're too intangible for the light. It's passing right through you. Your pupils and retinas can't capture it. That's why your vision is going dim. Now, I'm guessing you're floating in midair amid a vast swarm of confused bees?"

"That pretty much sums it up," I said.

"Anyway, ninety-seven percent chance of that, so I'll just assume it's happening. What I need you to do is not worry. Even though you're going to be largely intangible, the worst of the effects will pass soon enough. I hope you're floating over something soft."

I looked down. I was floating over a sidewalk, which would be described rarely as soft.

"How long until the effects pass?" I asked. Nate couldn't hear me. I just had to hope he'd know what I was saying. With anyone else, it probably wouldn't work, but with Nate . . . ? Well, one time when I was in his room I noticed a chart on his wall (he has charts on his wall . . . *all over* his walls . . . sometimes thirty or forty charts deep) that was nothing but the odds on what I might say at any particular time. I'd looked at it, then turned to him and said, "You have a chart that gives odds on what I'm going to say? That's creepy weird."

He'd only nodded, then tapped on the bottom of the chart, where "That's creepy weird" came in at 99.8 percent. So I figured Nate would know what I was going to ask, even though he couldn't hear me, and that he'd tell me how long the worst of the intangibility effects would—

"Five," he said.

"What?"

"Four, three, two, and . . . one."

I fell.

"Ooompff!" I said when I hit the sidewalk, which actually did feel softer than I'd feared. I suppose being partially intangible does have its benefits. I scrambled for my fallen phone, but the call had been lost and my mostly intangible fingers weren't doing so well with picking up the phone, and the touch screen was absolutely refusing to acknowledge that I was touching it. At least my vision was coming back. Colors were still oddly faded, but I could see I was in a residential area. Rows of houses. Nobody in sight. Betsy was speeding down the street, coming my way, screeching her tires. She came to a squealing stop right next to me, so close that I worried about my toes.

I looked down.

There was a note on the sidewalk. One of Nate's notes. A precisely folded triangle with "Delphine" written on top of it.

I opened it up, though it was a bit tricky, since the paper kept sliding partially through my mostly intangible hands. At least there was no chance of paper cuts.

The note read, "Hey . . . no chance of paper cuts, right? But, I should get to the point. If you find this note, you're only a few blocks from Tommy Brilp's garage. I need you to go there and disable the transmitter before these bumblebee swarms get even worse. And, no pressure, but it's probably best you hurry, because I can only hold off the attack on my house for so long. Also, if you look up, there are probably some bees about to attack you."

I looked up.

There were some bees about to attack me.

It was a huge swarm. The biggest one yet.

I leaped onto Betsy's hood (no way was I getting *inside* the car again) and yelled, "Tommy Brilp's garage, Betsy! Hurry!" Thankfully, she didn't argue with me or spend any time dreaming about Nate; she just zoomed off and away, leaving the bees behind. Her hood twisted a bit in order to form handles that I could hold, and I didn't bounce too much since I was still partially intangible.

But *only* partially.

That meant I could use my phone.

I called Nate.

I said, "How did you know where to leave that note?"

He said, "Because you wore a skirt yesterday, and there was an X19 solar flare measured this morning, and the prevailing wind is only gusting at seven miles per hour. It all adds up."

"Oh," I said. Nate's reasons rarely make sense to me. I've learned to accept that. Kind of.

Nate said, "Well, I should go. I'm being shot at."

"What?" I screamed.

"Yeah. Lots of shooting, here."

"Nate!" I absolutely screamed. And then I hung up the phone, because I'm one of those people who believe it's not safe to be on the phone while you're driving, and if you shouldn't be on the phone while you're driving, then you probably shouldn't be on the phone while you're being shot at.

I scowled at my phone.

Stashed it away.

Scowled some more.

Then I grabbed up my phone again and called Mom.

"Delphine," she said. "Where are you?"

"At the mall," I lied, because mothers almost never want to hear that you're fighting millions of bees that are being controlled by a menacing secret society. "How's the bee situation, Mom?"

"Oh. Much better. There were so many! Gone now, though. There's a peculiar gull flying over the house now. Just . . . circling and circling. I think it scared the bees off. Isn't that strange?"

"Weird," I said. Parts of me wanted to explain to Mom that Sir William was a robot, but then I'd have to tell her all about Nate, and I was worried Mom wouldn't want me to be friends with Nate anymore, because she would ridiculously overreact and think it was too dangerous.

"Gotta go, Mom!" I said, because it was time to fight the mysterious murder society and their insect horde.

"Delphine, you sound anxious. Is there something you're not telling me?"

"Huh? No! There's just . . . a sale here. At the mall. Where I'm at. A sale on . . . things I like."

"Well, that didn't make me suspicious at all."

"Good!" I said, pretending I didn't hear the sarcasm in her voice, which made me feel a little bit like Nate. "Talk to you later, Mom!" I ended the call just as Betsy screeched to a halt and screamed, "We're here!"

"Also," she said, "there are lots of bees here." I looked back the way we came, and there was an incoming swarm. Also, there was a swarm covering Tommy's garage. So, two swarms.

"I need to get in that garage!" I told Betsy. It didn't look possible. The garage was currently a garage-shaped mound of bees, with the bees scrabbling to get inside. I could hear Tommy yelling from inside, cursing at the bees, but at least it didn't sound like he was being stung.

"I'll spray sugar water to attract them," Betsy said. "And then you run into the garage while you have a chance."

"Good plan," I said. "Tell me when you're about to do it."

"Ready in three . . . two . . . one." A big cloud of sugary water sprayed out of her muffler, billowing into the air. The two bumblebee swarms both shivered with interest. Then, here and there, a bee peeled away from the garage to investigate the new and obviously interesting (to bees) cloud. Soon, like one massive creature, the entire swarm left the garage and buzzed toward the sugar-water cloud. The other swarm began heading toward it as well. This was my chance.

I leaped off the car.

Then, just before I could start running, Betsy's door popped open and one of her air-conditioning vents sprayed another cloud of sugar water.

On . . . me.

"Glack!" I said, as the sugary mist spilled all over me.

And then Betsy's door slammed shut and locked.

"Good luck!" she said.

"What? No! Are you *serious*? You just . . . *BETSY!*"

"I would advise you to run," she said.

It was good advice.

So, if ever there was a time to panic, I'd found it.

The bees were indecisively hovering between the two clouds of sugar water, meaning the one that was slowly settling to the street, and the one that was named Delphine Cooper and was kicking the side of a talking car. I was beginning to wonder if Nate had created Betsy on a Friday the thirteenth, the day he does really stupid things. Everything would make more sense that way.

I ran for the garage. It was challenging, because I was still partially intangible, not getting much traction. Melville flew next to me, unable to perch on my shoulder because she'd sink right through. She gave a buzz that I took as an inquiry, and I said, "Sure. Go ahead. Have some sugar water." She buzzed happily and began licking up some of the disgusting substance that was covering me. Because I was partially intangible, it was dripping off faster than normal, which was good, but it was also dripping *inside* me, because I was so porous that, in effect, I'd become a living cloud of sugar water.

The bees approved.

The two swarms had combined into one gigantic

swarm, hungry and impolite, and they were gaining on me, but I made it to the garage door first, frantically knocking and yelling, "Let me in!"

"Who's . . . who's out there?" I heard from inside. It was Tommy's voice.

"It's me! Delphine Cooper!" Behind me, I could hear the bees getting even closer.

"Delphine?" Tommy's voice was full of wonder. I should probably point out that Tommy has a crush on me. He's always asking if I'd like to go to the movies, or to the park, or to the roller derby (I honestly do want to go to the roller derby, but it would be more fun with Nate), and he tries to walk me home sometimes, even though we live in entirely opposite directions. Also, he wants us to form a band, with him on drums and me on guitar, but Tommy's already in a band called Captain Underworld's Circus of Breakfast Hellfire and I want to start a band called Unicorn Sparkle Boot, so I doubt we're compatible, music-wise.

"Let me in!" I said, intangibly pounding on the door. "It's me! Delphine! You know . . . the cute girl who doesn't like being trapped outside a locked door and getting devoured by bees? Remember?" I hoped that last part wouldn't throw him off, since we'd never talked about me being devoured by bees before, but while it's true that most boys are endlessly confused about girls, I think they're smart enough to understand that we don't want to be devoured by bees.

"Are there any bees with you?" He sounded scared. I couldn't help but think Nate wouldn't have asked that question. He'd have immediately unlocked the door. In fact, he'd have probably known I was coming, and the door would've been unlocked from the start, because Nate seems able to predict the future sometimes, with the way he—

I noticed a note taped to the garage.

It had my name on it.

In Nate's handwriting.

I tore it open and read it as fast as I could. It said, "I can't actually predict the future; I'm just really good with probabilities. Not the same thing. Anyway . . . don't forget you're partially intangible. You can just walk through the door. Like a ghost."

"Oh yeah!" I yelled, just as the first bees reached me.

"See you, suckers!" I said, stepping forward.

It felt somewhat like water. But very *dense* water. There was more resistance than I'd hoped, enough that at first I was worried I wouldn't be able to make it all the way through, and I'd have to turn around and apologize to all the bees for calling them suckers, and it would be really embarrassing because once you've said your exit line, you really *do* have to exit, or else it's awkward.

But I kept pressing onward, squeezing myself through the door, which groaned and moaned as the wood complained of my passing, like when you kick your way through a pile of leaves. As soon as I reached the other side, I waved hello to Tommy (he was hiding inside a stack of tires, with only his head and shoulders showing), and then I turned quickly around, unlocked the door (the bolt kept slipping through my hands, but I was growing more and more tangible), and opened the door just long enough for Melville to fly through.

"Bzzz!" she said in appreciation as I slammed the door shut behind her.

"Are y-you a g-ghost?" I heard Tommy ask with a whimper, hiding in his stack of tires. "Did the bees m-murder you?"

"What? No! I just swallowed an intangibility pill so that I could . . . well, it's complicated, but I'm not a ghost." Melville landed on my shoulder and only sank a little. The intangibility pill was definitely wearing off.

"Is that a b-bumble-b-bee?" Tommy shrieked. He tried to scramble away, but only managed to tip over the tires and fall. He looked like an enchilada, rolling around on the garage floor, encased in the tires with only his feet and head visible, yelling and cursing.

"Quit laughing, ghost!" he said. Boys don't like to be laughed at. Well, Nate doesn't mind, but that's because he enjoys my laugh, and also because he says he learns something every time I make fun of him. But, most boys hate it.

"Seriously, Tommy," I said. "I'm not a ghost." I was helping him out of tires. The pill had worn off and I was entirely solid.

"But you . . . phased through the door." He pointed to me, and pointed to the door. It was unfortunate. I'd been hoping he hadn't seen me do that.

"And you were . . . transparent," he said. "Ghostly." He was becoming confused. He poked at my shoulder, then let out a squeak when Melville buzzed in warning.

"Don't worry," I told him. "She's friendly. Her name is Melville. And you must have been hallucinating everything else. Maybe you were stung by the bees? Did you get some bee venom in your blood? That causes hallucinations, you know." I nodded in a knowing fashion. Nate tells me that most people will believe anything as long as you act confident when you lie.

"Oh," Tommy said. "Yeah. That's probably what happened."

I looked around, trying to think of a way we could escape. There wasn't much of anything in the garage that I thought could help us. There were the tires, a couple of bicycles, an assortment of household junk, but mostly it was a practice area for Tommy's band, meaning there was a drum set, a pair of guitars, some speakers, and lots of band posters on the walls.

I glanced at my phone, where I could see . . . via Sir William's radar . . . the swarms covering Tommy's garage. And there were several other swarms downtown, and another at the swimming pool, and all throughout the shopping district. There was another just outside my favorite comic book store, several at the police station, and basically there were swarms of bees . . . everywhere.

"We're stuck in here," I grumbled.

"Yeah," Tommy said, resigned. He'd gone to his drum set and was fiddling with the drumsticks.

"But I *can't* be. I need to get back to saving the city."

"Saving the city?"

"Yeah."

"Wow. You're like . . . a hero." He drummed a couple of riffs on his drums. I walked over to the window, which had a fine view of a swarm of bees covering the glass. I made a gesture to them, a rude one that I was hoping they'd forget if they managed to get inside the garage.

My phone buzzed in my pocket.

It was Nate.

He asked, "Have you disabled Tommy's transmitter?" I looked over to Tommy. He's maybe five foot three. His long hair is the color of fresh dirt. He has pronounced cheekbones and an equally pronounced nose. He's lanky.

He was wearing blue jeans and a T-shirt with an anarchy symbol, the one that always makes Nate laugh, because of the whole corporate structure that it took to sell Tommy a shirt about anarchy.

I told Nate, "So, in order to un-attune the transmitter, I could just get him *really* scared, right?"

"That would work, yes."

I looked to Tommy. He was playing his drums, nervously tapping on them, looking to the walls and the ceiling, swallowing repeatedly. After a bit he dropped the drumsticks and covered his ears. The relentless drone of the bees outside the garage was getting to him.

I told Nate, "I think I can handle this. He's terrified of bees."

"Oh. Bad time for him, then. Are you sure he's not facing his fears?"

"No. He's facing the wall." It was true. Tommy was now standing against the wall, mumbling to himself. I couldn't hear what he was saying over the roar of the bees outside.

"Hmm," Nate said. "Well, then, have Melville sting Tommy."

"Can do," I said. It was exactly what I'd been thinking. I wouldn't normally ask a bee to sting one of my friends, but not only were the bees starting to inundate Polt, but I could hear Bosper frantically barking in the

212

background of the phone, and there was also what sounded like occasional gunfire. *Not* good. Nate seemed calm, but he always does. The point is, there were already too many bumblebees in the city, and Nate needed me back at his house as soon as possible, and I needed to disable the bee-summoning transmitters, so . . . if having Melville sting Tommy would hurry that up, then so be it.

"Go sting Tommy," I whispered to Melville.

She did.

With permission granted, she eagerly whooshed closer to Tommy and then stopped, looking back to me. At first I didn't know what she wanted, what she was asking, but then I figured it out and pointed to my left forearm.

"Get him here," I said.

Melville turned, zoomed in, and stung Tommy on his left forearm.

"Gee-yarggh!" he yelled.

"Good," Nate said. "Sounds like she stung him on the left forearm. An excellent choice. That's one more transmitter disabled." I was watching Tommy. He was staring at me in outrage. And he was glaring at his bee sting in outrage. He was also staring at Melville, flying back to me, in outrage. I'd have to say that his general mood was outrageous.

"Who's next?" I asked Nate. "I could find Marigold Tina, or should I try to find Gordon Stott again?"

"I'd say Gordon. Since we didn't find him the first time, it's probably best that . . . that . . . Uh oh, that's nuclear."

"Huh? What's nuclear?"

"Oh . . . nothing. A development, here. Entirely unexpected. How exciting!"

"Nate, what's nuclear?"

"A weapon of Maculte's. The Red Death Tea Society is—" But at that point there was a strange keening whistle from my phone, and then silence except for Bosper barking, and after that we lost contact, which instantly made me sweat. Sweat even *more*, I mean. I was wishing I'd have stashed that whole bottle of "Shower Pills" in my pocket.

I immediately dialed Nate back.

Nothing. No answer.

I texted him, What happened?

Nothing. No return text.

Okay then, no reason to panic, besides having every reason to panic. I needed to help Nate, and that meant I needed to get out of the garage. I ran over to Tommy to find that he was clutching his forearm, where a big red welt was starting to form. It looked like he was growing a miniature volcano.

"Your bee stung me!" he said. He was angry.

"We needed to disable your transmitter," I answered.

"Oh," he said. But his expression was understandably confused. Then he brightened and asked, "Hey, would you like to go out sometime?"

"Yes."

"Whoa! Really? Excellent! We could go—"

"No. Shush. I meant that I want to go out of this *garage*. But I can't. Too many bees. Especially since I'm covered in sugar water."

"Is that what that is? Some new perfume? It smells like you put a lot on."

"A car accident," I said, which was almost true and sounded saner than the truth. By then I was pacing, walking the length of the garage, looking for anything that might help. But it was just the tires, the posters on the walls, the band equipment, nothing of any use. I might be able to outdistance the bees on one of the bicycles, but that wouldn't get me through the swarm in the first place, and the band equipment was useless, especially since I'm not all that talented of a singer, or a guitar player, as was so nicely (I mean *incredibly rudely*) pointed out by the rock camp instructor when she said that whenever I was really cutting loose it scared the bears, the deer, the raccoons, the squirrels, the turtles and . . .

. . . and . . .

. . . and . . .

"Hey," I said.

Tommy looked up and said, "What?"

I picked up the black guitar (because it looked the most hard-core) and slung the strap over my shoulder. I plucked on the strings, making sure they were properly tuned. Then I plugged the guitar into the amplifier and turned all the dials up as far as they would go.

I tapped my toes on the concrete floor and looked over to Tommy.

"Let's make some noise," I said.

🔆

The bees didn't know what hit them.

As soon as I was ready, I had Tommy fling open the door. He then immediately ran to his stack of tires and dove inside, covering the top with a blanket we'd found on the shelves.

A few inquisitive bees came in through the open door, then immediately left.

"Scouts," I told Melville. She was on my shoulder. I had my weight on one leg, guitar slung over my shoulder, waist cocked to the side, a sneer on my lips.

A mass of bees was now hovering just outside the door. A swarm so thick that I couldn't see through them. It was a solid wall of bumblebees.

"Free concert," I encouraged them. "Come on in."

The swarm moved a bit closer. But they were oddly timid. Can bees sense a trap? I tried to look afraid. It was exceptionally easy to do, because I was, in fact, afraid. What if my plan didn't work? How many bumblebees would sting me? Only a few hours ago, a single bee had swelled my forehead into a melon. This time, with so many bees, I could end up looking like a hot-air balloon.

The swarm moved closer. I adjusted the guitar strap on my shoulder.

"Are you guys music lovers?" I asked. The bees were invading the garage, marching across the floor like a thick and relentless tide, scuttling over the walls and the ceiling, creeping closer. And of course there were thousands of bumblebees in the air. Tens of thousands. Maybe *hundreds* of thousands.

"C'mon, girls," I said. "Get your front-row seats." The swarm was coming closer, closer. The ones on the floor and the walls were several inches deep. And the ceiling was forming stalactites, huge dripping columns of bees. The bumblebees were coming closer, closer, sharpening their stingers, probably already dreaming about the day they'd tell their grandchildren the story of how they'd stung Delphine Gabriella Cooper over one . . . hundred . . . *billion* times.

They came closer.

Closer.

They were a few feet away.

Even closer.

I cocked my hip even more to the side, delivered my absolute best sneer, and said, "Thank you for coming out tonight. The name of this band is . . . *Sugar Water.*"

Then I smashed my fingers against the guitar strings, strumming violently against them, and the speakers and the amplifiers did their job, and it was as if lightning had exploded inside the garage and I'd just become the sixth grade rock-and-roll equivalent of *thunder*.

"Thunder!" I yelled. Tommy peeked out from his tires, watching the first wave of pure noise drive the bees backward, sending them tumbling through the air, pinwheeling back over themselves, smashing into one another.

"Thunder!" I screamed, again strumming against the guitar strings, unleashing my entire repertoire of three notes. My fingers were flying against the strings, causing the guitar to shudder in my hands and the speakers to spark in the raging fury of the noise I was unleashing. Again and again I strummed against the strings, faster and louder each time. The speakers were screeching. The walls were shaking.

"Thunder!" I bellowed, and I started singing a song I'd written during Rock Camp, a song about a unicorn with a machete for a horn, and the army of tigers and lions it defeats, and how he sends them falling into a black abyss, and even though I didn't really remember many of the words (mostly just *"Unicorn strikes! Lion falls! Unicorn strikes! Tiger howls! Black abyss! BLACK ABYSS!"*), it didn't seem to matter very much, because the bees were too busy desperately fighting to get out of the garage, with the noise battering them against the walls, a roaring wave of concussive force smashing them out of the air, sending them tumbling away from me, like leaves caught in a rock-and-roll hurricane.

"THUNDER!" I shouted at the top of my considerable lungs, and as I crashed my fingers down against the guitar strings, all the windows exploded.

Betsy wasn't talking to me.

Not much, anyway.

She'd been waiting for me when I walked out from the garage, silently watching as I let the guitar fall to the ground, like rock stars do when they leave the stage. All around me was the broken glass from the windows, and huge piles of unconscious bees, all of them stunned by the sounds I'd unleashed. Tommy was following me, excitedly blabbering about how awesome I was, and I could see that he was crushing on me even harder now that I was the Queen of Rock-and-Roll Thunder, but I wasn't interested in him (or in any boy that I'd have to save) because all I wanted to do was get back to Nate's house and stop the Red Death Tea Society.

"Hmm," Betsy said, opening her door so that I could get in.

"What?" I said.

"Nothing."

"Whatever," I said. "Betsy, we have to get back to Nate's house. There's been a change of plans, and Polt will have to worry about the bees itself for a bit, because Nate and I talked on the phone and he said something about a nuclear weapon." I was breathless from talking so fast and being so nervous.

"Hmm," Betsy said, speeding off.

"Bzzz?" Melville said, crawling out of my hair, where she'd hidden when I was bringing the thunder.

"We're going home," I told her.

"Bzzz?" she said.

"Yeah. I *know* Nate wanted us to disable the transmitters, but that was before the Red Death Tea Society went nuclear."

"Bzzz," she said, agreeing with me.

"Hmm," Betsy said.

"What *is* it?" I asked her. "Why do you keep grunting like that?"

"I believe . . . I just thought I should tell you, you see, the bees, in the garage."

"Yes? What about them?"

"There were four hundred seventeen thousand six hundred and twenty-one of them."

"Okay," I said. I didn't understand why that was important.

Betsy said, "Delphine, this means you've defeated one hundred thirty-three thousand nine hundred and ninety-four more bees than I have."

"Oh," I said.

Together, in silence, we sped off to Nate's house.

chapter
11

There wasn't anything wrong at Nate's house.

Nothing I could see, anyway.

That made me more nervous than if I'd seen a whole herd (flock? swarm?) of Red Death Tea Society assassins. Where were they? Why were the house and even the entire neighborhood so *quiet*? Proton, Nate's exceptionally irritating cat, was walking across the lawn, entirely unconcerned about anything. That, of course, meant nothing, because cats never truly concern themselves with anything beyond naps and food, neither of which I suspected the Red Death Tea Society would use in an attack, and certainly neither of which were known to go nuclear.

"Go take a nuclear nap," I told Proton as he walked past me. He made the slightest of hisses. We haven't been on very good terms since we first met, when he'd grown into a monster and tried to murder me.

I made it to the front door with nobody shooting at me, or doing anything at all. There was simply no one to be seen. No attack in progress. I could hear a television from inside the house. The living room is right off the front door, and a window was open. I snuck around the house and peered inside, to where I could see Nate's dad, Algie, dusting the frames of the paintings that hang on the wall. The television was playing a game show from Japan, one where oiled-up contestants in bathing suits were seeing how far they could slide across a room without falling into a pit. Algie was watching the show, dusting the paintings, chuckling whenever one of the contestants tumbled into the pit.

"Nothing seems wrong," I told Melville. She'd taken her perch on my shoulder.

"Bzzz," she buzzed. I couldn't tell what she meant.

"Do you think Nate lied about the house being under attack?" I asked. I should mention that it's not like I thought a bumblebee could answer my questions; I just needed someone to talk to, to work out my thoughts. And I didn't really think Nate would lie about the attack, but maybe it was possible that he'd fibbed on the actual location, so that I couldn't find him? He might've thought he was protecting me, keeping me from showing up and getting into trouble. If he'd wanted to protect me from trouble like that, then *he* was the one who was going to be in trouble.

I knocked on the door.

It was only a few seconds until Algie opened the door. Mr. Bannister is tall, a couple of inches over six feet. He has Nate's brown hair, although not as floppy, and they have the same nose, meaning Algie's nose is too big. Still, instead of looking out of place, Algie's nose, like Nate's, only seems to accentuate his eyes, which are wide and intelligent. Mr. Bannister works as a mailman and keeps very fit. I can remember Nate telling me his dad often wishes he could just strap a mailbag to his back and jog his delivery route.

Oh, and he skateboards, too, and there's a full sleeve tattoo on his right arm, one in the style of the old Japanese prints, a tattoo of an entire fishing village trying to fend off an attack from a giant squid. It's quite bizarre and I like it a lot.

"What's up, Delph?" he asked, moving aside to let me in. He's the only one I allow to call me Delph. My brother Steve calls me Delph, too, but he is not allowed.

"Looking for Nate," I said. I stretched out the words, looking for evidence of tea drinking, of Red Death Tea Society members, or for anything that appeared out of the ordinary, especially if it was nuclear.

"He's in his room," Algie said. He turned down the hall and yelled, "Nate! Delph's here!" Proton the cat took advantage of the open door and tried to get into the house, but Algie nudged him back outside and closed the door, saying, "Stupid cat's been howling and hissing for the past couple of hours. Scratching at nothing." He shook his head.

"Cats will do that," I said, pretending that the cat's behavior didn't mean anything, but wondering if it did. I could hear Melville buzzing softly in my hair. She'd hidden when Algie opened the door.

"Can I get you anything?" Algie asked. "I just made sandwiches if you're hungry. Cookies, too. Fresh baked." He gestured to the kitchen.

I said, "No thanks. I'm good," mostly out of habit, but then my stomach rumbled (apparently paying attention to the conversation) and I said, "Oh. You know what? A sandwich would be great."

We walked to the kitchen, with Algie leading the way. At one point he seemed to stumble, and he frowned at the hallway floor. There wasn't anything there.

"I've been clumsy all day," he said, mostly to himself, scowling. Then, before I could comment, he yelled down the hall again. "Nate! Delph's here! Come out of your room! Go rock climbing or something! It's a beautiful day!"

We'd made it to the kitchen, where Algie tried to open

the fridge, but it seemed to be stuck. He struggled with it a bit, frowning. "It's been sticking all day," he said. "Might have to get it looked at." He took a covered platter of sandwiches from the now-open refrigerator and said, "You like rock climbing, right?"

"I guess."

"It would do Nate a world of good to get out more." Algie reached up to the cabinets to get a plate, but because he was talking to me he was absently reaching for the wrong cabinet. He was, in fact, reaching for the cabinet that I knew hides all the computerized equipment Nate uses to control every aspect of the house. There was more computerization in that cabinet than in a NASA control room. There were strange buttons. Levers. Dials. Keypads. Nate's mom and dad are never supposed to look in there. Nate keeps his amazing genius secret even from his parents.

Just as Algie was reaching for the cabinet, a small valve opened and a spray of gas whooshed out. It momentarily enveloped Algie's head, and for one second it was as if he were a robot, acting very mechanically, turning away from Nate's secret cabinet and opening the adjacent one to take out a plate. He clearly didn't even notice what had happened.

"Turkey, Swiss cheese, and guacamole," he said. "That work for you?"

"Sure," I said. Where was Nate? Where was the Red Death Tea Society? Was I too late? Had they already taken him and gone? Is that why everything was so quiet? My stomach was rumbling with anxiety and hunger.

Algie set me up with a plate of oatmeal cookies and a sandwich, plus a glass of lemonade. I sat at the table, eating, waiting for Nate. The sandwich was delicious. As were the cookies. Algie went to check on Nate, and while he was gone Melville crawled out of my hair and flew down to the table. I could hear Algie moving down the hall, and there was a soft thump, and then his voice quietly murmuring, "Again? Why am I so *clumsy* today?"

I just chomped on my sandwich. Wondering. I was thinking about what Nate had said about Maculte, how the man wanted everyone to have an assigned number, a set value of their worth, and I knew that it would all be based on pure intelligence. There would be no room for creativity, for dancers or actors or comic book artists. There would be no room for people who just wanted to laugh or swim or hang out with their friends. Those people . . . to Maculte . . . were small numbers. It would be a bleak, gray world if the Red Death Tea Society won. But where *were* they? I'd come to Nate's house for a fight, but all I was getting was a sandwich. To say that I was confused and tense would be an understatement.

Case in point, I almost screamed when my phone buzzed on the table, and Melville must have been feeling the same way, because she nearly stung my phone, as if fighting off an attacker.

It was a text, from Liz. It said, Where are you?

I texted back, At Nate's. Again.

Oh. *Again*? I could say some things about you being at Nate's *again*, but won't, because . . . this. That was the whole of the text, but only a couple of seconds later an image popped up. It was Liz, looking thoughtful. And winking.

Seriously, nothing between us, I wrote back. I thought I heard a noise behind me. It was a . . . a . . . thumping noise of some sort, but I looked back and there was nothing there. Weird.

We're still at the mall, Liz texted. But we were just thinking of you. There are bees here. Flying around.

Bees? I wrote.

Bees, Liz wrote. They're insects. Like the ones that stung you.

Yes. Thank you. I know.

Bees in the mall, Liz wrote. It's abysmal. Get it? "A bee's mall." Abysmal.

That's very clever, Liz.

I know. Listen, seriously, you okay?

I'm okay.

Polt seems . . . weird today. Dangerous. Where are all these bees coming from? Be careful.

You, too, Liz. I put the phone down. Melville landed near it, as if keeping watch, perhaps wary of it buzzing at her again. Bees must hate being buzzed at.

I was just finishing my sandwich when I again thought I heard that noise behind me. I quickly turned around, but there was nothing.

"Did you hear that?" I asked Melville. She buzzed in a noncommittal fashion. I don't even know if bumblebees hear very well. I kept an eye behind me as I munched on a cookie.

There was a loud thump from beneath the table. I gasped and pulled my legs back so quickly that I almost fell over, scrambling out of my chair to look beneath the table.

Nothing.

"What's going on?" I murmured. I'm not prone to hearing things, or being paranoid, so I couldn't chalk it up to that. I drank more lemonade and chomped on another cookie, chewing and crunching, eating so fast that my teeth were clicking together. It was delicious, but I barely noticed. Then, after I swallowed and I was no longer making all the chomping noises, I thought I heard . . . voices?

I concentrated on the sound as hard as I could.

Melville started to buzz but I held up a hand to silence her as she flew up from the table to land on my shoulder. She stayed quiet.

There was definitely thumping from somewhere. Right in the kitchen. Was somebody hiding? I opened the kitchen cabinets, the cupboard beneath the sink, everywhere, but there wasn't anybody tied up or anything like that, which is what I'd been expecting, so maybe I was paranoid after all.

Then . . . something brushed against my leg.

But there was nothing.

Nothing.

"Nate?" I called out. I was now officially nervous. And absolutely paranoid.

Algie walked back into the kitchen and saw me. There was a moment when he was a bit startled, but he immediately relaxed.

"Oh," he said. "It's you. You startled me, Delph. How long have you been here?"

"Umm, maybe five minutes?" Didn't he remember?

"I think Nate's in his room," he said. "I'll see if I can rouse him." Algie turned toward the hall and called out, "Nate! Delph's here!" Melville crawled around to my back, hiding herself in my hair.

"You want a sandwich?" Algie asked, moving past me.

"No. I'm . . . good?" I didn't mean to make it sound

like a question, but Algie clearly didn't remember having let me into the house. Something was definitely strange.

"Cool," Algie said. "Help yourself if you change your mind. There's some sandwiches on a plate in the refrigerator. The door's been sticking today, though, so if you need help, just holler. And, speaking of hollering . . ." He turned to the hall again and bellowed, "Nathan Bannister! There's a beautiful young woman here to see you!" He looked back to me, winked, then said, "That should do it. I'd have been out of my room in a flash, at his age, and Nate can't be all that much different than I was." I just smiled, thinking that Nate was vastly different from not only Algie but, well, *everyone*.

Then I frowned, because something brushed against my back, but when I turned around there was nothing.

Nothing.

Wait.

There *was* something.

One of Nate's notes. On the floor. With my name on it.

I picked it up and was hurriedly unfolding it as Algie walked out of the room. Just before he reached the open doorway he seemed to trip on something and he almost fell over.

"What *is* it with me today?" he murmured, scowling at the floor, where there was absolutely nothing to be seen. I barely paid attention, because I was too busy reading the note. It didn't take long.

The note read, "Delphine. You need goggles. Third cabinet from left."

"Goggles?" I said aloud. "Third cabinet from the left?" I was already in motion, heading toward the cabinet. It was another of Nate's "forbidden" cabinets, the ones he doesn't like anyone else opening. I put my hand on it for a moment because I knew it needed to scan for my palm print. There was a brief glow and then it clicked open, revealing a small refrigerator with several bottles of root beer, a selection of Nate's invention-pills that needed to stay refrigerated, and then a pair of goggles that looked like swim glasses, except with black lenses.

I picked them up.

I put them on.

They were cold.

I said, "Brrr," and shivered, with goose bumps rising on my arms, and then I looked around the room and I said, "GAHHH!" and my goose bumps got about ten times worse.

My vision was now in shades of blue. Everything was blue, just darker in some areas, lighter in others. And I wasn't alone in the kitchen. There was a man just running out of the room, leaping over an unconscious man on the floor. And there was another unconscious man slumped against the refrigerator, which likely explained why the door was so hard to open.

There was also an unconscious woman beneath the table, and yet another man, dazed and senseless, struggling to get up from the counter, where he was stretched out with his head in the sink.

There was even an unconscious man floating above me, bumping along the ceiling like he was an errant balloon.

They were all wearing red suits.

They were assassins from the Red Death Tea Society.

I took off the goggles.

Everyone disappeared.

I put them back on.

"There you are," Nate said. He was standing right in front of me, and let's just say that there's a possibility I screamed and punched him. The chance of that possibility is, well . . . one hundred percent.

And let's just say that as Nate was saying, "Gahhgg!" I was trying to run past him, because he'd *really* startled me. And let's just say that when I punched him in the shoulder, it twisted him around a bit, so that when I was trying to run past him we knocked our heads together, and let's just say that this impact staggered me and that it knocked Nate unconscious.

Let's just say all that.

Because it's all true.

Nate went limp and fell to the floor, and I tripped on him and sprawled just as the man I'd seen running out of the room came back.

He was maybe six feet tall and was built like a bulldozer.

He had a smirk, and he had one of those strange glass ray guns, and he said, "What happened?" when he looked down at Nate, who was entirely unconscious.

"I accidentally knocked him out," I said. "It's . . . a thing I do."

"Thank you," he said, and he leveled the disintegrator gun at Nate, and I scrambled to my feet and leaped in front of Nate, because it was all my fault and I was yelling something, not sure what, mostly just yelling out of fear . . . and then Melville stung the man on his butt.

"Wharrgg!" the man yelled, just as he pulled the trigger, and the shot went whooshing past me, hitting the sink and absolutely disintegrating the faucet, which began spraying water all over the room.

Luckily, "all over the room" included Nate, with the broken faucet spraying water like a small but enthusiastic hose, and Nate began sputtering and trying to push the water away, but of course water is rather insistent, so it kept spraying all over his face.

"Guhh," Nate said, coming to his senses. "Blarrg!

What's with the *water*? Oh. I get it. Delphine, did you knock me out again?" Luckily, I didn't have to answer, because, unluckily, Nate's attention became more focused on an immediate problem.

The man with the gun.

"Look out!" Nate yelled, pushing me to the side just as the man once again pulled the trigger, and this time he hit Nate right in the chest with a full blast of disintegration. There was a huge flash of light.

I screamed in horror.

Melville buzzed in dismay.

The man laughed an evil laugh, displaying tea-stained teeth.

And Nate Bannister said, "Nice try."

He was fine. Nate hadn't been disintegrated at all. I did notice that one of the buttons on his shirt was glowing. It faded as I watched, and then I decided that it was stupid for me to be looking at buttons when I could be much more actively engaged in far more interesting pastimes, such as kicking an assassin in his shins.

So I began kicking him, and as it turned out I was pretty good at it. And Melville, who has many times proven that she's a world-class stinger, began stinging him in a variety of sensitive places, as if at some point in her past someone had given her a precise map of areas where humans would rather not be stung. The man was shrieking in pain and bellowing interesting curses, hopping on one foot and then the other, trying to aim his disintegrator pistol, but every time he did Melville would sting him or I would kick him and then Nate stepped forward with a spray can shaped more like a pencil than a regular can, and he spritzed the man in the face and the man's eyes immediately rolled back in his head and he toppled to the kitchen floor.

"Don't breathe that," Nate told me, pointing to the small blur of mist in the air. "That's my special brand of knockout gas. You'd be unconscious for hours."

I hugged Nate.

Hard as I could.

"You scared me," I said.

"I had everything under control."

"You did? Then what did you mean on the phone when you were talking about something being nuclear?"

"Oh. That. Okay, I had *most* things under control."

"That sounds ominous," I said, stepping back from him. We paused as Algie walked back into the kitchen, completely oblivious to everything. He grabbed an orange juice carton from the refrigerator, having to tug at the door a bit until the man who was slumped against the refrigerator (who Algie clearly didn't see) fell to one side. Algie, now with the orange juice, sloshed his way through the water on the floor to grab a glass from a cupboard. He poured the orange juice in the glass, drank it, then put the glass in the sink and the orange juice carton back in the fridge.

He left.

"Manipulating his mind?" I asked Nate.

"Yeah. Mom, too. She's gardening out back. Bosper is protecting her."

"Why weren't you disintegrated when that man shot you?"

"Force field," Nate said, tapping on one of his buttons. "But . . . why are you here? I thought you were disabling the remaining transmitters?"

"Your 'nuclear' call scared me, so I decided you needed help."

"Thanks. You might be right. I should show you the nuclear thing. Come with me."

We started walking down the hall to his room. There were more unconscious members of the Red

Death Tea Society slumped against the walls, sprawled out on the floor, and one woman was even halfway through a wall. The wall wasn't broken or anything like that; it looked like she'd been intangible, passing through the wall like a ghost, but had somehow fallen unconscious.

Also, there were teacups just *everywhere*. Broken ones, for the most part, and the smell of spilled tea filled the hall.

"You've been busy," I said.

"Some of this is me," he said, gesturing to the various unconscious Red Death Tea Society assassins slumped here and there in their red suits. "And some of this is doorknobs."

"Not even remotely understanding what you mean, Nate."

"Doorknobs," Nate said. We were walking past the door to the laundry room, and Nate tapped on the doorknob. "Extreme defenses. I've installed Category Seven Comprehension Distorters in each of them."

"Still. Not. Remotely. Understanding."

"They emit signals that interfere with the synapses in your brain. You know how your senses work? Things like light and sound make signals that your brain understands, signals that travel through the air. My doorknobs emit signals that *turn off* your understanding.

Interfere with it. So you don't hear some sounds, or see certain things. You're partially immune because of the nano-bots you inhaled, and then those goggles give you the rest of the real view of what's going on."

"You know, since I met you, I'm not sure I've *ever* had the real view of what's going on."

"Well, we can never be entirely sure of anything. That's what's so exciting, right?"

"Right," I said, entirely sure that Nate wouldn't detect the sarcasm in my voice. We were on our way to his room, and having to step over five more members of the Red Death Tea Society, three women and two men, all jumbled together in an unconscious pile. Nate held my hand, steadying my balance as I stepped over them. He gestured to them with a nod.

"It's been interesting," he said. "A full Red Death Tea Society assault on the Infinite Engine. Their attacks have been surprising, innovative. I have no idea what they might do next. Usually I know everything, so having no idea is fun."

"Yeah," I said. "It's great. I do it all the time. Even more since we became friends. What's all this stuff?" We'd made it into his room, which was a mess. There were strange instruments and small inventions tossed all over the place. Nate doesn't usually have them in plain sight because he doesn't want his parents to know about them.

Nate said, "The assassins were looking through my rarest inventions, searching for the Infinite Engine."

"They're not exactly *tidy* burglars, are they?" I asked. Nate just shook his head, and we started putting things back in place. There was a Sonic Fork (which jiggles the calories out of food) and Nate's Mighty Underwear (they allow Nate to levitate, although the wedgie problem is still eluding solution), and I saw his Carrot Jet, which allows carrots to fly, which was apparently something that Nate felt needed to be done. Discarded on Nate's bed was a tube of Ape Balm, which can turn you into an ape with a one hundred percent chance of success, and right next to it was a jar of I Shouldn't Have Made That Ape Balm ointment, which turns you *back* from being an ape, with a forty percent chance of success, so there's still some work to be done there, obviously.

"What are those?" I said, pointing to a pair of athletic shoes with metallic sides.

"Swagger Shoes," Nate said. "They turn you into a better athlete, but also into kind of a jerk."

"Oh," I said. "And . . . how about this?" I was holding up a bolt of cloth. It felt like silk but looked like . . . wood, maybe? Or . . . metal? Denim? Maybe leather? It was constantly changing, fluttering back and forth.

"That's nano-clothing," Nate said. "The same

material I use to make all my clothes, so I can turn my clothes into anything I want."

"Wait a second, are you saying that you *mean* to wear those clothes of yours?" Nate had changed from his vintage clothes into his more-than-a-bit-messy pants and his customary checkered shirt.

"Yes," Nate said, confused. "Why?"

"That's not important, Nate," I said, patting him on the back of his ugly checkered shirt. Melville made a buzz of fashion judgment, but luckily Nate didn't understand what she was saying.

"Oh," Nate said. "Okay." He was reaching inside a small piggy bank, pulling out an invention that couldn't have possibly fit within, but Nate has always been on very good terms with the impossible. The invention he was holding was a circle of metal about the size of a baseball, but with what seemed to be five glass chopsticks stuck through it. The whole thing was softly humming. Melville began buzzing along in harmony.

"What's that?" I asked.

"This is it," Nate said. "My Infinite Engine. An engine with unlimited energy. The math was very difficult, owing to how it exists in fifteen dimensions, three of which need to be anti-structural, but Bosper and I were able to work through all the calculations and now this has the power of hundreds of thousands of suns, or even more."

"Neat," I said, a little scared of getting a sunburn. "No wonder Maculte wants that thing. With that much power he could control the whole planet. He'd be unstoppable. You'd better hide it again. Hide it where nobody would ever find it."

"Right," Nate said. He looked around for a moment, and I could see his brain working. I could see perhaps the greatest mind in all human history calculating the very best hiding place, with Nate's vast intellect weighing the various possibilities and working on a scale that I couldn't even possibly comprehend.

And then he stuck the Infinite Engine under his pillow.

"There," he said. "That should do it."

"What? Under your *pillow*? Are you serious?"

"Here," he said, waving off my concerns and also waving me toward a wall. "This is what I really wanted to show you." I was still staring at Nate's bed, and that obvious lump under the pillow. Nate, meanwhile, was looking at a poster of Nikola Tesla, the amazing inventor, that he'd put up on the wall. Tesla *is* pretty interesting, but I wasn't paying attention to a poster . . . not when the fate of the entire world was resting on Maculte and the Red Death Tea Society *not* looking under Nate's pillow for an engine with infinite power.

But out of the corner of my eye I noticed Nate putting a finger on Tesla's mustache, and Nate twirled his finger and the mustache on the poster twirled around like a dial, and a door opened in the wall.

"You have a secret room?" I asked, seething with jealousy. I've always wanted a secret room.

"Sure," Nate said, walking through the secret doorway, which led almost immediately to some metal stairs leading down. "I have lots of secret rooms. You sound jealous. Do you want me to build you one?"

"Oh. Yes. Please. Nate. Secret room. Me." I'd lost all power of speech. The human mind only has so much capacity for thought, and I was using almost all of mine to design a secret room.

"Put this on," Nate said. It was a hard hat. There were three of them hanging from hooks on the wall.

I said, "Uh, okay." Saving the city was apparently about to get dangerous.

"Stand like this," Nate said. He was standing with his legs wide and arms outstretched. So, saving the city of Polt was about to get . . . silly, I guess?

Suddenly, jets of mist starting coming from everywhere around us on the walls, from the ceiling, and even from the floor. Jets of *cold* mist.

"Yi-yi-yiiiii!" I said, because it was cold and wet and Nate *really* could have warned me it was going to happen.

"I should have warned you that was going to happen," Nate said, and I had an amazing comeback for him (it mostly involved me punching him in the arm), but he was already thumping down the stairs, disappearing from sight.

Which meant that I . . . dripping wet and shivering cold, had little choice but to follow.

💡

"Down here is Project A," Nate said. His voice was coming from the darkness.

"Project A?" I asked.

"The Red Death Tea Society's infiltration plan," Nate said. "You're not going to like this."

"I do not like this," I told Nate.

More insects.

Ants, this time.

We were in an underground tunnel, and it was filled with ants.

Filled with them.

They were each at least an inch long, and they were everywhere, at least a foot deep on the floor and several inches thick on the walls and the ceiling, blocking out so many of the lights that the tunnel had a horrible gloom, and also a constant seething clamor that was something like stomping on dry leaves and brittle sticks, magnified a thousand times over.

Luckily, the ants couldn't touch us. The spray valves had doused Nate and me with ant repellent. Each time we stepped forward, the ants would back off, staying a good two yards away from us, as if Nate and I were in the eye of an ant hurricane.

"Project A," Nate said, gesturing to the ants.

"*A* for 'ants,'" I said. "Very inventive. But what are they doing here?"

"Infiltrating. Trying to find a way into my house. They were able to breach a lot of my defenses, just small cracks, but that opened the door, so to speak, and that's why the Red Death Tea Society is in my house now."

"What can we do?"

"Convince them to leave," Nate said. "I've already been working on it. That's why there aren't very many ants here anymore." I looked around. I would have guessed that the number of ants was at something verging on infinite. Nate noticed the look I gave him.

"Okay," he said. "You're right. This is a lot of ants, but not as many as before. I created tiny robot ants that emit the proper chemicals to blend in with the regular ants. And my robots are emitting other chemicals that are chasing the real ants away. Anytime now, we should reach the tipping point."

"The tipping point?"

"If my robots persuade enough ants to leave, then at some point *all* the ants will become collectively convinced."

"How soon do you think that will happen?" I was scratching at my arms. I was scratching at my legs, my stomach, and my back. I was using my fingers to comb through my hair. I knew there weren't any ants on me, but it *felt* like there were.

"According to my calculations, that should happen in five . . . four . . . three . . . two . . ."

All the ants shuddered. Shivered. And then they turned back down the tunnel, suddenly racing away.

"Hmmm," Nate said. "I was a little bit off, there."

"I'm just glad they're leaving," I said, only then noticing there was a greenish tint to the walls, but only where the ants had been. It was almost as if they'd been painting the walls. And the floor. And the ceiling, too.

"Oh, that's nuclear," Nate said.

"What?"

"Nuclear."

"What?"

"Nuclear."

"Ahhhhhh! Nate, don't tell me what you *said*. Tell me what you *meant*!"

"Oh, I see." Nate adjusted his glasses, referred to an equation he'd written on his pants, and gulped. There was something he didn't want to tell me.

I said, "Melville, sting Nate if he doesn't tell me what he's talking about." Melville rose up from my hair (she'd been hiding from the ants, because she thought they were creepy) and went to hover next to Nate.

Nate said, "Hey! No fair. I'll tell. Each of the ants was applying micro-thin nuclear components to the tunnel's walls, ceiling, and floor. With enough of them in place, a nuclear event could be triggered by remote control."

"A nuclear event," I said.

"Yes."

"You mean a nuclear explosion."

"Yes."

"*Parades* are events. *Birthday parties* are events. Explosions are *explosions*."

"Technically, an explosion could be—"

"Technically, a sixth grade girl named Delphine Gabriella Cooper could explode in an arm-punching fury if some genius doesn't do *something* about the nuclear bomb that she's apparently standing *inside!*"

"Oh. I see. You're worried about a nuclear explosion." Nate stopped and looked at me, as if waiting for me to say, "No, you're entirely wrong . . . I'm not worried about standing at ground zero during a nuclear explosion. Who *would* be?"

Instead, I said, "Yes. That's true."

"Oh. Well. It shouldn't be a problem. I can just realign the atoms so they refuse to enter a critical density stage."

"Great. Any way I can help?"

"Ooo! I was hoping you'd ask!" Nate reached out and took my hand. He wasn't holding it in a "we're dating!" manner; it was more of a "this is cool that you're helping me defuse the scariest bomb in all existence" gesture. I swallowed. Heavily. Nate's hand was warm. Mine felt cold.

Nate asked, "Is there any way you could go hold off the Red Death Tea Society's full scale assault for . . . maybe an hour?"

"Ooog," I said. It wasn't a word. But I pronounced it very clearly.

"What?" Nate asked.

"Piffle," I said. Also not technically a word, but it's a word that I say. It means bad things. I was not thinking good thoughts.

Then I said, "Yes. I can do this."

"Get Bosper to help if you need him!" Nate called out, as I began trudging back down the tunnel, the way we'd come.

Nate, scratching a fingernail through the apparently nuclear ant paint that was covering the tunnel wall, said, "Sorry I can't help, but there are quite a lot of atoms down here, and my nano-bots and I will need to reconfigure a few hundred trillion atoms in order to keep levels below critical."

"Okay!" I said. I tried to smile, but to be honest, my panic levels were reaching critical.

chapter 12

Sssst!" I whispered, trying to get Bosper's attention. The terrier jumped and twisted in midair, landing facing me. We were in Nate's backyard, somewhat under his tree house, next to the garden where Nate's mom grows a selection of flowers and vegetables and a few other things. Bosper had a stalk of rhubarb in his mouth when he saw me, but he spit it out. He's very good at spitting.

"Delphine the red-haired girl!" Bosper said.

"Ahhh!" I gasped. But it was a whispered gasp. Bosper is *not* supposed to talk around Nate's parents. They're not supposed to know he *can* talk. But there was no way that Maryrose, Nate's mom, didn't hear him.

But . . . she didn't. She was on all fours, working slowly along a garden row, pulling weeds from a patch of carrots. She was pulling a few carrots, too, putting them in a basket to be cleaned later. They were nice and ripe, covered in splotches of dirt. There were five of them. Speaking of the number five, that's how many unconscious members of the Red Death Tea Society were in the backyard. There were three women and two men slumped in various areas. One of them was crumpling a row of rhubarb, fallen atop the plants. Another was draped across the branches of a tree, dangling twenty feet over the ground. Sir William, the robot gull, was perched next to him. Seeing Sir William worried me. If he'd left my house, that meant my family was unguarded. And . . . speaking of family . . .

"Don't talk around Maryrose," I whispered to Bosper.

"Nobody hears!" the terrier said, burying a carrot. "The dog can be talking and farting and there is no trouble!"

"There's lots of trouble!" I said. "Nate's figuring out how to disarm a very strange nuclear bomb, and there are assassins in the house searching for Nate's Infinite Engine, and you and I have to fend off the Red Death Tea Society for an hour."

"Bosper will be a good dog!" the terrier said. He was digging up the carrot he'd just buried. Sir William came floating down to the lawn, skipping with the landing until he was at my feet. He made the gull sound a few times, apparently trying to tell me something.

"Ah," Bosper said. "The bird makes discontent."

"Huh? What's up?" Bosper seemed to have understood whatever Sir William had said.

"Bees," Bosper said, "Here comes a big visit!" I realized that Sir William must've been tracking more bees by his radar, and now they were on their way here. So, that's why he'd left my house.

"How many bees?" I asked Sir William. He made the gull noises again. I looked to Bosper for translation.

"Seventeen!" Bosper said.

"Seventeen?" I said. "That's not so bad. A can of bug spray and a tennis racket, and I'll be more than a match for—"

"Seventeen swarms," Bosper said. "Millions of bumblebees! Who likes pudding?"

It was at that moment that I first began to hear the dull roar. It was like the sound of the ocean's waves when you're a mile away. But the noise was growing, building in intensity until it sounded like the ocean's waves were only a half mile away. Then a quarter mile away. A hundred yards away. And then I could see masses of blackness in the sky, swarms of bees converging on Nate's house, millions upon millions of bees like black clouds roiling through the sky, undulating, writhing, twisting, soaring ever closer. The lawn began shaking with the thundering roar of the oncoming bees, and I began to feel like I should run, just run anywhere, simply hide until everything was over and the darkness was gone, because there were so many bees that they were blotting out the light from the sun.

"The dog is someone who likes pudding!" Bosper said. He was jumping up and down, scurrying about, bounding all around.

"I'm not sure we can fight this," I told Bosper.

"We should not fight the pudding," he said in a serious tone. Then, in a whisper, he added, "It is our friend."

"No. I mean . . . the bees." I was looking to Bosper, hoping he would come up with some great idea (which might not have been my best moment, looking to a terrier for guidance) when I noticed there was a note on the ground. One of Nate's notes. With my name on it.

I leaped for it.

It read, "Delphine. Tell Sir William to sing. Tell my mom that she should pick the sweet peas. Also, there's a friend ray in Betsy's glove box. And watch out for Luria. She'll probably attack you with bees."

There was a drawing of a bee on the note. It was quite well done. It had human hands and was holding a huge bomb over its head, with a word balloon of "We can do this, Delphine!"

I told the note, "That's really great that you remind me of the nuclear bomb because it doesn't make me nervous at all." Then I crumpled up the note and tossed it at one of the oncoming seventeen swarms of bees.

The paper arced through the air.

The bumblebees simply parted around it, so that it traveled through a tunnel of bees, not hitting any of them.

"Piffle," I said. I'd been hoping to take down a few of them. Was it so much to ask that a couple of bumblebees would be knocked out? Even momentarily dazed? That way, there would be two less bees to worry about, leaving only infinite bees to deal with.

I sighed.

Time to get to work.

I told Sir William, "Nate says you're supposed to sing."

I told Maryrose, "You should pick the sweet peas!"

"Ohh," Maryrose said, completely oblivious to the bumblebee danger, shuffling along on all fours past the carrots and along the edge of a rhubarb patch to reach the sweet peas. "You're right, Delphine. These do look ripe." She began plucking the peas from their stems. She was humming. The noise was a comforting accompaniment to the roaring swell of the millions of buzzing bees.

And then Sir William began to sing.

I suppose I should've expected something along the

lines of the robot gull's singing voice and what it would do to the bumblebees. After all, I'd been able to knock out two swarms of bees using only my skills as a rock diva, and the robot had far more control of its voice.

The bees wavered when Sir William first began singing. And by "singing" I mean emitting a noise like when you flip through a huge pile of papers, or when talented card dealers shuffle the deck.

The noise was, *"Flapp flapp flappity-flap."* And then it was the same noise, but much quicker. And then the same noise, but much lower in tone. And then even faster and faster until Sir William was racing all along the yard, "singing" in a voice that was similar to the snarling drone of the oncoming bees.

And they began to waver.

They were flying erratically. Losing altitude. Swerving around. Veering sharply in one direction and then another.

"What's happening?" I asked Bosper. The terrier had one of his ears against the ground and a paw over his other. Dogs hear at different audio ranges than humans. It was clear that Sir William's "singing" was not to the terrier's liking.

Thousands of bumblebees were falling to the ground like plump fuzzy raindrops.

Millions of them, even.

But I didn't know what was happening. Bosper hadn't answered me. The bees were struggling to regain the air. Crawling all over one another. Fighting to reach me. It was a yard-deep wave of bees, an insect tsunami that was advancing across the lawn. They were moving slower than they had been in the air, but they were definitely getting closer, and being stung by millions of crawling bees isn't really all that much different from getting stung by millions of flying bees.

"Bosper," I said. "What's happening?" But the poor terrier couldn't speak, too overcome by the noise coming from the robot gull. Then, a bee stung me. It had reached my foot. Crawled up my leg. Stung my shin.

"Piffle!" I said. The crawling swarm surged closer, and I realized I'd been standing there like some terrified nitwit rather than a sixth grade girl on whom the entire city of Polt was depending, a girl who needed to hold off the Red Death Tea Society for another fifty-three minutes so that Nate could deal with the threat of the nuclear bomb in the tunnel beneath my feet. So I ran as fast as I could through the edges of the crawling bees, darting through an area where they weren't very deep, like just the shallowest advance of a wave, all the while trying not to think of the depths of the bumblebee ocean. I was stung five or six times and screamed in pain a similar number of times, give or take an extra ten.

I ran right for the tree with Nate's tree house.

My speed enabled me to run a good five feet up the trunk, far enough that from there I was able to jump up and grab the lowest branch. The sudden addition of my weight jiggled the branch, and then the unconscious man in the tree, the assassin from the Red Death Tea Society, fell off his branch and disappeared below, sinking into the seemingly infinite bees that were covering Nate's lawn.

Hand over hand, I began moving along the branch. My feet were hanging just a few inches above the bees, and even then just because I was holding my feet up, shimmying along the branch as it stretched out toward the street, across Nate's fence, and to the sidewalk. The bees were surging below me, trying to fly up to me, but something about Sir William's singing was keeping them grounded. Still, they tried to build themselves into a big-enough pile to reach me, and they almost did, but I managed to stay one step ahead of them, or rather one frantic branch-swinging grab ahead of them.

"Made it!" I said, dropping to the sidewalk. The bees were already turning my way, beginning to crawl in my direction, but I had a relatively straight run to the curb where Betsy was parked. I very much needed that friend ray from her glove box.

"Arrgh!" I said. And, "Piffle!" And, "Seriously?" I said

these assorted things because I was being stung by a few advance bumblebees as the giant swarm readjusted. I'd only given myself a few moments. More bees were on the way. Millions of them. I flung open Betsy's door and frantically grabbed the friend ray from the glove box.

"Great!" I said. I'd made it. Everything was going great.

Then the noises changed.

Sir William quit singing.

For a second there was complete silence.

Then the bees started to take to the air again. First one. Then another. Then about ten million of them. The roar of their wings and the clicking irritation of their voices washed away the silence. The combined swarm was as big as an ocean liner. With stingers.

"Piffle!" I said. "Sir William? Why aren't you singing?" I whispered this, to tell the truth, because I was rather nervous. Also quite terrified. And seeing as how nobody else was around, I didn't expect any answers to my question.

But I got one.

"He isn't singing because I shot him," Luria said. I gasped. I screamed. I spun around so quickly that I almost fell over. Luria was standing in the middle of the street, holding one of those strange glass pistols. She was wearing a black dress with hints of green. Black sandals with green stockings. A gray cloche hat. Her silky red hair looked dramatic against the black of her dress. Her wide mouth was curved into a smile, bunching up the freckles on her cheeks. Her green eyes were glinting whenever the sunlight managed to filter through the dense cloud of the bees overhead. She began walking closer.

Did I mention the gun?

"Shot him?" I asked. It came out as a whimper. She'd *shot* Sir William? I quickly turned toward where I'd last seen the robot and . . . he was still there.

Except he didn't have a head.

He was crumpled on his side, one wing beating feebly, and his head had completely vanished. It was gone. The disintegrator ray had simply erased the robot's head from existence.

I turned back around, ready to unleash a volley of my most remarkable swear words at Luria, as angry as I've ever been and already stomping in her direction before I noticed that her glass handgun, the disintegrator pistol, was now aimed at . . . me.

Me.

I gulped.

And flung myself to one side.

A huge swath of the asphalt just vanished, revealing packed soil beneath. I barely had time to register it before I heard the hum of the gun charging again. I leaped up and over Nate's fence, even as Luria's disintegrator pistol was erasing the fence from existence.

"Ackk!" I said. I turned to run for the house, but the bumblebee swarm was blocking my path and I really didn't think they were going to give me permission to pass. Bumblebees are rude that way.

So . . . there I was. You know that saying about being between a rock and a hard place? Well, I was between millions of bees and a disintegrator pistol, and that's much worse.

Luckily, I had the friend ray.

"Hah!" I said, pointing it toward Luria and pulling the trigger just as she walked through the gap in the fence. A brilliant kaleidoscope of colors washed over Luria in waves, in concentric circles of various colors.

"Hah!" I said again. "Now you're my friend and you have to do what I say!" I should point out that I don't really believe friends have to do what you say. That's nonsense. Friends just have to be friends. I was only caught up in the moment. That said, I suppose I could argue that while friends *don't* need to do what you say, they *do* need to do what you say *if* you're saying, "Don't attack me with millions of bumblebees or shoot me with a disintegrator pistol." Really, I think you can expect at least that much out of a friendship.

Luria watched all the colors playing over her. She frowned at me. She raised an eyebrow.

"Really?" she said. "A friend ray? How cute. Did you really think that would work?"

"I really did," I admitted. Then I rolled to the left because she was trying to shoot me. After that, I rolled to the right because she was still trying to shoot me. Then I leaped over a patch of potatoes in Maryrose's garden, because Luria was extremely insistent about shooting me, while I wasn't very much into that at all.

The final result of all my rolling around and leaping was that I ended up quite dirty and tremendously winded and splayed out on my back at the edges of the garden, where Maryrose had been growing some tomatoes. Several of the tomatoes had squished beneath me, making me look like an accident victim, but it was unfortunately no accident that Luria was standing over me, aiming the pistol at my heaving chest.

"Good-bye," she said.

And pulled the trigger.

Which is when Bosper bit her on the rump.

"Squaaa?" she said, her shot going wide.

"Grrrr!" Bosper said.

"The dog?" Luria screamed.

"Who's a good boy?" Bosper said. The words were muffled because he was very busy with the biting.

I scrambled to my feet, trying to think of what to do. Bosper lost his grip and he fell to the lawn. Luria immediately tried to shoot him, but he was too quick for her, jumping here and there, scrambling to one side or the other, all the while talking about mathematical concepts that I simply could not understand, lecturing Luria about triangles and swath arcs, and other things, explaining that he was too mathematically talented to ever fall into the range of her shots. And while I didn't understand the math, I *did* understand how close I'd come to being nonexistent, and how very lucky I was to have a friend like Bosper.

Wait.

Oh yeah.

Friends.

I was holding a friend ray.

"Hah!" I said, shooting the friend ray into the huge swarm of bees that was descending on the yard, the one that was cutting off Bosper's escape routes, narrowing the areas where he could run. The colors from the friend ray permeated the entire swarm, washing over them, the colors flickering over each of their little insect bodies.

"Hah!" I said again, because I was certain the tide of the battle would change, now that I had about twenty million new friends.

A bee stung me.

I said, "Hrrgggh!" And then, "Hey! Friends shouldn't do that!" I was outraged at the bee.

Luria asked, "Did you use the friend ray on the bees? Really? Did you think that would work?"

"Yes," I admitted. "Again, I thought that would work."

"What a foolish girl. I confess that it was clever to use the oscillations of that robot's voice to rob my bees of their flight by vibrating at the same frequency as their wings, thereby canceling the lift and causing them to plummet to the ground, but—"

"Oh. That's what happened?"

"Yes. That's what happened. One of Nate's ideas, then? That boy is a genius. He would never be so foolish as to believe that a friend ray would work on me. Or on my personal swarms of bees."

"I am *exactly* that foolish," I admitted. "Why wouldn't it work?"

Luria was walking closer. Bosper was near her, ready to bite at a moment's notice. We all stared at one another in menacing fashion, ready for the fight to break out again, but taking a short break when Maryrose, carrying a basket of freshly picked carrots and sweet peas, walked past us to the house.

Luria said, "A friend ray won't work on me because I

would never be friends with you. We're too different. You stand against everything I believe in."

"Really? Piffle. You must suck." A bit harsh, but I was telling the truth. If she was against everything I believed in, then she was against *cake*, and *science fiction movies*, and *comic books*. Of course I already knew that she was against being friends with Nate, and that's one of my favorite things in my life.

Luria said, "And since Nate's friend ray works by establishing a rapport, an empathy, between each side, of course it failed." She was getting closer. About ten feet away. Easy shooting range. Bosper was growling at her, standing in front of her, backing up with every step she took.

"But why wouldn't it work on the bees?" I asked. I'd really thought it would work. That said, there was a little buzzing in my brain, telling me I was forgetting something.

"Easy," Luria said. "Their insect minds are too foreign. Again, no link could be established. You might be able to turn bees when I'm not nearby to guide them, but these bees"—she gestured to the millions of bees—"are too well trained. By my chemicals. They're beyond your power to control. They're my robotic slaves, and they will never be your friends."

"Oh," I said. "So you're just too horrible to be friends

with, and the bees are too alien, meaning I would either need to use the ray to make *you* friends with *somebody else* that was horrible . . ." My words trailed off. There was that buzzing in my brain again. Right at the back of my head. There was an idea forming. But . . . having Luria become friends with another horrible person would be . . . even more horrible. Then they'd just be horrible together, against me.

"Bzzz," went my brain.

I said, "Or . . . couldn't I have the bees, the millions of bumblebees, be friends with somebody who I'm *already* friends with?" Even as I spoke, my brain was going off like a buzzer. Like I'd hit on the right answer.

"Hah," Luria laughed. "That's absurd. You're an idiot, Delphine Cooper. Do you happen to be friends with any insects?" She was taunting me. Laughing. And then I realized the buzzing in my brain was . . . not in my brain.

It was in my hair, actually.

It was Melville.

She flew out from my hair.

Luria's eyes narrowed in concern, then went wide as I said, "Remember Melville? She's my friend."

Then, before Luria could do anything, I bathed the huge swarm of bumblebees with the friend ray again, but this time I included Melville in the color bath, so that I wasn't trying to be friends with the bees, but rather making Melville friends with each and every last one of them.

And you know what they say about "the friend of a friend."

The bees all pivoted in the air.

Hovering in precise formation.

Staring at Luria.

Bosper said, "Oh boy!"

Luria said, "Oh no."

"Oh *yes*," I said. "Get her, girls."

The roaring sound of the swarming bumblebees rose to unimaginable levels. The leaves in the trees were whipping about, like during the heaviest of storms. Even the trees themselves were shaking. The house was shaking. The very ground was shaking. There were so many millions of bees. So many friends . . . of Melville.

Melville zoomed forward and stung Luria, setting an example.

"Grgargh!" Luria screamed. And then she looked up to the darkening sky, and she said, "No. Oh. Oh no."

And the swarm descended.

We took it easy on Luria.

I mean, sure, the bumblebees stung her a couple of hundred times on her arm so that she'd drop the pistol.

And they stung her maybe a hundred times on her left leg, because she kept trying to do some martial arts moves and she actually managed to smack Melville at one point, momentarily dazing my bee and incensing all of her friends, so that the bees stung Luria on her back, and on her butt, and . . . well . . . they stung her *everywhere*, I guess.

Come to think of it, we really didn't take it easy on her.

-𝕔-

Bosper and I ran into the house.

And left the door open.

There were two members of the Red Death Tea Society just inside the door, near the stairs to the second floor. One was going up the stairs, and the other was using a wall socket to charge one of the bizarre glass handguns. They both looked up when I entered, first to me, and then to Bosper. They smiled, but they did not look nice.

"Hello," I said.

"I'll take the dog," the man on the stairs said. He was ridiculously huge, maybe seven feet tall, dressed in the suit that the Red Death Tea Society favors, red with black trim. He had a full beard. Massive arms. A cup of tea in his large hands.

"That leaves the girl for me," said the other man,

unplugging his handgun from the wall socket, keeping it pointed at me the whole time. He was dressed in a similar suit, but with the addition of a red baseball cap. He wasn't nearly as tall as the other man and not as muscular, but he had a wiry athletic quality about him, and a cup of tea in one hand. I couldn't help but admire how, despite quickly turning to me, he maintained his balance so perfectly that he didn't spill a drop.

"Hello," I said again. Neither of the men had bothered to respond the first time I'd said hello, which is rude, especially if you're an uninvited guest in somebody's house.

"Good-bye," the shorter man said, obviously about to pull the trigger.

"Hello," I said yet again, but this time I wasn't speaking to the assassins, I was speaking to approximately twenty million bees.

That's why I'd left the door open.

To let them in.

Melville was in the lead, and she was the first to sting the men, both of whom quickly vanished under the great roaring wave of my invited guests. By that time I was already running into the kitchen, where two women in tracksuits were setting up some sort of strange device on the table. It looked like a laptop computer with miniature satellite dishes and a holographic display of numbers floating above. Also, it had a cup holder, suitable for cups of tea.

The women weren't alone in the kitchen. Maryrose was there, too. She had a paring knife and, completely unaware of the others in the kitchen, was slicing off the tops of the carrots she'd picked from the garden.

"She's a good person," I said, pointing to Maryrose.

"But they're bad," I said, pointing to the two women setting up the strange device, the ones who were looking up to me in shock, possibly because I'm so incredibly awe inspiring, or perhaps because I was accompanied by a few million bees that were swarming into the kitchen, bees that were pausing, listening to what I had to say, and then choosing their victims accordingly.

"Bosper!" I said, pointing to the device on the kitchen table. "Chew on that until it breaks!"

"Good boy gets to chew?" he said. His voice was full of

anticipation. Nate doesn't usually let him chew on things.

"Go ahead!" I said. "Chomp, even!"

"Oh boy, chomping!" Bosper said, jumping up onto the table. I was already running into the hall, where Nate's dad, Algie, was walking along, carrying a skateboard, spinning one of the wheels, checking to make sure it was properly aligned.

"Oh hi, Delphine," he said. "You looking for Nate? I'll tell him you're here."

"Good guy," I whispered to the bees. They looked to Melville for confirmation. I assume she nodded. Anyway, the bees didn't attack Algie, not even when he yelled, "Nate! Delph's here!" at the top of his lungs. Then he patted my shoulder and said, "Help yourself to some sandwiches if you like. They're in the refrigerator. Door's been sticking today, though."

With that, Algie turned and went up the stairs, accidentally tripping on the huge man writhing at the bottom of the steps, the one who was still half-covered in bees.

"Why am I so clumsy today?" I heard Algie muttering as he walked up the stairs, but by that time I was already on my way through the rest of the house.

There were five members of the Red Death Tea Society in the living room.

"All bad guys," I said, waving my hands at the men. The assassins frowned, then their eyes went wide when they saw the bees. I left a fair number of the bumblebees behind, and continued on.

There were three members of the Red Death Tea Society in Nate's parents' bedroom.

"Bad guys," I said. The bees went in.

The door to the downstairs bathroom was closed. I knew Maryrose was in the kitchen, and Algie was upstairs, and Nate was somewhere below the house, hopefully well on his way to diffusing a nuclear bomb. I knocked on the bathroom door.

"Occupied!" a man's voice responded.

"We're serving tea," I said. It was a test.

"Oh! Excellent! Be out in a second!"

"Ahhh, sorry about this," I said. He'd failed the test.

"Sorry about what?" he asked.

But by that time I'd pointed to the crack at the bottom of the door, the crack that was easily large enough for bumblebees to crawl under, and I said, "Bad guy."

Probably a few thousand bees snuck under the door. And then I could hear the man yelling and, honestly, I really did feel bad about it, but ... more work to be done!

There was a man in the laundry room. I set the bees on him.

There was a man searching through a closet in the hallway.

More bees.

And so we moved through the house, uncovering the various members of the Red Death Tea Society and stinging them a few thousand times each, stinging the man in Maryrose's computer room, the woman in the spare bedroom, the four men searching Nate's room, and all the rest of the assassins who were all over the house.

The bumblebees seemed to be enjoying themselves.

The assassins were not.

As for me, I was decidedly enjoying myself, at least as much as you can enjoy yourself when you're standing atop a nuclear bomb that's set to explode in the next few minutes, because such things are well known to put a damper on even the best of all parties.

"Bosper has been biting!" the terrier said, bouncing along next to me as I pointed out a few more people for the bees to sting. He had a shred of red cloth hanging from one of his teeth.

"The dog enjoys the biting!" he added. Then, realization hit him. His tail went lower, and he could barely look at me. "The dog is not supposed to be biting," he said. "The dog has gone bad."

"No worries," I said. "Dogs are supposed to bite bad guys. Go ahead and keep biting!"

"Good boy!" Bosper said, brightening immediately. He went bounding off down the hall while I checked my cell phone for the time. It was 5:17, meaning it was fifty-seven minutes since Nate had asked me to hold off the entirety of a deadly secret society for an hour. I'd almost made it! But . . . then . . . I started to hear a strange noise.

The bees.

The bumblebees.

They had been making a sound like *buzzz buzzz buzzz*, but now they were going *brrrz brrrz bruzz*. Entirely different. This new sound was uneasy, full of tension.

"What's going on?" I asked Melville.

"Bzzz?" she said. She didn't know. But then, only a moment later, she made a little coughing noise and . . .

. . . she flew out the window.

Leaving me behind.

The other bees quickly followed.

All of them.

Millions of bees went rushing out of the house as quickly as possible, funneling through the windows and doors. I hurried to look out the window, and with all the bumblebees rushing past me it felt like I was in a windstorm full of fluffy sand. Horrified, I watched as my bumblebee bodyguards flew high up into the sky, far, far away, disappearing into the distance. One after another, millions after millions, they all flew away.

Leaving me alone.

"Delphine Cooper," I heard a voice say behind me.

Meaning, as I expected, I wasn't *exactly* alone.

Also as expected, the voice sounded a lot like that of Maculte, the man in charge of the super-secret society bent on world destruction, the man who was not afraid to make his enemies disappear by means of . . . well, *death*. Death is, after all, right there in their name: it's the Red *Death* Tea Society, not the Red *Ask-You-Nicely-to-Go-Away* Tea Society.

So I turned around, and, yes, it was Maculte. He was standing in the middle of the hallway dressed in his immaculate suit and carrying the finest of tea sets atop a silver serving tray.

"I have enough tea for two," he said.

"Piffle," I squeaked.

ⵜ

Maculte was eerily calm. My heart was thumping like a train engine, and it didn't help when every single one of the doors in the hall suddenly slammed shut, as if enraged ghosts were at work.

"Did that scare you?" Maculte said. "I was hoping it would. I've hacked into Nathan's controls for the house. But, far more importantly, would you like tea?"

"I—"

"I had to send your friends away, Delphine. All those bees. It was simple enough to induce an overwhelming fear into their primitive minds. Speaking of minds, it was quite admirable how you managed to outwit Luria. She's livid. Furious. I've promised she can have you. For experimentations."

"That's—"

"Do you know the proper components of a tea set?" Maculte asked. He held out the serving tray, smiling at me. He did not have a particularly winning smile, not unless the competition was for Smile Most Likely to Spell Doom for Sunshine, Puppies, and Red-Headed Sixth Grade Girls.

I said, "Uhh—"

"First, you want the dishes to be made of bone china. Do you know what bone china is made of?" He was stepping closer. I began stepping backward down the hall, wishing I was small enough to squeeze under the doors, like the bees had done.

I said, "Bone?"

"Correct," Maculte said. "But *whose* bones?" There was that smile again. I reached out and tried one of the doors in the hall, the one that led to Nate's library. It wouldn't budge.

"They're really made of bones?" I said, continuing my backward walk down the hallway. "You're not just saying that the way an evil guy says things?" I could hear Bosper on the other side of a door, scratching and barking, saying, "Door? Could door open? Delphine needs the dog!"

"They really are made of bone," Maculte said. He took a sip of his tea. Sighed. His eyes closed in pleasure. I tried another door in the hall. It wouldn't budge.

"They won't open, Delphine," Maculte said. "You're trapped. But at least you're learning about tea sets. Here, this is the teapot." He pointed to the teapot. "They should be short, but stout. The tea leaves need room to expand in order to properly flavor the hot water."

"That's—"

"And here's a tea caddy for holding the leaves before they're brewed. And a sugar bowl for those who want their tea sweetened. And here's a waste bowl, for depositing the used tea leaves. Do you know why the tea leaves are thrown away?"

"Because—"

Maculte grabbed my hair and slammed me back against the wall so hard that the paintings on the wall jiggled and I lost my breath. He leaned in closer, staring me in the face. His eyes seemed black. His teeth were stained a horrible yellow, and his breath was that of rotten tea and burnt honey.

"Because although the tea leaves brought flavor to the drink, we don't need them anymore. And what we do not need, we *remove*. We *eliminate*. Do you understand?" Still holding my hair, Maculte put the tray down on a small display table in the hall, the one where Maryrose always has dried gourds and pictures of Nate with his friends. Well, with his *friend*. With me. Singular. Everybody else in school thinks he's too weird.

There was a syringe on the tea tray. Maculte picked it up, smiled at it, and slightly depressed the plunger. A bead of dark liquid formed at the end.

"Tea," he said, tapping a finger on the syringe. "My

own brew. I call it Maculte's Finale. An acquired taste, I admit. I find it delicious. Deadly delectable. You will likely only find it . . . deadly."

The needle moved closer to my arm.

I said, "I . . . I thought you promised Luria she could have me?" I didn't really want to be given over for experimentation, but considering the alternative . . . ? Best to stall for time.

"Oh, Delphine," Maculte said. "Do I look like a man who keeps my promises?"

The needle came closer.

I was thinking of how, if Nate and I couldn't stop Maculte, he'd find the Infinite Engine and then he'd have all the power he'd ever need. Enough power that a single one of his disintegrator pistols would be enough to wipe out the entire world. He'd have a threat that nobody could stop. Everything would be lost. Everything would just be the dark, gray world of Maculte, devoid of art, passion, love, and friendship.

The needle came closer.

It touched the skin of my arm.

And all the doors in the hallway opened.

"I wouldn't touch her, if I were you," I heard. It was Nate's voice. And he sounded colder than he normally does. It wasn't an "it's snowing and I'm accidentally outside in my underwear" type of cold, but the good kind of cold, an "action-movie" voice, at that moment where the hero's eyes narrow and the villain knows he's in trouble.

"Nathan?" Maculte said. He still had the tip of the needle against my arm. My arm felt cold. The "please don't inject me with that needle" kind of cold.

"It's me," Nate's voice said. I still couldn't see him, but then, of course, ever since I became friends with Nate, I've learned that there are a lot of things I can't see. Nate says it's because our eyes can only perceive certain wavelengths, meaning that if light hits them with longer or shorter waves, then we just don't see them. They're effectively invisible. I won't pretend to understand it. I can only deal with what I *can* see. Like, for instance, Maculte's leg.

I kicked him.

"Arghh!" he hissed. I quickly jumped away from the range of his needle, but he was coming closer, lunging for me, hopping on one leg. He jabbed at me with the tea-dripping point of his needle, but I managed to grab the silver tray and use it to block the attack.

The needle broke.

And so did all the teacups and the teapot as they fell from the tray, shattering on the floor as they hit, as if they'd been just waiting for their chance to explode.

"No!" Maculte yelled in dismay. It was clear that the

serving set had meant something to him. He went down on one knee and started scrabbling at the remains of the teacups as if they were a puzzle he could simply piece together. I almost felt sorry for him.

"Guhh!" he said, when I hit him over the head with the silver tray, which was quite heavy. It looked like it hurt. Once again, I almost felt sorry for him. You might note that I'm not saying I *did* feel sorry for him; I'm saying that I *almost* felt sorry for him.

There's a difference.

There's also, unfortunately, a difference between how hard I hit Maculte and how hard I needed to hit him in order to knock him out. He was reeling, but managed to get to his feet. When I tried to hit him again with the serving tray, he blocked it, then he pressed a button on his cuff link and the serving tray just weirdly . . . melted. I mean, it didn't get hot or anything; it just . . . went liquid. Like it was thick water. Maybe yogurt? Pudding? Whatever it turned into, it splooshed all over my arm and down onto the floor.

Maculte pressed another button on his cuff links. There was a hissing noise, and then the air all around him began sparkling. Like glitter. Maculte straightened his tie, smiled at me, and made a slapping motion with his hand, slapping at nothing but air.

He was five feet from me.

But the air around me went . . . hard . . . and I whooshed up into the air and was flung backward.

"Brute force," Maculte said. "I normally abhor it. Removing an opponent from the playing field should be done with finesse. But, that said, there's a certain primal satisfaction in crushing a pawn with a club." He waved his hand again. The air swirled around me. A gust of wind picked me up and slammed me to the floor. I was dazed. Out of breath. I couldn't seem to inhale. It felt like the air was avoiding my nose, remaining just out of reach. I was starting to choke.

And then I saw Nate run past me.

He wasn't wearing a shirt.

Also, he wasn't wearing any pants.

Nate was only in his underwear, which had a picture of Isaac Newton on one side of his rear, and on the other side was Rosalind Franklin, meaning the woman who was instrumental in the discovery of DNA. It was odd underwear, but of course Nate is normally quite odd, and right then he was as odd as I'd ever seen him.

Because he was entirely painted green.

"Nate?" I said.

"Nathan?" Maculte said. He was pressing his vest buttons, tapping on the knot of his tie, using a small bottle to spritz some cologne onto his cheeks, and he'd taken a flask of tea from inside his jacket and was gulping from it. He was a flurry of activity.

"Why are you green?" I asked Nate, struggling to my feet. I expected Nate to help me up, but he was avoiding my touch.

"Green?" Maculte said, staring even more intensely at Nate. He made the color sound ominous.

Nate said, "Well, I had a thought." He grinned. Maculte frowned. Nate's thoughts can be a pretty big deal.

Nate said, "As I was working on the nuclear paint, down below in the tunnel, I determined there was a 98.7 percent chance that Delphine could defeat everyone in the house. She's that resourceful."

"Thank you," I said.

"But if *you* were here"—he pointed to Maculte—"then the odds went down to a 21.8 percent chance of her lasting for the full hour I needed, and there was even a 17.2 percent chance that she would not survive. I found that unacceptable."

I said, "I also find that unacceptable."

Nate said, "So I needed to do something drastic, because it was likely that when I came up from the tunnels we would be at a disadvantage."

"Do something?" Maculte laughed. "What could you possibly do? You're just two children." He took a step forward.

"That's true," Nate said.

Maculte took another step forward.

"And you're not even carrying any weapons," Maculte said.

"That's also true," Nate said.

Maculte took a step forward.

"And I've sent away all your friends," Maculte said. "The bees are gone."

"So I see," Nate said.

Maculte took a step forward.

He was only about four feet away, and he'd reached into his jacket and pulled out another needle.

"And I'm protected by a force field now," Maculte said.

"Absolutely true," Nate said.

Maculte took a step forward. I bent down, all without taking my eyes off Maculte, and grabbed up a few shards of the broken teacups. I tossed them at Maculte, curious to see what he was talking about. The shards hit the area where the air was sparkling, and the sparks went brighter and . . . sizzled. And then the shards were gone. Simply gone.

"You can't hurt me," Maculte laughed.

"Now *that*," Nate said. "That's *not* true."

Maculte stopped. He considered what Nate had said. He took a sudden breath, but then . . . with eyes narrowed . . . he calmed himself and took a step forward.

He reached inside his suit and brought out one of those strange glass handguns, meaning he now had the gun in one hand and the needle with the poison tea in his other. And there was madness in his eyes. But his lips . . . they trembled.

"What do you mean it's not true?" he asked Nate.

"I could easily hurt you," Nate said. "It's not like I painted myself green because I have incredibly poor fashion sense."

I coughed discreetly.

"The nuclear paint, then?" Maculte said, as if admitting something he already knew.

"Yes," Nate said. "The nuclear paint. Of course."

"It's so obvious," Maculte said, nodding.

I held up my hand.

They both looked at me.

I said, "I have a question. What's all this about nuclear paint?"

They both looked at me.

I said, "Look, maybe it's obvious to two geniuses, but I'm a fairly common sort of sixth grade girl and I don't understand what you're talking about."

"I'm not sure I'd categorize you as common," Nate said. "For instance, only 3.8 percent of the world population has red hair. And you've fought a giant cat, and commanded a horde of bumblebees. That's uncommon."

"Nate," I said. Just his name. But I used the voice that my mom uses on my dad. It never fails to make him blush and stammer an apology.

"Oh," Nate said. "Sorry. You're not talking about the law of averages, you mean common like ... not a genius. Meaning you want me to explain why I'm wearing the green paint, owing to how you're nervous about Maculte because he has a gun and a poison needle, and now I'm babbling because I think you're going to be mad at me when I tell you that I scraped off all the nuclear paint from the walls down below and covered myself with it, so that I've become a walking nuclear bomb, and the temperature of my own body could trigger an event if it rises too high."

All I'd done was say his name and he'd gone off babbling. Had he blushed? It was hard to tell, since he was covered in green paint. Or he was covered in a nuclear bomb. Your choice.

I said, "When you say, 'trigger an event,' you're still not talking about a party, are you? You're talking about explosions again, right?"

"That's correct," Maculte said. "A nuclear explosion." He had his gun trained on Nate. The needle was pointed toward me. "But such an action is madness. You simply *must* be joking, Nathan. It's true the explosion would stop me, easily overcoming my force field, but even a contained nuclear explosion would destroy this entire block, including you and that uncommon redhead." He shook the needle at me. A droplet of tea was flung off the tip of the needle and splashed onto the wall. It sizzled.

"It was the only way to stop you," Nate said. He reached into a hall closet and brought out his dad's favorite broom and dustpan, the ones painted with racing stripes, and began to calmly sweep up the remains of the tea set as if we were in no danger at all. "If I don't stop you, I calculate a 97.3 percent chance that you'll take over the world, which would be a disaster."

"A 98.87 percent chance," Maculte said. "And it would not be a disaster. It would be good for the cattle that you call humanity to serve me, to show me the respect I deserve. Most humans, after all, are little more than the greedy termites you set on my tea crop. Termites that I've now eliminated, Nathan. Termites that—"

"You're ranting," Nate said. "Please don't. My point is, I knew I had to stop you, even at the cost of my own life, so I covered myself with nuclear paint, and now if I get too stressed my body temperature will rise and the heat will act as a catalyst, causing a detonation. Hold this, will you?" He held out the dustpan to Maculte.

Maculte stared at the dustpan. His eyes narrowed. He looked to Nate. Then to me. I could almost see the calculations being worked in his head. Odds were being weighed. Actions considered. At several points he opened his mouth to speak, but then his mouth snapped closed. And through it all, Nate, with that smile of his, was just holding out the dustpan with a steady hand.

"You would sacrifice your own life for the good of others?" Maculte finally asked. Nate nodded. The dustpan didn't waver.

"Not something you understand, is it?" I asked Maculte. "Self-sacrifice? Doing something for others?"

"It's absurd!" he said. It came out as a snarl. He glared at me, and then at Nate. There was so much hate in his eyes that I had to look away, but Nate only cleared his throat in a meaningful way and gestured with the dustpan. The air in the hallway seemed heavy, thick as water. Being so close to Nate, I could smell the paint on his skin. It was like the smell of a gas station, or of spilled lemonade, and it burnt my nose, a little.

With a grunt of rage, Maculte pulled the trigger of his gun and the table in the hall burst into . . . nothing. It simply disintegrated. Maculte hissed with fury, and I jumped a bit, but Nate didn't so much as shiver. He simply gestured with the dustpan, again.

"You're nothing to me!" Maculte said. "Nothing!" He stomped on the floor. The sound echoed down the hallway. I could hear myself breathing. I could hear the electric hum of the strange glass gun in Maculte's hands. There was a breeze coming through the open window, making the nearest door creak an inch or two, back and forth, swaying. *Creak. Creak. Creeeeak.*

Nate gestured with the dustpan.

He said, "I'm getting tired of holding this out. It's a lot of effort. Hope it's not too much exertion, raising my heart rate."

Maculte looked to his gun. To Nate. He turned and kicked the wall in a childish display of temper. He started to say something to me, but I shook my head and reached out to tap on the dustpan in Nate's hand. *Tap. Tap. Tap.*

Maculte let out a long, disgusted, *heaving* sigh, and he took the dustpan from Nate's hands, and that's how I found myself watching the most dangerous man in the entire world, a supreme genius unrivaled by anyone except Nate, bending down to hold the dustpan while my green-painted classmate whisked the shards of the broken tea set into it.

"This is humiliating," Maculte complained.

"What's humiliating is a tea leaf tattooed on your rump," I said. It just sort of slipped out. I have a habit of saying what's on my mind, of speaking up at the wrong time, and a further habit of not feeling sorry about it. "Do you guys really do that?" Nate had told me that every member of the Red Death Tea Society has a tea leaf tattooed on their bottom.

"It's a show of solidarity," Maculte said. "A badge of commitment." I could tell I'd offended him. He was trembling with fury, holding the dustpan, looking for a wastebasket. I knew there was one in Nate's room so I ducked inside and grabbed it, then came back out and held it for him. With a look of anguish, Maculte allowed the debris of his tea set to fall into the trash.

"Still pretty silly," I argued. Maculte turned to face me, shivering with rage. I could tell he wanted to press some of those buttons on his cuff links again, but he didn't dare. Attacking me would make Nate angry, and Nate's body temperature would rise, and . . . well . . . boom. Not good. Of course, it wouldn't be good for me, either.

"What now, Nathan?" Maculte asked. "Do you allow me to be further tormented by this crimson-haired girl, or am I free to go?"

"Put your gun and that needle in the trash can, please," Nate said. Maculte had put his weapons on the floor when he was helping Nate to sweep. Now, he picked them up again and . . . with a moment of hesitation . . . dropped them in the wastebasket.

"There's a button on the side of the wastebasket," Nate told him. "Press it." The wastebasket was made of metal and had an image of Cookie Monster from Sesame Street. The button was right on his nose. Maculte pressed the button, and there was a brief flare of light from inside the wastebasket and then it was empty. Everything inside was just . . . gone.

"Hmpff," Maculte said. "And, now what?"

"I've called the proper authorities. You and Luria are going into custody."

I thought Maculte would get mad when Nate said that, or become nervous, or do anything but softly smile. But softly smile is what he did. He tried to hide it, but he wasn't a very talented actor.

"Something amusing?" Nate asked him.

"No. Of course not. I'm to be taken into custody, then?"

"Yes," Nate said. "Please step outside." He used the broom to point down the hall, toward the front door. Maculte went first. Nate and I followed at a safe distance, although of course I was walking next to a nuclear bomb, so my idea of "safety" was perhaps a bit off.

"I have to say, this is well done, besting me like this," Maculte said, looking back. "Are you sure you won't reconsider my offer to join my society?"

"I'm sure," Nate said.

"And how about you?" Maculte said, looking back to me.

"Me? I'm not into getting tea leaves tattooed on my butt. Or being evil."

By then we'd reached the yard. I could hear sirens in

the distance, and a strange sort of rustling in the hedges next to the house. Splitting a bit off from Nate, I investigated the rustling, cautiously peering through the thick branches of the hedge along the house, and then yelping when I saw two eyes staring back at me.

"Ahh!" I blurted.

"The dog is here!" Bosper said.

"Bosper?"

"The dog is stuck," he whined.

"Stuck?" Now that I could see him better, I could see how he was hanging in the branches, two feet off the ground, all four of his feet wiggling in midair.

"Door was not opens," he said. "Dog leaped through window! Heroic drama! Then . . . stuck." I reached inside the hedges and rescued the terrier, telling him, "The police will be here soon. We've caught Maculte. Nate is a nuclear bomb."

"The dog does not understand," Bosper said.

"Me, either, really. But . . . we win anyway." Bosper and I hurried to catch up with Nate and Maculte. They were standing on the sidewalk. I could hear the sirens getting closer, closer. They were only a few blocks away.

"Sounds like they're almost here," I said. A couple of cars drove by. I was nervous. Maculte was sneering. Nate was just . . . Nate. Bosper sneezed a couple of times, and then moved upwind of Nate. I could understand that, since Nate's nuclear body paint reeked like a gas station even to my nose, and Bosper's nose was a few thousand times more sensitive.

"Urggll," I heard. I looked beneath the tree house, from where Luria was staggering closer. The bumble-bees had really done a number on her. A *big* number. She basically looked like a pumpkin patch.

"What's happening?" she asked. She probably narrowed her eyes, but it was very difficult to tell.

"You lose," I said. "Nate called the police. You're going to jail." Luria looked to me, and she probably sneered (again, it was hard to tell), and then she looked to Maculte, who shrugged in return, admitting the truth. Luria, with a few moments of hesitation, shuffled over and stood next to him. I would've felt some pity for her, but . . . she'd shot Sir William.

"I can repair him," Nate said.

"Huh?"

"Sir William. I just saw the worry in your eyes and calculated you were thinking of him, right?"

"Uh, right." Nate's uncanny, sometimes, with his ability to know what's going on in someone's mind. I myself always find it hard to guess what people are thinking about, other than . . . just then . . . it didn't look like Maculte was at all worried about being given to the police.

"And you can repair Sir William?" I asked Nate.

"I can. I *will*. I have some ideas for new capabilities that—"

"The police sure are taking their time," I said. It's important to stop Nate before he starts talking too much about working on robots. He can go on for hours. And . . . what I'd said was true. The sirens were closer, maybe, but still a ways off. What was taking so long?

Nate only smiled. Shrugged. I couldn't begin to guess what he was thinking.

We were all standing there, together, on the sidewalk, in the sunlight. It was warm. Hot, even. I reached out to Nate, put a finger on his upper arm, and pushed him a couple of steps into the shade of his tree house. I did this because direct sunlight can actually be harmful to your skin, especially if it raises your body temperature enough to trigger the nuclear bomb you're wearing.

"You, uhh . . . sure you made that call?" I asked Nate. It seemed like the police should've already arrived.

"The proper authorities are on their way," Nate assured me. He scratched his chin. A bit of paint flaked off. I watched the flecks waft down to the sidewalk. They hit with a *PFFFT!* sound effect, like the sidewalk had been shot.

"Probably shouldn't scratch anymore," I told Nate.

"Probably not," he agreed.

A crow was in the street, pecking at nothing, barely

moving aside as another car approached. It was Liz Morris and her mom. They slowed down, then stopped.

"Hey, Delphine!" Liz yelled out.

"Hi, Liz!"

"What are you guys doing?"

"Nothing."

"Okay. I asked because it seems like Nate is painted green and standing there in his underwear, so when I asked what you were doing I thought maybe your answer would be more interesting than you saying, 'nothing.' Is this something we can talk about later?"

"This is something we can talk about *never*."

"Hmm," Liz said.

"Sorry," I said.

"Hmmmm," Liz said.

"Maybe next week," I said.

"I'll call you later tonight," she said, and the car drove off, startling the crow. I couldn't hear the sirens anymore. Where had they gone?

"This is useless, you know," Maculte said. He was far more relaxed than I personally felt he should be. He should have been *un*-relaxed. *Anti*-relaxed.

"Orgoble," Luria said. Her word (words?) was unintelligible, thanks to all the bee stings distorting her lips. The only thing I could tell for sure was, *she* wasn't nervous about the police, either.

Maculte said, "It's true you've caught us, but we'll escape from police custody within two hours." My eyes went up with this. Was he serious? Just two hours, and then the leaders of the Red Death Tea Society would be free again? No way!

Nate said, "Less than two hours, by my estimate. I personally calculate one hour seventeen minutes and twelve seconds, but that's of no matter. I never said I called the police. I said I called the proper authorities. I have someone else in mind."

"Someone . . . else?" There was the first hint of anxiety in Maculte's voice.

"Yes," Nate said. "Someone else."

And it was at that moment that I heard the helicopter. It started with that distant *whuum whuum whumm* noise, but quickly changed to a *WHUMM WHUMM WHUMM* noise, and then the helicopter swept up over the rooftops, sending shingles sailing away from the Greans' house, and then the helicopter was right above our heads, blowing dust all over the street. The crow in the street was buffeted by the strong winds and swept up into the air, tumbling for a bit before righting itself, squawking in indignation before flying off into the distance. Bosper was running around beneath the helicopter, barking at it. Betsy was parked on the street, but the helicopter clearly made her nervous, because she started her engine all by herself and drove halfway down the block before parking.

The helicopter landed.

It was huge, painted an unreflective black, and mostly looked like a prehistoric insect. There was a gunman with a mounted rifle that looked like it could shoot through a mountain, and I noticed it was glowing with electricity, sending out bright red sparks. The soldier in charge of the weapon was wearing thick rubber gloves.

The weapon was trained on Maculte.

"Ahh . . . *them*," Maculte said. "I . . . see."

Seven soldiers dressed in tight-fitting black clothing came leaping out of the helicopter almost before it settled on the street. Bosper was occasionally barking at them, but mostly yelling about hoping he could have a ride in the helicopter. The soldiers quickly searched the surrounding area, looking everywhere, putting on a variety of oddly colored goggles, scanning each of the nearby yards. One of the men had a spray bottle that he used to spritz some sort of liquid into the air, a liquid that spread out in a thick mist. Another of the soldiers set up an antenna in the middle of the street, and it began to hum. One of the women opened a metal box, no more than a few inches square, and a metallic eyeball whooshed out of the box to hover in the air. Everything was quick and efficient. In less than a minute, their search was over and they fanned out in a line, facing us, their weapons trained on Maculte and Luria.

"All clear!" one of the soldiers yelled.

A gray-haired man in a bright green suit stepped out of the helicopter. He was chewing bubblegum. He blew a bubble. Looking at me.

"Delphine Cooper," he said.

"Reggie Barnstorm," I said. It was the leader of the League of Ostracized Fellows, the man who'd kidnapped me only that morning. I didn't even try to hide my frown. I'm not one to hold a grudge, but it really *had* been a kidnapping, and it really *had* been only that morning.

"Dog rides in helicopter?" Bosper said, jumping up and down. It ruined a lot of the drama, and drama there was, because Maculte had grown tense. Luria was fuming.

"You're giving me to *them*?" Maculte said, barking the words as loudly as Bosper was begging to ride in the helicopter.

"I'm giving you to them," Nate said. "And then I'm washing off this nuclear paint and putting on some pants." The soldiers had surrounded Maculte and Luria and were snapping handcuffs on them, handcuffs made of metal, and a second pair of handcuffs made of circular beams of light (no idea what *that* was about), and the hovering metal eyeball had zoomed to a position only a few feet above their heads, keeping watch. Reggie strode purposefully over and used a strange device (it reminded me of a magnifying glass, but the lens was black) to look over both Maculte and Luria from a yard away. Several times the device flashed for a second, and Reggie would reach over and grab something from Maculte's suit, or use a laser to cut away the cuff links, and so on. Then Reggie repeated the process on Luria, all while his soldiers were carrying the various unconscious assassins of the Red Death Tea Society away from Nate's house and yard.

"Dog?" Bosper said. "Helicopter?" Nobody was answering him. The poor terrier was almost pleading.

Nate, talking to Reggie Barnstorm, said, "We didn't have much of a chance to talk earlier."

"No. Your dramatic rescue of Delphine was—Wait a moment. Is that *nuclear* paint? Are you an *active nuclear bomb*?"

"Sort of," Nate said. He shrugged. Some of the paint flaked off his shoulder. The breeze wafted the paint chips a few feet into the grass, where they exploded like a string of firecrackers and started a small fire. I smiled at Reggie while stomping out the flames. No big deal. Just one of those things, like when a friend sneezes and needs a tissue, or when a friend accidentally farts and you pretend to agree with her that the noise was only a squeaky floorboard, or when nuclear paint peels away from a friend's shoulder and you need to stomp out the resulting flames. You know, the basics of friendship.

"Hmmm," Reggie said. "Well, I won't claim to know how your mind works, so if you felt the need to paint your body with nuclear material, I'll assume it was necessary."

"Seventy-one percent necessary," Nate said. "And forty-two percent fun."

"Umm," I said. "I know I'm basically the only non-genius here, but, that's more than a hundred percent, right?"

"Of course," Nate said. "But fun doesn't play by math's rules." I thought Reggie and Maculte were going to faint when Nate said that, but I wanted to hug him. It was one of the main reasons why he was better than them, meaning that he wasn't just some cold computerized version of a person, that he—

"Delphine?" Nate said.

"Yes?"

"I'm calculating a ninety-seven percent chance that you want to hug me now. Please don't."

"Oh?" I was a little disappointed. He usually isn't bothered by my hugs. Maybe he *was* growing more impersonal? Maybe being around these other geniuses would turn him into—

"Because we'd explode if you hugged me," Nate explained.

"Oh, right. That."

"I assume this fulfills my obligation?" Nate asked Reggie. "I've given you Maculte."

"Just so," Reggie smiled. "We at the League of Ostracized Fellows will no longer badger you to join us. Though, we're having a dance mixer next Tuesday, and it would be grand if you and Delphine could attend. I'll be reciting my poetry and playing the xylophone!"

"Ooo," I said. It was basically a verbal grimace.

"The dog knows how to be in a helicopter," Bosper pleaded. "The dog can *show* you!"

By then, the soldiers had loaded all the members of the Red Death Tea Society into the helicopter. All of them except Maculte, who looked back to us just before stepping up into the vehicle.

He said, "Nathan, a request, from one genius to another. I give you my word of honor that I'll never bother you again, *if* . . . you tell me where you hid the Infinite Engine."

Nate, looking as proud as I've ever seen him, said, "Under my pillow, in my room."

"Ingenious!" Maculte said, with awe in his voice.

"Brilliant!" Reggie Barnstorm said. More awe.

"*Really*, guys?" I said. "It's brilliant to hide something

under a *pillow*? That's really stupid! That's . . . ahh, you know what? Forget it. Never mind. Maculte, it's been horrible knowing you, but I guess we'll never see you again."

"Yes, you will," he said. "And next time, this ends differently." With his smug smile in place, he stepped up into the helicopter.

"Next time?" I said. "What? No! You *promised* you'd quit bothering Nate. You . . . you *lied!*"

"Not really," he said. "Nathan knew I wasn't telling the truth, and if a lie isn't *believed*, then it was never a lie in the first place."

"Don't try philosophy on me. You promised on your honor!"

"It's fine," Nate said. "I did know he was lying, and as far as Maculte promising on his honor, he has none. And I knew that, too."

With that, the sliding door on the helicopter began to shut. As it slid closed, I could see the usual smile of arrogant amusement on Maculte's face. But, then, just before the door closed, and when he probably thought we couldn't see him anymore, I saw the hate.

Pure seething hate.

And then the door closed, and the helicopter rose up into the sky and was gone.

Poor Bosper was baying at the disappearing helicopter, like a dog barking at the moon.

chapter

13

So we're safe?" I asked as Nate and I were walking back to his house.

"Safe? No. It's true that the police couldn't have held Maculte and Luria, but the League won't be able to, either. Frankly, they're out of their mental league. I calculate thirteen days, six hours, and fifteen minutes until Maculte and Luria escape."

"Guhh," I said. I pulled out my phone and looked at it. I went to my alarm app and set the timer for thirteen days, six hours, and fourteen minutes. I showed it to Nate and said, "Really? Only this long before they escape?"

He nodded.

"Then . . . why even give Maculte to Reggie and the League? Why didn't we just . . . send Maculte off into space or something?"

"I thought about it, but sending someone into space requires several days' notice."

"Are . . . are you being serious?"

"Of course. You should never send someone into space without preparing."

"No, I mean . . . we *really* could have sent Maculte into space?"

"Sure. But I couldn't have done any of the necessary preparations while also keeping Maculte in custody. So I decided to do it this way, because giving Maculte to the League will allow us enough time to send the *Infinite Engine* into space, where it can't hurt anyone. It's simply too dangerous to have around, and I can't destroy it without catastrophically releasing all the energy, but I *can* send it off into the deep, dark depths of the universe, where nobody can possibly steal it ever again."

"Oh," I said, thinking it *was* good that the Infinite Engine would be safe, but not thinking it was good that *we* wouldn't be safe, because I was looking at the timer on my phone, to a remaining countdown of thirteen days, six hours, and thirteen minutes.

-☀-

An hour later, Nate had used a bath of subatomic particles to wash away the nuclear paint. I wasn't really sure what "a bath of subatomic particles" meant, other than it made Nate's skin a bright pink, and for some reason he smelled like a lightning strike.

❦

Three hours later, Nate had repaired all the damage to Sir William. He was as good as new, or even better, because this time Sir William's screech was a recording of *my* voice instead of Nate's, and I do a much better imitation of a gull.

❦

Eight hours after Maculte was gone, it was the middle of the night and I was staring at my ceiling, trying to sleep. That is also what was happening nine hours after Maculte was gone, and ten hours after he was gone. Eleven hours after he was gone, I was having a dream about cake that I'd best not describe.

❦

Fifteen hours after Maculte had been taken away, I was back at Nate's place, where he'd temporarily converted Betsy into a helicopter. We were soon flying high above Polt, whooshing through the skies, with Bosper hanging half out of the open door, and his tongue hanging all the way out of his mouth.

"Good dog!" he was saying. "Good dog!"

I felt sorry for everyone down below, because the weather report had a high probability of *drool*.

🔅

Sixteen hours and one minute after we'd watched the League of Ostracized Fellows take Maculte away, Betsy was admitting defeat. Between all the bees that I'd stunned with my musical brilliance and the ones I'd turned into friends during the battle with Luria,

I'd easily won our contest to see which of us could defeat the most bees, and therefore win the prize. And by "prize," I mean the kiss from Nate.

"It's mine?" I asked.

"I guess," Nate said. He was confused. He hadn't truly understood that Betsy and I had been in a competition, or that his kiss was the prize. It was . . . *interesting* to see Nate confused. He's so smart that he almost *always* knows what's going on. It made me almost sort of maybe want to kiss him.

I said, "If the kiss is mine, then I can do whatever I want with it."

"True," Nate said.

I pointed to Betsy and said, "Kiss her."

Betsy's paint turned bright red.

"Ooo!" she said.

🔆

Twenty-seven hours after Maculte was taken away by the League of Ostracized Fellows, Tommy Brilp called to ask if I wanted to go out with him. I said, "*No.*"

🔆

Three days after we defeated the Red Death Tea Society, Melville landed on the windowsill outside my bedroom when I was doing my homework.

"Bzzz?" she said, which I translated as, *"I'm sorry that I flew off with all the other bees, but now I'm back and I hope you'll forgive me and we can be friends, and if you need me to sting somebody that wouldn't be any problem."*

I opened the window. She flew inside and landed on my math homework. I went to the hallway and yelled downstairs, saying, "Mom! Can I have a pet bumblebee?"

"Yes!" she called up.

"Great! Thanks!"

"Sure! Hey . . . were you serious?"

"Yes!"

"Oh. Huh. Well, what do bumblebees eat?"

"Honey, I guess? Potato chips? Nectar? Pizza? I'm not sure. I know she likes sugar."

"Does she eat much?"

"Mom! Her name is Melville and she's my friend and she's a bee. It would take her, like, ten days to eat a single sugar cube."

Silence.

"Mom?"

"Okay, Delphine. But make sure she doesn't sting your father."

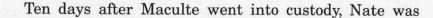

Ten days after Maculte went into custody, Nate was

looking through my adventure kit and telling me there wasn't enough.

"Not enough adventure?" I said.

"Not enough tools," he said. "Let me work something up for you."

Twelve days after Maculte and Luria were gone, and only a little more than a day before Nate had predicted they would escape, Nate brought me a new and improved adventure kit. It still had my favorites, like the first aid kit, a few candy bars, my good luck charm, some bottled water, a jar of peanut butter, a compass and a whistle and a flashlight and so on, but now there was *more*.

Much more.

Because Nate said we needed to be ready for anything. That it was impossible to predict what the Red Death Tea Society might do next. That he'd been preparing a few surprises of his own, and that I needed to be prepared as well.

So my new adventure kit had a miniature flame-thrower. And a cell phone that Nate said would work underwater, or in space, just in case. And there was a wide range of the strange pills that Nate has created, in case I ever need to do such things as turn invisible, or be able to understand a dolphin's speech, or turn any animal into a zebra.

There was even a pill I could take to make my fingers glow bright pink if anybody was drinking tea within fifty yards.

I looked at the tea-detecting pill, and then to Nate. I could tell he was worried. Then, together, we looked at my phone, where the timer was still counting down. Nate's predictions are uncannily accurate. I've grown to accept them as simple truth.

Twenty-six hours to go.

Thirteen days, six hours, and fifteen minutes after Maculte and Luria were taken into custody, Nate and I were sitting in my room, having just fired the Infinite Engine off into space.

We had ice cream. But I was far too nervous to eat.

We were watching the counter clicking down to zero.

Five seconds to go.

Nate and I hadn't really been talking for the last half hour. We were too anxious.

Four seconds to go.

Bosper had come along with Nate, and he was chewing on the edge of one of my blankets. I'd told him to stop, but he'd kept right on chewing. Terriers are naturally nervous dogs, and the tension in the room wasn't helping.

Three seconds to go. Melville landed next to my phone, staring at the numbers.

Two.

One.

Zero.

My phone rang.

Melville flew away from my phone as I, after a long and worried sigh, picked it up, and clicked it to speakerphone.

"Hello, Delphine," a voice said. "And, hello, Nathan. This is Maculte. Would you care to guess what's next?"

Acknowledgments

Even though this book was written as I sat alone in a variety of places scattered throughout Portland, Oregon, no book is ever truly written alone. There's an army of people who inspire each and every step, and who help take the necessary next steps after the manuscript is finished. I always feel their presence next to me as I write in my cafés. Each time I finish another chapter, I can almost feel this vast crowd smiling, and hungrily eyeing the cookies next to my computer.

To Thierry Lafontaine, who probably just ADORES how much I have Nate and Delphine change their clothes, forcing him to revise his artwork.

To Cindy Loh and Brett Wright and everyone else at Bloomsbury, so many of them employed in the job of *Being Better Than Paul with Grammar and*

Punctuation, making them a part of America's largest workforce.

To my agent, Brooks Sherman, who is the first line of defense against my many . . . many . . . many ellipses. Take a bow, Brooks . . . you deserve it.

To Colleen Coover, who never gets annoyed when she's trying to talk to me, but I ignore her completely because I'm writing.

To *Monty Python's Flying Circus* and the *Goodies* and *Benny Hill*, three shows that taught me my great love for pure absurdity.

To my dad, Charles Tobin, who was always tinkering with this and that, taking things apart and putting them back together, and who never blamed me for my own enthusiastic hobby of taking things apart . . . even though I combined it with my utter lack of interest or ability to put them back together.

To my brother, Mike, for his childhood vow to beat up the dentist who had injected me with enough anesthetic to render me into a babbling idiot flopping about in the backseat of the car, uttering insensible pleas for us to stop and pick up some comic books on the way home.

To my mom, because she taught me the value of the long game.

To Red and Spook and Ginger. They were dogs. That meant they were friends. I've never shaken finer paws.

To my grandmother Steinberg, who had an obsession with garage sales and who stuffed her house with an incredible array of dubious treasures, and actual treasures, the comics and the books of my childhood. It was such a joy to dive into those rooms, like a pig in mud, except somewhat more cultured and literary. Maybe.

To Jerry and Mike and Bill, for all the times we got together in high school and played Dungeons and Dragons and other role-playing games, inadvertently teaching me how to create and tell stories, and also for the times we'd get together and craft potions and weapons gleaned from "how to be a spy" books available only from certain underground dealers. Mike, I'm sorry about that time we were making a poison in Bill's basement and the fumes knocked you out. Bill, I'm sorry about that little rocket bomb we made that exploded on your leg.

To all the Nates and Delphines and Bospers of the world, no matter what your names might be. Go out and build a better world.

It's Friday the thirteenth again, and things are about to go very, very, wrong . . .

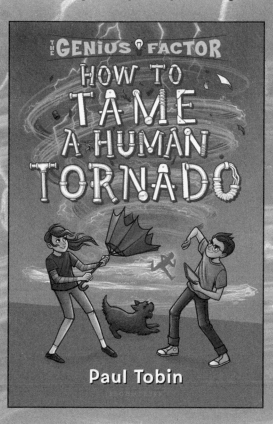

THE GENIUS FACTOR

HOW TO TAME A HUMAN TORNADO

Paul Tobin

Nate has not-so-wisely hidden science vials full of his inventions throughout the town of Polt, and now Nate and Delphine are facing lots of new problems, including an overwhelming amount of toads, zebras running wild through the streets, and lightning storms that won't quit!

This is their most disastrous Friday the thirteenth yet . . . Will they get out of it alive?

Read on for an excerpt of the next book in Paul Tobin's hilarious Genius Factor series.

I was on high alert.

Ready for anything.

It was the middle of the afternoon and I was in the center of the sidewalk in the heart of downtown Polt. There were people everywhere. Everyone else was walking casually, but I was on tiptoes, looking in all directions, and knowing that it was almost entirely useless.

My phone rang.

It was Nate.

"Do you see him?" Nate asked.

I looked around at all the people. There was a college-age couple walking by. He had huge sideburns and she had pigtails and they were looking at something together on her phone. There was a businessman in a striped suit, balanced on one foot, checking the bottom of his left shoe to see if he'd stepped in something unpleasant. There was a group of three high school boys kicking a soccer ball. There was a man with a remarkable mustache just ahead of me on the corner, holding a signboard advertisement for a mattress store, bellowing "hello" to everyone and trying to shake their hands. There was a very young girl holding her mother's hand and *earnestly* explaining the differences between apes and monkeys. There was a woman trying to text with one hand while eating a meatball sandwich. Her blouse was white. She was holding the sandwich away from her, worried about stains.

The meatballs smelled *so good*.

"I don't see him," I told Nate, on the phone. "What should we—?"

But it was at that moment I heard the roaring hum. The air began to vibrate. There were crackling noises from everywhere, like tinfoil being crunched. A Corgi began nervously barking. An old woman in a blue hat clutched a tiny dog to her chest, saying, "Hush, Jeremiah. Hush." Even so, I could tell she was worried. The air didn't feel right. There was . . . too much of it. Pigeons were suddenly flying away. A crow that was on the awning for the All-Winners Art Museum began cawing, hopping along the awning, head swiveling nervously. The hum was growing louder. The crackling rising in intensity.

It felt like the whole world was starting to shiver.

And then . . .

. . . I saw him.

He was only there for a second.

Moving much too fast to see.

He was a blurred line, a thousand flickering images, racing around everyone, racing past them, the air sizzling around him. A few bits of trash . . . newspapers and fast-food wrappers . . . simply burst into flame.

The couple toppled over in the sudden gust of wind. Their shared phone dropped to the sidewalk, tumbling along, bouncing again and again, caught in the blustering wake. The businessman's shoe was ripped off by the pure force, so that he was hopping on one foot, gazing around, bewildered. The high school boys were frowning at their soccer ball, which had popped from the intense air pressure. The woman with her meatball sandwich was looking at her blouse in horror, because it had been simply *painted* with meatball sauce in the sudden wind that'd lasted for less than a second, but had been faster than any tornado, stronger than any hurricane.

The man with the signboard was frowning at it, clearly puzzled. The edges of his sign were tattered and smoldering. And . . . written on the sign with the remains of a meatball sandwich . . . it said, "Nate! Delphine! Help me! *Please!*"

I looked down the street to where the blur had disappeared, then picked up my phone from where I'd dropped it in the sudden chaos.

"Nate," I said. "Chester was just here. We have to save him."

Two hours previously I'd been in the Next Page Bookstore on Trillip Avenue and Nate Bannister had been chastising a confused employee because the quantum physics section had fewer books than the one for celebrity diet tips. The clerk's name was Lucy and she was at least thirty years old, meaning almost twenty years older than Nate and me, so you'd think she'd be wiser (my mother *assures* me that wisdom comes with experience), but Nate, as it so happens, is the smartest person on earth. His IQ is immeasurable. His hair is brown and flopping. There's no connection between these two facts, at least I don't *think* there is, though Nate says there's a connection between ALL facts, if you know how to find them.

Anyway, poor Lucy was just staring at Nate and his

floppy brown hair, which he kept having to brush out from behind his glasses, because he has a big nose, meaning that it holds his glasses too far out from his face, meaning his hair can fall behind them. There *is* a connection between all these facts.

"I was hoping you'd have *Brinkman's Theory of Transitive Kinetics in Orbital Molecular Vectoring*," Nate complained.

"Maybe . . . we could order it?" Lucy said. Her blond hair was almost as curly as my red hair. She was tugging on a few strands, looking around in that manner people have when they think they're being pranked. Her lips (she was wearing green lipstick, which made me jealous) kept squinching up like chewed bubblegum. There was a computer terminal just a few feet away, and she beckoned Nate and me closer to where she typed for a moment before saying, "Oh. Oh, *wow*."

"What?" Nate said.

"That book is, like, really expensive."

"It is?" Nate asked, clearly disappointed. "But I've seen it listed for cheap. Only around four thousand dollars."

"Four thousand dollars is *not* cheap," Lucy said. Her eyes were wide and her lips became chewed bubblegum again.

"Knowledge is worth any price," Nate said. "I'd like the signed copy, if one's available. It doesn't matter if it costs more." He was taking his gold elephant credit card out from his wallet. It's the rarest of credit cards, only three of them in the entire world, because Nate is apparently one of the richest people on earth, though he won't tell me *how* rich. As for me, I have a part-time dog-walking job. I make seven dollars an hour. Per dog. Sometimes three or four dogs at a time. I do okay.

"Here," Nate said, holding up his credit card. "Do you know what this is?"

"Uh, a shiny credit card?" Lucy said, clearly not impressed.

But, then . . .

"G-GOLD! G-g-gold ELEPHANT CARD!" the store manager shrieked, bellowing out from three aisles away. He not-very-adeptly leaped over a display of books on Greek mythology, scurried through an aisle of romance books, then skidded to a stop in front of Nate. He trembled. I thought he was going to salute.

It was at that moment, when everybody else was watching the commotion, that I saw Bosper sneak in through the front door.

Bosper is Nate's Scottish terrier.

Bosper is also the smartest mathematician in the world, excepting only Nate, and possibly Jakob Maculte, the leader of the Red Death Tea Society, a cult of super-smart villains who do super-evil things. Maculte's top priority is to take over the world, and his credo is . . . *Whatever works, as long as it's EVIL.* (I made that last part up, but it's basically true.)

Anyway, we weren't talking about the Red Death Tea Society, even though Maculte had recently escaped from custody and was calling Nate multiple times every day, swearing all sorts of revenge, making an amazing array of threats, and sporadically inviting me over for tea, invitations which I have *politely* and *not-so-politely* declined.

No. We were talking about dogs.

Nate's dog, in particular.

Bosper can talk.

And he was *not* supposed to be in the store.

Because he forgets he's not supposed to talk when he's in public.

I had to do something.

"Be right back," I told Nate.

"Oh, okay, Delphine," he said. The bookstore manager was stupidly grinning at Nate and babbling about how it was an honor to have him in the store, meaning it was an honor to have a *gold elephant card* in the store. Some people are *way* into money. It's kind of sad, really. They're so focused on money, they miss the bigger questions in life, like . . . is there anything better than climbing a tree to watch a sunset with a friend? Or, why do some people think *pie* is better than *cake*? Or, of course . . . why was a talking dog sneaking into a bookstore?

And Bosper *was* sneaking. No doubt about it. He was darting between bookcases, peering around them, acting like a spy. Like an especially *incompetent* spy. You know that thing in horror movies when people are scared of the monsters, so they tiptoe into rooms or along darkened corridors, but they never look *up*? That's what Bosper was doing. Forgetting to look *up*. Which isn't very smart if you happen to be a Scottish terrier and therefore only about a foot tall.

I secretly started following him.

It wasn't very hard to do.

All I had to do was stay behind the bookcases, one aisle over, because he was in the children's picture book section where the shelves were only about three feet high. I could easily peer over them at Bosper.

He was whispering, "The dog is quiet. No barking for Bosper! I am a sneaker." I should've mentioned that while Bosper can do math and can also talk, he's much better at math than he is at talking.

I followed after him, keeping out of sight, listening to what he had to say.

"No time for farting," he said. "Because Bosper is a sneaky dog." He stopped at the end of the aisle and looked left, and right, and then he farted.

"This has happened and the dog has regrets," he said. His tail slunk low. But, then he regained his composure and scurried forward as fast as he could, dodging a group of children looking through picture books, then skidding out on a tile walkway at the edge of the carpeted children's area and thudding into a bookcase, knocking over a display of Robinson Crusoe books and a cardboard pirate ship.

"The dog has tumbled," Bosper said. "But no one has noticed." This was decidedly untrue. Several first graders had been listening to a bookstore employee (Ms. Chrissy) reading from the *Polka Dots vs. Angry Spots* picture book, but had turned around to stare at the Scottish terrier. Those who were close enough had even heard Bosper speak. They were staring at one another in amazement, but it wasn't very *deep* amazement, because first graders still believe that everything is possible and therefore aren't too surprised when they hear a dog talk. I still remember being that age. It was fun. It was only later that I began to understand how the world works, and that dogs do not talk, which is why it was such a shock the first time I heard Bosper speaking on the day that I met Nate and discovered that everything *was*, in fact, possible.

Bosper was again trotting through the bookstore. Now and then he would look back to make sure he wasn't being followed, but he would always murmur, "Bosper is checking for spies," before turning around, giving me ample time to hold a book in front of my legs so that Bosper wouldn't recognize me. I wasn't holding the books in front of my face, because Bosper still wasn't looking up.

We moved through all the math books, just an aisle away from where Nate was talking with the store manager. Bosper pawed at some of the books, whispering about "inter-universal Teichmüller theory," but then moved on.

I followed him through the romance section.

And the section for westerns.

And into world history.

I was only a few feet behind him when he turned into an aisle, let out a happy yelp, and said, "The dog discovers you! His tail goes wagging!"

I couldn't see who he was talking to.

I edged closer.

I was in a shelving area for bookstore merchandise. There were various coffee cups and water bottles and shirts emblazoned with the store logo, as well as other items like action figures of famous authors and an assortment of calendars, including a display calendar turned to the proper date.

Saturday the fourteenth.

Wait.

What?

Uh-oh.

COLLEEN COOVER

Paul Tobin is the award-winning author of the Genius Factor series and numerous comics for such publishers as Marvel, Dark Horse, and DC Comics, as well as the novel *Prepare to Die!*, which earned a starred review from *Publishers Weekly*, *I Was the Cat*, which was nominated for an Eisner Award, and the graphic novel series Plants vs. Zombies. Paul and his wife, artist Colleen Coover, have won multiple Eisner Awards for their ongoing series Bandette, which also placed on YALSA's Great Graphic Novels for Teens list. He lives in Portland, Oregon.

www.paultobin.net